After
the Dawn

ALSO BY FRANCIS RAY

A FAMILY AFFAIR
When Morning Comes

AGAINST THE ODDS SERIES
Trouble Don't Last Always
Somebody's Knocking at My Door

INVINCIBLE WOMEN SERIES
Like the First Time
Any Rich Man Will Do
In Another Man's Bed
Not Even if You Begged
And Mistress Makes Three
If You Were My Man

THE GRAYSONS OF NEW MEXICO SERIES
Until There Was You
You and No Other
Dreaming of You
Irresistible You
Only You

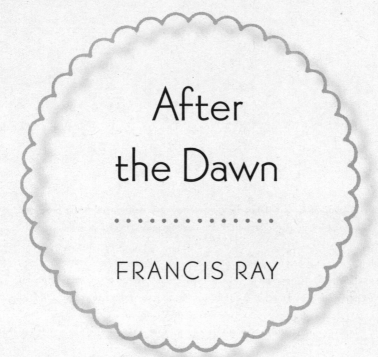

After the Dawn

FRANCIS RAY

St. Martin's Griffin

New York

AFTER THE DAWN. Copyright © 2013 by Francis Ray. All rights reserved. Printed in the United States of America. For information, address St. Martin's Press, 175 Fifth Avenue, New York, N.Y. 10010.

www.stmartins.com

ISBN 978-0-312-68163-0 (trade paperback)
ISBN 978-1-250-02481-7 (e-book)

St. Martin's Griffin books may be purchased for educational, business, or promotional use. For information on bulk purchases, please contact Macmillan Corporate and Premium Sales Department at 1-800-221-7945 extension 5442 or write specialmarkets@macmillan.com.

First Edition: June 2013

10 9 8 7 6 5 4 3 2 1

To my loyal readers.

You make the long, solitary hours

at the computer worthwhile. Bless each of you.

Acknowledgments

Many thanks to Richard South, manager of Regogo Racing Team for Vintage Car Racing. His expertise was invaluable. I'd also like to thank Lisa Williams South, his gracious and charming bride, for the introduction.

After
the Dawn

Prologue

. . . .

In Abe Collins's eighty-one years of living, he'd made his share of mistakes. Believing he had time to correct them, he'd pushed matters to the back of his mind. Six days ago he'd been given a fast reality check, and it wasn't pretty.

Propped up on pillows, wearing an oxygen mask, and hooked to two annoying machines, he was as weak as a baby.

He'd always taken his health for granted. After all, he'd never been sick with more than a cold. His cholesterol might be a little high, but whose wasn't over the age of fifty? So he forgot to take his high blood pressure medicine. He was president of Collins Industry.

His company manufactured and shipped close to two hundred turbochargers a day. He arrived at work an hour before the shift started and was usually the last one to leave the factory. He believed in letting his people do their jobs, but they also knew he kept an eagle eye on productivity.

Odds weren't in his favor that he'd be able to continue. He'd built Collins Industry from the ground up. It was as much a part of him as his hands. The thought that his company wouldn't continue was unthinkable. To make sure that didn't happen, he had to own up to his mistakes. He just hoped and prayed he had a chance to correct the biggest one before it was too late.

He'd passed out talking to the manager of his plant and awakened in the hospital fighting to breathe with an elephant sitting on his chest. He'd had a heart attack.

Abe was alive by the grace of God, but he wasn't out of the woods yet. The doctors wanted to do a quadruple bypass. They'd given him the odds at his age of getting off the table. They weren't good enough for Abe . . . at least not until he had all of his ducks in a row.

Slowly, Abe twisted his head toward his nightstand. He saw the first things every morning, the last things he saw each night—the grouping of family pictures. Family had always been the most important thing in the world to him. To his everlasting shame, he hadn't always shown it.

There was his wife, Edith, beautiful and vibrant at her sixtieth birthday party before cancer took her from them nine short months later. Next were their sons, Evan and William, in their varsity football uniforms in high school. Abe's eyes misted.

William, their youngest, had also been taken. When Abe heard the news that his son's plane had gone down in a thunderstorm, killing him and his wife, Abe hadn't thought he could go on. His heart had actually ached; it still ached.

Despite knowing you should love your children equally, Abe had always favored William, the child of his heart. Smart, funny, and as stubborn as his father, William rarely backed down, and they'd butted heads a time or two. One of those regrets was that they'd had an argument before William had flown off to Austin for a meeting with one of their suppliers.

He and his young wife, Gayle, never made it. Abe swallowed the sorrow, the regret. His gaze moved to the smiling picture of William and Gayle's only child, Samantha, when she was sixteen. Abe added her to the growing list of regrets.

Samantha had wanted her parents to stay and see her in the lead part of the high school senior play. Abe had told her and his son there'd be other plays—the trip was important to the company.

Abe's punishment was having to tell her that her parents weren't coming home. She'd thought he meant they were spending the night in Austin and had said she guessed the company still came first. Explaining that their plane had gone down was the hardest thing he'd ever done. She'd fought him when he'd tried to hold her, her anger and misery making her uncontrollable. He'd accepted the pelting of her small fists against his chest, held her when she'd finally begun to sob.

That was the last time he remembered holding her.

Four months later, she was in Stanford University in California. She always had excuses for not coming home. His other two grandchildren from his oldest son, Evan, didn't even pretend he was important in their lives. Shelby, the oldest at thirty-two, had been married twice. Her brother, Ronald, was thirty, working on his second marriage, and as lazy as they came. As far as Abe knew, they'd called once since his heart attack and then had gone on with their lives.

What gave him hope that it wasn't too late for him and Samantha to find common ground was that she had come from Houston the same day he was admitted to the hospital. She was still here, sitting with him, ready to fluff his pillow, give him a sip of water, reassure him, hold his hand.

The smile forming on his lips faded. He'd missed so much

in his life because of his stubbornness, and he was paying for his know-all attitude. His hand swept across his chest. William had wanted to modernize the factory, but Abe had stubbornly refused.

He'd started the company in 1972 with an idea that he could invent a turbocharger with more power and half the size. He'd had a thousand dollars and the unfaltering faith of Edith. They'd both scraped and saved to get the money— which wasn't easy with two boys in college. But it had paid off.

Collins Industry made the best turbochargers in the Southwest. He saw no reason to change. What was good thirty years ago was still good.

Yet he was alive because of the remarkable changes in the medical profession. He had a chance for even more years. He wanted to ensure that Collins Industry had the same chance— and it would take new thinking and modern technology to do it. That required the right people in charge.

What he was thinking would cause problems and hurt, but Abe didn't see any other way. His callused hand felt the wires and leads connected to his still muscled chest, and he grudgingly accepted he was on the downside of his life. He dared not put off the conversation that would tear his family even further apart. His eyes closed, then opened.

Stretching out his left hand, he picked up the picture of his oldest son, fifty-nine-year-old Evan, and his wife, Janice. They were in evening attire; Evan wore a black tuxedo, and Janice had on a shiny silver gown that probably cost half as much as one of his workers' yearly salary. They'd been at the Cattleman's Ball in Dallas. Tickets were six figures, but Evan said it was good for business. He said the same thing whenever he spent lavishly. And he spent a lot.

Sadness had Abe's hand gripping the silver frame. It was hard to admit that his remaining son might not be the man to run the factory. Evan didn't put the time or the effort into the company. William never paid any attention to the time clock—unless his family needed him. Evan left most days promptly at five. He was vice president, liked the title, but did little to help the company's bottom line if it didn't mean socializing or traveling.

Abe acknowledged that it might have been his fault. He'd always run the company his way, seldom asking for guidance or a second opinion—one of the things William didn't like. While William kept trying to get his father to change, Evan cashed his paycheck and went about his business. But therein lay the problem: Profits were way down. Collins Industry was in a fight to survive.

Abe had to accept that a man he'd ordered off his property years ago might be the one to save his company. It was hard for a man who'd once thought he and the Man Upstairs controlled his destiny, thought that he didn't have to ask any man for anything, to admit just how wrong he had been.

Abe wouldn't blame the man if he laughed in his face. He certainly didn't need the headache or the money, but Samantha would need help to pull the company out of its tailspin and, sadly, that help wouldn't come from Evan—especially once the contents of Abe's new will were known.

How had it come to this? He loved his family, did his best to see that they had more than just the necessities, that they would be people you could count on, proud to know, and capable of carrying on the family company. He'd failed.

Emotions clogged his throat. He thought of his wife, the only woman he'd ever loved. Perhaps if she had lived, he would have learned to bend a little. Perhaps not. She'd called him bull-headed on more than one occasion, but she'd loved him just as he'd loved her. He still did.

A soft knock sounded at the door. "Granddad?"

Even with the difficult task before him, the mistakes and regrets, he thanked God he heard the love and concern in Sa-mantha's soft voice. Despite his overwhelming blunders, he hadn't killed her love for him.

"Baby girl, come in," he said, then cursed his body because his once booming voice now trembled in weakness.

"I'll let her in, Mr. Collins." Bertha Scott, the private duty nurse the doctor insisted come home with him, rose from the nearby chair and went to the door and opened it.

"Hello, Ms. Scott."

"Come on in, Ms. Collins," the nurse greeted her.

Samantha took a hesitant step into the room. He under-stood why. The trip from the hospital yesterday put more strain on his already weak heart. His doctor, who had ridden in the ambulance with him, had wanted to take him back and sched-ule surgery immediately. Abe had refused but had to agree to no visitors until late the next day.

He motioned her closer, annoyed that just that bit of move-ment made his heart act up, the monitor to increase its annoy-ing noise. His nurse was back by his side, checking his vitals, studying him as much as the machines. It was useless to tell her that he was all right. They both knew he wasn't.

"Can—I have a—word alone with my granddaughter?" he asked. The nurse hesitated. "Please."

"I'll be outside." She closed the door softly after her.

Samantha slowly approached the bed, her light brown eyes,

so much like her father's, watching him as closely as the private duty nurse had. "It's good to have you home, but—"

Abe held up his hand. Samantha had been the most verbal against him putting off the surgery. "My heart attack made me realize that I'm not indestructible. I needed to get things in order."

He watched her swallow, blink her eyes rapidly, and catch his hand. "Granddad, you're going to be fine."

He nodded, breathed in the oxygen flowing from the nearby tank. He wished he could take the mask off. He didn't want her seeing him like this.

"Why don't you rest and we'll talk tomorrow?"

As much as he could, he tried to tighten his hand on hers. Tomorrow wasn't promised. "I—I want you to run Collins Industry."

He watched shock widen her eyes, lines form in her otherwise smooth forehead. She was as beautiful as her mother and probably just as sweet. She'd be lost and overwhelmed if the man he'd selected didn't help her. "Collins Industry needs . . . needs you to keep it going, keep it the company your father believed in."

Her hand holding his clenched, then relaxed. She glanced away, then back. Tears shimmered in her eyes. "He loved the company."

Abe tried to sit up and only managed to cause his breath to shorten, his heart to pound wildly in his chest. Samantha curved her arm around his shoulders and eased him back against the bed. "Breathe. Just breathe and relax."

When Abe felt as if he had enough strength and breath, he said, "He loved his f-family. Don't ever forget that."

Samantha nodded. "I won't. Now breathe and relax. We all need you to get well."

"I loved him best." Tears formed in the corners of Abe's eyes that he was unashamed of. "Losing him and your mother—"

Samantha gently dried his tears. "He loved you too. He was proud of you. He called you stubborn, but I heard him say more than once that if he was half the man you were, he'd— he'd die a happy man."

Abe's eyes shut. Tears seeped anyway. He let Samantha dry them, watched her dry her own. Nothing she could have said would have eased his heart more. And she had to have known it.

She'd forgiven him. He'd made the right choice. "Any special man in your life?"

Something flickered in her eyes, and she glanced away. "No."

She'd been here since his heart attack, and as far as Abe knew, no man had visited her. Houston, where she lived, was less than three hours by car, an hour by plane. She didn't have the look of a woman missing a man. Good. One less obstacle. "Five years, with triple your salary. You'll have help."

Samantha wrinkled her nose, the action reminding him of his late wife, who'd stand toe-to-toe with you and didn't take crap from anyone. "Uncle Evan and I have different opinions on things."

An understatement. "Won't matter. He—he won't be the one helping you run the company."

"What? Who, then?" she stammered in bewilderment.

He took a few more breaths before he could answer. "I have a call in to him now."

She looked confused and unsure. He hadn't expected it to be easy.

"Ask me again when you can reveal who the other person running the company will be." She kissed him on the forehead. "Now, please rest. If the nurse okays it, I'll come up and sit with you in a couple of hours."

"You gonna do it?" He had to know.

She patted his hand. "Let's talk more when you feel better."

His baby girl hadn't given him the answer he wanted. Abe just prayed he had time to convince her. Now, for the worst part. "Please ask Evan to come see me."

She hesitated. She and his son were never in the room with him at the same time. Neither ever mentioned the other.

"Please," he asked.

She nodded, and then left.

Before the door closed, the nurse was back in the room, checking him, the monitors. "I think you've had enough visitors for the day."

Abe wasn't going to argue, but there was one more person he needed to see alone. If he had to lie to do it. . . . "I could have some broth."

The nurse straightened. His appetite hadn't been worth warm spit. "I can't leave you alone."

"Evan is coming in a bit."

The nurse hesitated. "We'll see. Just rest."

Abe closed his eyes and tried to relax. His baby girl, Sammie, would send Evan. Abe just hoped his eldest would understand why he wasn't leaving him in charge. But he was afraid he wouldn't.

Outside her grandfather's bedroom, Samantha hung her head briefly and said a silent prayer for him. Each time she saw him, he was weaker. He needed the surgery, but for some reason he was putting it off. The doctor had warned them that he was playing with a loaded gun. Despite everything that had happened in the past between them, she loved him, regretted that she had stayed away so long. She'd blamed him, blamed Collins Industry, for taking her parents.

She'd missed so much with him, wasted precious time that she might not get a chance to have in the future. Straightening, she stared at the closed door, then started down the hall toward the stairs. Her uncle and his wife lived on the third and top floor. She wasn't looking forward to the conversation.

For some odd reason, her aunt and uncle had never liked her. Even as a child she had sensed their animosity. Her parents, her uncle and aunt, their children, and her grandfather lived in the same house. The three-story Georgian manor had ten bedrooms and had over twelve thousand square feet. It still seemed small at times because of her aunt and uncle's attitude.

Which was going to get worse once he learned his father didn't want him running Collins. Since her grandfather's heart attack, Evan had spouted a lot about "when I'm in charge." He fully expected to step into his father's shoes. It wasn't going to happen.

But did she want the job?

She massaged her temple. She wanted to be passionate about something, but she wasn't sure what it was. She certainly wasn't thrilled with her job as a feature writer at the *Houston Sentinel*. She'd majored in journalism because it had nothing to do with the automobile industry.

She'd been an average student, graduated, and bounced around a lot until she'd landed a job as a feature writer at the newspaper in Houston. The pay was horrible, the hours worse.

If not for the trust fund her parents left her, she would have never made it financially.

She thought she'd found love with Mark Washington, the sports reporter at the same newspaper. They'd dated for three months before she'd ended things six months ago. Mark wanted her back, but as she'd told her grandfather, for her it was over. Worse, she was tired of trying to avoid him at work. Perhaps if she were more forceful, he'd leave her alone. There was nothing to keep her in Houston. But did she want the responsibility for over two hundred people and a business she had only a basic understanding of?

No matter how she'd felt as a teenager, her father had loved the company *and* his father. He would have done—had done—whatever it took to ensure both were served well.

Could she walk away knowing her grandfather and Collins Industry needed her? She wondered, going up the flight of stairs to the top and third floor. She hoped she never had to find out. Tonight, if the nurse allowed her to visit, she was going to encourage her grandfather to schedule the surgery as quickly as possible. They all needed him.

She knocked on her uncle's door. He and his wife had the entire floor of eight rooms since their children, Shelby and Ronald, were grown and gone. From what she'd been able to learn from the housekeeper, her cousins came home less than she did. They'd called but hadn't come to visit their parents or their grandfather.

The door opened and her uncle stared down his nose at her, his eyes as unwelcoming as ever. "Yes?"

Not even a semblance of a smile, of warmth. Once her grandfather went back to the hospital for his surgery, she was moving into the guest cottage in the back of the house. She would have already been there if she hadn't wanted to be near her grandfather. It was obvious no one wanted her here except him.

"You wanted something?" he asked. He'd been home from work since a little after five, yet he still had on his white shirt and red silk tie. It was almost six. He and his wife both had a fondness for designer clothes and fine jewelry.

"Granddad wants to see you."

"He must be feeling better." He spoke over his shoulder. "Janice, Daddy wants to see me. I'll be back and we can go down to dinner."

Dinner was always served when Evan wanted. The kitchen was closed otherwise. Her uncle liked being in charge. She just hoped her grandfather didn't intend to tell him about his plans to put her in charge until he was stronger.

Tall and trim, Evan stepped into the hall. "Was there something else?"

She'd rather do anything than have a confrontation, but she forged ahead. Her grandfather's health was too fragile. "He's still weak and shouldn't be upset."

Dark eyes glinted with malice. "I know how to treat my father. Unlike you, I've been here." He brushed past her and continued down the hall.

Samantha slipped her hands into the pockets of her jeans, stared after him, then headed for the stairs. Looked like she was eating out again. There was no way she was going to sit through another dinner with her aunt and uncle.

Abe heard the knock on the door and said a prayer he'd find the right words. His nurse opened the door.

"My father wanted to see me."

Abe briefly shut his eyes. Evan hadn't even looked at Bertha. How could his flesh and blood be so uppity and condescending?

"I was just going down to heat up some broth. Just sit, no exertion. His granddaughter left a short time ago."

Abe saw Evan's mouth tighten. The boy never liked being told what to do. Or perhaps he recognized that Bertha had snubbed him by not looking at him just as he had her. "Of course."

"I'll be back as quick as possible, Mr. Collins."

Abe didn't try to acknowledge her in any way. Bertha would understand. He would need all of his strength in the coming minutes. Unlike Samantha, his oldest son didn't approach the bed. Abe couldn't help but think nothing would have kept William away.

"Need to talk to you," he managed. He had to get this said.

Evan cautiously approached the bed, then slipped his hand into the pocket of his slacks. "Daddy, maybe you shouldn't talk."

Abe finally saw that Evan was scared and unsure of himself. Unfortunately, Abe had seen the furrowed brow and darting gaze before. "Company in trouble."

His son's brows drew together. His hand came out of his pocket. "What kind of trouble?"

"Losing business. My fault. Wouldn't listen."

Evan braced one hand on the side of the bed near his father's arm and leaned closer. "Listen to whom?"

"William. Dillon."

Evan's shoulders snapped upright. Anger flashed in his dark eyes. "You're dwelling in the past. It's the effect of the lack of oxygen when you had the heart attack."

"No. Wrong. I asked Sammie to help run the company."

"What?" Evan yelled. "Are you crazy? She's a reporter, for God's sake! You must be senile!"

"No. Try to understand."

"Understand that you always loved William more and, since you can't have him, you want the daughter!" Evan yelled, leaning closer to his father. "You can't do this to me!"

All wrong. All wrong.

Abe struggled to lift himself from the bed to somehow reassure Evan, who had always been insecure. His son kept yelling, pacing, shutting his father out.

Abe couldn't understand the words because the pain in his chest was too severe. He was having trouble catching his breath. He fought to ignore the pounding in his chest, the dizziness, the sense of falling, of darkness.

Somehow he had to fix this. He— Abe slumped back on the bed and didn't move. The monitor wailed long and loud.

Evan spun. Horror and fear gripped him. "Daddy!" He rushed to the bed.

The beeper screamed. Evan screamed louder. "Daddy! God, no! I didn't mean it. Please, no!"

The nurse burst into the room and rushed to the bed, but even as she grabbed the automatic electronic defibrillator and ordered a hysterical Evan to call 911, she knew that it was too late.

Abe Collins wasn't going to cheat death twice.

One

· · · · · · · · · · · · · · · ·

Most of Elms Fork had turned out for Abe Collins's funeral, Dillon Montgomery noted. Two hours ago, they'd spilled out of the largest church in town. There were so many flowers, it had taken two black vans to carry them to the cemetery. The slow procession of cars behind the hearse had been two miles long. Most of the businesses—except for the gas stations and a couple of restaurants—were closed in honor of a man who had made Elms Fork more than a dot on a map.

Muffled sniffles came from beside him. Feeling helpless, Dillon tightened his arm around his mother's slim shoulders. She wasn't a woman who cried easily. They both had reasons to hate and love the man being slowly lowered into his final resting place. Abe had stuck by Dillon's mother when half the town and many of the employees at Collins Industry turned their backs on her because she'd been unwed and pregnant with Dillon.

Twenty-three years later, he'd fired Dillon and ordered

him off the company's property. At sixty-nine, standing six feet, he'd still been a man who could win against another man half his age and win. At twenty-two, brash and arrogant, Dillon might have taken him on if his mother, Abe's secretary at the time, hadn't come into the office when she'd heard them arguing.

"Dillon," his mother said softly, bringing him back to the present, "I can't believe he's gone."

Dillon patted her arm awkwardly. It was just him and his mother. He had no idea how to deal with her grief. She'd lost friends, of course, but none had affected her as much as Abe's passing.

"I feel sorry for Samantha," his mother continued. "She'll have no one now."

Her uncle and aunt certainly wouldn't be there for her, Dillon thought. They were as selfish and snobbish as they came. Although Dillon didn't associate with them, they probably hadn't changed much in twelve years.

Dillon couldn't see Samantha for the crush of people, the towering hats the women wore, but he could visualize her face—hurt and embarrassed after he'd rebuffed her awkward attempt to seduce him.

That had been twelve years ago. His mind shut down from going further. Those thoughts weren't appropriate at a funeral. He hadn't seen or heard from her since. "She'll be fine."

"I hope you're right. Abe loved her so much," his mother mused. "I'm glad she came before we lost him."

Dillon wasn't sure if his mother expected an answer or just wanted to talk. He'd come as soon as he'd heard The Old Man, as Abe was called behind his back, had died. Listening to the

strong voice of the minister Dillon couldn't think of one reason why Abe would have called him the day he'd died. Dillon
had been in Canada working on a Lotus for the Formula One
vintage car racing competition.

His mother had mentioned Abe's heart attack when they'd
talked the day before but said he was recovering at home.
When the call came, Dillon had been in the middle of getting
the car ready for a trial run and hadn't been able to talk.

An hour later, when Dillon had been able to take a break,
he'd called his mother to check on her. She was his and Abe's
only connection. Once he knew she was fine, he'd decided to
call Abe later. When he'd called later that night, the housekeeper
said Abe was dead. He'd taken the first flight he could get to be
with his mother. He would regret for a long time that he hadn't
taken Abe's call.

"Ashes to ashes. Dust to dust."

"Come on, Mama," Dillon said, gently urging his mother
toward the car parked a quarter of a mile away on the narrow
two-lane road. There was no way they would get near Samantha to offer their condolences. His priority, as it had always
been, was taking care of his mother.

They'd been at his mother's home an hour when the phone
rang. Dillon grabbed the receiver. His mother was watching a
sappy Lifetime movie in the den. He hadn't wanted to leave
her, but the movie was making his eyes cross.

"Hello."

"May I speak with Dillon Montgomery and Marlene
Montgomery?"

Dillon frowned at the strange wording. "Who is this?"

"Samuel Boswell, Abe Collins' lawyer. Is this Mr. Montgomery?"

Dillon's stocking feet came off the cushioned hassock, hitting the area rug beneath. "Yes."

"Is Ms. Montgomery there as well?"

Dillon cut a look at his mother. He thought she was deep into the story, but obviously he'd been wrong. Sitting on the sofa across from him, she muted the sound on the built-in TV and watched him.

"Abe's lawyer wants to speak to us."

"Put him on the speaker," she said, folding her hands in her lap.

Dillon hit the speaker. "We're here."

"Excellent. I'm sorry to disturb you at the time of your grief and appreciate you taking my call."

Dillon rolled his eyes. Lawyers wasted so much time trying to make you know how important they were.

"Thank you, but what is the reason for your call?" his mother asked.

Dillon grinned. His mother was as straightforward as he was.

"The reading of Abe's will is tomorrow morning at the Collins mansion. Abe requested you both be there."

Dillon and his mother shared a look of surprise.

"I can't imagine why," Dillon said.

"What time?" his mother asked.

"Eleven sharp, Ms. Montgomery. Can I expect the both of you?" the lawyer asked.

"We'll be there," his mother said. "Is there anything else?"

"No, thank you. Good-bye."

His mother came to her feet, hung up the receiver, and

headed for the kitchen. Dillon followed, hoping she wasn't going to cry again. "You all right?"

"Yes." Using a potholder, she removed the baking dish with a rump roast from the warming oven. He'd wanted to eat when they returned from the cemetery, but since she wasn't hungry, he'd pretended not to mind waiting.

Dillon grabbed the plates, set the table, and filled two glasses with iced sweet tea. His mother had picked at her food for the past two days. Today, that stopped.

"Abe and I settled our differences years ago." She put the mashed potatoes in the microwave, then turned the gas burner on under the green beans. "I called the hospital when I heard about his heart attack, but was told only family members were allowed in his room. I spoke with Samantha once and asked her to tell him that I was praying for him."

"He called me the day he died," Dillon said quietly.

His mother placed her hand on his arm. "Perhaps he had a premonition he wasn't going to make it, and wanted to make amends."

Dillon lifted a dubious brow. "He'd choke first."

Shaking her head, she turned at the ding of the microwave. "He was a hard man sometimes, but he was there when I was pregnant. I'm not sure if we would have made it otherwise."

"And fired me when I wanted to make improvements on the turbo," Dillon recalled, the incident no longer stinging. Because of that one event, he'd gone on to become a successful businessman with three garages for regular cars and a fourth for high-performance cars. He was also an in-demand mechanical consultant for vintage racing cars.

"You succeeded, as I always knew you would."

She was probably the only one. She'd raised Dillon by herself. She'd never done anything but love and encourage him,
even when the town called him a jailbird-in-waiting. He'd
lived in the moment, doing as he pleased, and he'd done some
crazy things.

One of those times he'd come home buzzed on illegal
cheap booze and rammed his car into the garage. He recalled
waking up to his mother's tears, thankful he was all right, and
the neighbors standing around sneering and predicting he'd
kill himself one day and they just hoped he didn't take them
with him.

His mother had somehow gotten him inside, but he'd
passed out on the living room floor. He'd come to when he
heard her crying. She'd sat by him all night, scared he'd throw
up and choke on his vomit. He finally realized he was hurting
the only person who loved him completely. That was the last
night he'd come home blind drunk. He'd been a senior in
high school. He'd started hitting the books instead of the
bottle, and he'd stopped chasing easy women.

His mother had saved him. There wasn't a thing on God's
green earth that he wouldn't do for her.

"You're the strongest woman I know. You would have
made it," he finally said.

"Spoken like a son who loves his mother. Now sit down
and eat. You have to be starving." She filled his plate with beef,
creamy potatoes, and green beans with real bacon bits. She
placed a basket of soft rolls in front of him.

Dillon looked from his plate to her. Sighing, she picked up
the plate he'd placed on the table for her and prepared her own
plate. Seated, she said the blessing and picked up her fork. "I'm
eating."

"About time." House rule: They both ate or they both went hungry. Dillon dug into his food with relish. He'd eaten in some of the finest, most expensive restaurants in the world, but his mother's cooking beat them all.

"I wonder if there is someone to take care of Samantha. She sounded . . . alone and scared when we spoke briefly," his mother mused. "I'm glad we'll have a reason to see her tomorrow."

Dillon said nothing. He wondered if Samantha remembered the searing kiss that had made him rock hard and ready. She'd had on a ruffled pink prom dress that stopped inches above her knees. She and her friends had tumbled out of a limo into the bar where he'd been drinking, trying to get over Abe's firing him. He'd been in a foul mood.

Samantha hadn't seemed to mind. She'd come on to him as soon as she'd seen him. If he hadn't known she was half drunk and the reason she was trying to seduce him, he might have taken her up on her offer.

He'd never forget her clinging to him, murmuring that she just wanted to forget. Well aware of her parents' death two weeks earlier, he'd held her, then taken her home instead of to the motel as she'd suggested.

Once at the Collins mansion, he'd expected to find someone waiting for her. Or Abe with a shotgun. There hadn't been anyone. His mother never went to bed until he was safely in his.

Samantha had the saddest look he'd ever seen when she'd looked over her shoulder at him, then closed the door of the mansion. He'd made sure no one took advantage of her, but he'd always felt as if he'd let her down—which was idiotic because they'd barely known each other.

Adjusting his position in the chair, he kept his head down. Women. You could never please them.

Five minutes before eleven, Dillon and his mother arrived at the Collins mansion—there was no other way to describe the magnificent Georgian structure. It was the only three-story house in the town and sat on five acres of manicured lawns with its own small lake and eight-hole golf course.

Dillon pulled up behind a late-model Mercedes and cut the motor of his Ferrari, one of four cars he owned. It was part of his image as the go-to guy for automotive problems of high-performance cars. The other part, he freely admitted, was showing Elms Fork that the guy they'd written off was wealthier and more successful than they'd ever be.

His mother smoothed her hand over the straight black skirt of her suit. It had a designer label, but she had selected it for comfort and style. And at his insistence. She'd done without when he was growing up so he wouldn't have to. That was never going to happen again. Unlike Dillon, she had no desire to rub people's noses in his success. That was okay. He'd do it for both of them.

He reached for her hand and found it steady, but her eyes were troubled. "You all right?"

She gave him the warm, loving smile that had bolstered him time and time again. "You know the only reason Abe wanted us here is because we're in his will."

"The thought had crossed my mind." Dillon opened his door and came around to open his mother's. Still slim and agile at fifty-seven, she gracefully swung her feet out and stood. At five foot four, she came up to the middle of his chest. She pushed strands of blackish-brown hair that brushed her shoulders off her cheek. She remained a beautiful woman. Many of his friends didn't want to believe she was his mother when they met the first time.

"Maybe he wants me to restore his wife's Mercedes. I understand it hasn't been driven since she died."

Marlene adjusted the hem of her short jacket. "She became ill the year Collins Industry took off. Abe would have given it all to have her well and by his side. Theirs was a love that everyone should have."

Dillon caught his mother's arm and started up the curved bricked steps. The kind of love that she probably had thought she had. Instead, Dillon's father had deserted her. Times like these, Dillon wished he had ten seconds with A. J. Reed, his no-good father. But they'd made it without him.

One of the double twelve-foot oak doors opened. Dillon wasn't prepared to see Samantha standing there. She was draped in a simple black dress and misery. Lips that had boldly promised to fulfill his every fantasy, trembled. Black gave a haunting, fragile quality to her beauty.

"Hello, Samantha. You probably don't remember me. We spoke on the phone when Abe was in the hospital. I'm Marlene Montgomery, and this is my son, Dillon."

Samantha's startled eyes snapped to him the second his mother mentioned his name. He saw heat flush her cheeks. So she hadn't forgotten.

Samantha simply stared. Dillon Montgomery was easily the handsomest and sexiest man she had ever seen. He was six feet two of mouthwatering temptation. Twelve years ago, she'd been miserable enough to throw herself at him and risk the fires of hell. If rumors were right, he was related to her.

His sensual mouth curved knowingly. Butterflies fluttered in her stomach. She was definitely flirting with fire for her sinful thoughts.

"Abe's lawyer asked us to come," his mother said in the lengthening silence.

Samantha flushed. What was the matter with her? At a time like this, no matter how enticing, she shouldn't be ogling Dillon. "Please, come in."

Perhaps it wasn't a rumor after all that Dillon was Abe and Marlene's son. Why else would they be there? Her grandfather's lawyer said they were waiting on two other people. "We're in Granddad's study."

"He loved you," Marlene said as she entered the wide marble foyer. "I know he was glad you were able to be here with him."

Samantha's hand clenched on her damp handkerchief. "Thank you."

"Samantha, we're waiting. Bring them—" Evan Collins, in another of his tailored suits, this one gray pin-striped, stopped abruptly on seeing Dillon and Marlene. "What are you doing here?"

"Abe's lawyer asked us," Dillon said with entirely too much satisfaction, Samantha thought. "Since you sound anxious to begin, I suggest we go into Abe's study so Boswell can get started."

"I don't want you in my house." Evan blocked their entrance.

Samantha's gaze bounced from her angry uncle to Dillon, his easy smile gone, his black eyes narrowed.

"That's not what Abe wanted and, as everyone in town knows, this was his house, not yours," Dillon said.

Evan's face flushed. Samantha had never heard anyone talk to her uncle that way.

"You must be Ms. Montgomery and Dillon." Samuel Boswell, her grandfather's lawyer, joined them, acting as if nothing were amiss. He was barely five feet, with a receding hairline and sharp, intelligent eyes behind his wire-framed eyeglasses. "I was hoping that was you." He stuck out his hand. The handshakes were brief.

Samantha noted Dillon smirking at her uncle. Her uncle glowered back.

"Please follow me so we can begin," the lawyer said.

Evan caught the lawyer's arm. "Why are they here? I know what's in Dad's will, and they're not in it."

The man shifted uncomfortably in his shiny wing tips. "All your questions will be answered momentarily. Let's go in."

Ignoring Evan, Dillon caught his mother's arm and Samantha's without thinking. She looked as if she were at her breaking point. Living with her contentious uncle and aunt, Dillon understood why.

He found he wanted to comfort her as much as he did his mother. She had grown into a beautiful woman and was just as tempting now as she had been twelve years ago.

And just as off-limits. He never dated women from Elms Fork anymore. In the small town, people were too nosy and into everyone else's business. Besides, there were only so many free women to choose from. He'd never traveled the same path, dated friends or their relatives. Plus, he didn't want the woman bothering his mother when he moved on—and he always would.

Inside the study, Samantha stepped away from him, then

she introduced him and his mother to those already seated. "This is Ms. Montgomery and her son, Dillon. Granddad wanted them here. This is my aunt Janice, and my cousins, Shelby and Ronald."

Dillon nodded. His mother spoke, but the only response she got was a hostile glare from Janice and bored looks from Shelby and Ronald. Dillon ignored the speculative once-over from Shelby. He'd steered clear of her in high school for good reason. Too much drama and possessiveness for his taste.

Samantha flushed and turned to them again. "Can I get you anything?"

"They aren't guests," Evan snapped. "Sit down so we can get this over with."

Dillon stiffened and was moving before he realized it. Someone needed to put a muzzle on Evan's loud mouth. His mother's hand on his arm stopped him.

"Thank you, Samantha. We're fine." His mother sank grace-fully into a love seat, pulling a taut Dillon down next to her.

Twisting the handkerchief in her hand, Samantha took a seat in a high-backed chair near them. Dillon noted she hadn't sat with her family. His mother had been right. She had no one.

"Now that everyone is here, we can proceed." Samuel Bos-well picked up several sheets of paper, adjusted his eyeglasses. "I had hoped, as we all did, that this day was many years away. Abe Collins was a good man."

Marlene nodded. Samantha bit her lower lip. Dillon noted that no reaction came from the other family members.

"Abe made an unusual request in the reading of his will. There will be two readings with only the people involved. I'm meeting later with the house staff, several lifelong employees of Collins Industry, and the pastor of his church. He wanted family matters kept private."

Translation. The shit was about to hit the fan, Dillon thought. Apparently Evan had the same thought. He glared at Samantha, then at Dillon and his mother.

Dillon grinned. This was about to get very interesting.

"'I, Abraham Lincoln Collins, being of sound mind, do bequeath my home located at 1927 Pecan Place in Elms Fork to be equally divided between my son, Evan Emerson Collins, and my granddaughter Samantha Ann Collins.'"

Evan jerked upright and glared at Samantha. Since she was looking at the lawyer with a shocked expression on her face, she missed it entirely.

"Me?"

Boswell smiled kindly at her. "You. I believe his next statement explains better than I could. 'I want Sammie, my baby girl, to always have a place to come home to, to know I loved her parents, and mourn their loss daily.'"

Tears seeped down Samantha's cheeks. Dillon didn't expect her family to try to comfort her, and he wasn't disappointed. His mother rose, pulled a nearby chair closer to sit next to Samantha, then gave her a fresh tissue and curved her arm around her trembling shoulders.

Dillon had countless reasons to be proud of his mother, but this was one of the proudest.

"'To ensure she has the funds to maintain the house and grounds, I'm leaving her all of my assets, including cash, stocks, annuities, and bonds, in an irrevocable trust.'"

"What?" Evan came to his feet. "That can't be true." He crossed the spacious room, and reached for the will.

Samuel drew the papers to his chest. "Mr. Collins, please take a seat. I'm not finished."

Heaving with fury, Evan didn't move. "When was this will written?"

"The day your father was released from the hospital."

"Then that explains it," Evan announced with a dismissive shove of his hand at the will. "His lack of oxygen after his first heart attack must have affected his brain. He wasn't himself."

"Abe was seen by a psychiatrist less than an hour before he changed his will, which was witnessed by his doctor and his private duty nurse."

"Checkmate," Dillon said, and laughed. "This is really getting interesting."

Evan pivoted and snapped. "You think this is funny?"

"No, I think it's sad," Dillon said slowly.

"Please, Mr. Collins, take a seat so I can finish."

Evan retook his seat. The lawyer flashed a worried look at him, adjusted his glasses. " 'To Marlene Montgomery, the most efficient secretary a man could ask for, but just as importantly, a kindhearted woman who forgave when she didn't have to, I bequeath the sum of two hundred and forty thousand dollars—the salary she would have earned if she hadn't quit when I fired her son. I paid for my rashness ten times over. You were irreplaceable and I was too stubborn to ask you to come back. I know Dillon can take care of you, but I'd like for you to have the money to do something fun and then come by the grave site and tell me.' "

Although tears rolled down her cheeks, Marlene smiled.

Dillon started to rise and go to her, but she waved her hand to indicate she was all right. He noted that her other hand was wrapped around Samantha's. He couldn't tell who was holding whom.

The lawyer cleared his throat. "'Collins Industry was founded on a vision and succeeded because of hard work and determination. I want to leave my company in the hands of people who will value it just as much and work tirelessly for it to succeed. Therefore I leave joint ownership of Collins Industry to Samantha Collins and Dillon Montgomery—if they agree to jointly run the company for five years.'"

Dillon was stunned. There was no other way to describe his reaction.

Evan was on his feet again. "That's bullshit! Collins Industry is mine! I don't care what some quack psychiatrist said, Daddy must have been senile. He wouldn't have left the company to an outsider."

"Uncle Evan," Samantha said quietly when he stopped to take a breath, "Granddad asked me the day we lost him to consider taking over the company." She looked across the room at Dillon. "He mentioned there was another person he wanted to help."

"If there was another person, it was me," Evan said. "There must have been some mistake in drawing up the will."

Boswell looked offended. "There was no mistake."

"Mr. Boswell is right," Samantha said. "Granddad said I would be working with someone else. Don't think harshly of him," she rushed to say at her uncle's angry expression. "He was worried. The company is in trouble. He wanted to save it, and he thought Dillon and I could pull it off. I think that's why he put off his surgery."

Hands on his hips, her uncle snorted dismissively. "And how do you propose to do that? I've been here, helping run the company while you've been off playing and drawing the money from my brother's trust fund. You have no clue how to run Collins Industry. Dillon has even less. More importantly, Daddy fired him."

On an apparent roll, Evan swung to Dillon. "Just because Daddy was feeling sentimental that he never claimed his bastard is no reason—"

Dillon shot out of his seat like a bullet. He grabbed Evan by the collar of his tailor-made white shirt and drew back his fist.

"Dillon," his mother called, catching his arm with both hands. "Stop it."

Dillon's chest heaved with barely controlled rage. "Bastard" was the one word that he would never take easily. He was called that too many times growing up, taunted, not allowed to associate with the "good kids" because his mother wasn't married when she had him. Abe wasn't his father, but Dillon had no intention of telling the loudmouthed Evan.

"Dillon, please." His mother's voice trembled.

Dillon cut a look at his mother. While he'd been called bastard, she'd been called much worse. She wasn't turning loose of his hand. He'd walk through burning coals before he hurt her. "Apologize to my mother."

"I won't—"

Dillon's fist tightened, cutting off the flow of oxygen, then relaxed only marginally. "Do it!"

"I apologize, Marlene," Evan said with a nasty sneer on his face.

Dillon shoved Evan distastefully away from him before he hit him anyway. Evan staggered, then straightened. His face promised retribution. "I'll have you arrested for assault."

"Go ahead and try," Dillon told him, noting that Evan's

family had stood but none had tried to help him. "I'll put my lawyers against yours any day. I was provoked. You're lucky my mother was here or you'd be picking your teeth up off the floor."

"Come on, Dillon. Sit down." His mother tugged his arm.

"Cross that line again and nothing will save you." He finally allowed his mother to lead him back to the love seat he'd been seated on.

Samantha felt helpless and miserable. This wasn't what her grandfather wanted. "Uncle Evan, what we don't know, you can teach us. The company is slowly dying. If that happens, the employees and town will lose as well. Together we can make Collins Industry a top contender with turbo engines again."

"The company is fine!" Evan shouted, his chest heaving. "I'll get an injunction if I have to! I'll sue! I'll lock the doors!"

"Perhaps I should finish," the lawyer said quietly. "If you start any legal proceedings to contest the will, your salary at Collins Industry will be frozen until the case is settled. If you'll recall, Abe left all of his personal assets—with the exception of the house, which you and your niece own jointly—to Ms. Collins. If you want to fight this, you'll do it with your personal funds. Since Abe was deemed sane by a notable psychologist, the case could take months, especially if Mr. Montgomery and Ms. Collins decide to fight."

"I'll fight," Dillon promised, for the hell of it. He planned to sign over the company before the day was over.

Boswell cleared his throat. "However, if you accept the will, Mr. Collins, you're to remain as vice president with your salary."

"That's blackmail," said Janice, his wife, coming to stand by her husband. "Do something, Evan! What will people say when they find out?"

"That—" Dillon stopped abruptly as his mother shook her head. He leaned back in the seat.

"Abe knew it wouldn't be easy, but he hoped you'd come to see that the company needs to change or it won't survive," the lawyer said.

"I see all right. And all of you can go to hell!" Evan stormed from the room with his wife on his heels.

"Is there any mention of his other grandchildren?" Shelby asked.

"No, I'm sorry." Boswell slowly shook his head. "Just Samantha Collins."

"So am I." Shelby stood and left the room. Her brother followed.

Samantha's emotions had never been so chaotic. She wasn't sure about working with Dillon, but she didn't have a choice. He still looked as if he'd like to rip someone apart. She liked things orderly and calm, nonthreatening. They wouldn't be that way with Dillon. Then, there was this attraction she couldn't control.

She flexed her toes in her black heels. If she didn't want them hanging over a very hot fire, she'd do well to remember that Dillon could be related to her.

"Dillon, I'm not sure what your schedule is like," she ventured. "I'm available anytime you'd like to meet tomorrow to discuss our next step in running the company."

He aimed that laser-sharp gaze at her. It was all she could do not to shrink back in her chair.

"You don't think I'm going to go along with this farce, do you?"

"Farce? Granddad left half of the company to you because he believed in you," she returned, anger creeping into her voice.

"Yeah." Dillon laughed without humor. "A company he took great pleasure in firing me from. I have no intention of helping Collins Industry. I have my own life. I wish you well." He approached the desk the lawyer sat behind and braced his hands on top.

"Draw up the papers, and I'll sign over my half of the company to her."

"I'm afraid that's impossible." Boswell folded his hands on top of the will. "Abe took into account that you might not be amenable to this initially."

"He was right." Dillon straightened. "If you can't do it, my lawyers can."

"Mr. Montgomery, it's not a matter of can't. Abe's will specifically stipulates that neither you nor his granddaughter can sell or give away your half of the company for five years. Whether you want to or not, you're half owner of Collins."

"We'll just see about that."

Turning, he took his mother's arm and walked away, leaving Samantha and the lawyer staring after him.

Two

· · · · · · · · · · · · · ·

S amantha won't be able to run the company by herself,"
his mother said from beside him as he started the motor
of the car. "She'll have no one. Her uncle certainly won't
help."

Angry at Abe for placing him in such an unwanted situation, at Evan for being such a greedy, unfeeling ass, and at
Samantha for looking at him with a mixture of fear and hope,
Dillon shifted the gears of the Ferrari. In a squeal of tires, he
pulled out of the long driveway, easily controlling the low-
slung sports car as it rocked, then straightened.

His mother didn't seem to notice as she continued. "Without you, she won't make it. That means the people working
there will be without jobs. It's not like you to walk away from
your responsibility."

Dillon recognized that his mother was doing a number on
him, but she was right. He did take his responsibilities seriously. He might have been all about himself once, but he now

realized it might be trite, but no man made it on his own, and
when you could, you reached out and helped someone else.

But he liked his carefree life, the financial freedom to go
and do as he pleased. If he took the job running Collins, he'd
be tied down for five years in a town that had treated him like
dirt. "Not my problem."

"Hmmm."

Dillon tossed his mother a look. He didn't like the sound of
that.

"Why don't we drive by the complex before you take me
home?" she suggested mildly. "I've seen all of your other prop-
erties; I wonder if Collins Industry will look any different now."

"I know what you're doing," he said, taking the left turn
that led out of town. "It's not happening. I have too many
irons in the fire, plus I like my life the way it is. I don't want to
be tied to a company that's having financial trouble."

"I imagine neither do the people working there."

He'd never been able to win an argument with his mother.
She tended to be logical and thought things through. That
didn't mean he wouldn't keep trying. The law of averages said
he was due.

Neither said anything else on the short drive. In less than
three minutes, they topped a hill. On the left side of the road
a large sign read: COLLINS INDUSTRY, FOUNDED IN 1972 BY ABE
COLLINS. In the parking lot were a mixture of old and new,
economy and expensive cars and trucks. A large metal two-
story building attached to a long one-story structure backed
up to scrub brush, oak, and crabapple trees.

"Two of the women in my book club work there. One is a
divorced mother of a five-year-old. The other one, she and her

husband both work there. They have two children in college. She's so proud. They'll be the first college graduates of the family."

Dillon shifted uncomfortably as he pulled up into the paved road leading into the complex. He'd always had a soft spot for single parents.

A stout man with his belly hanging over his belt stepped out of the manned booth. Dillon recognized him as one of the men who, as a teenager, had taunted him. There were probably other bullies working there as well. They'd never left Elms Fork.

"I wouldn't feel bad if Sparks got laid off."

"But how do you separate the good from the bad? Unfortunately, if the company closes, no one will be spared." She glanced at him. "We both know what it's like to live from paycheck to paycheck. But thanks to Abe, there was a paycheck."

Putting the car in reverse, Dillon backed up and took the highway back into town. They didn't have to worry about money now, but there had been some lean years growing up. It wasn't until he was older that he'd realized his mother had gone without, saying she'd eaten already or that she wasn't hungry, so he'd have enough to eat, enough clothes, toys.

She had a steady job, but the small house she'd bought always seemed to have something that needed to be repaired. She could have rented an apartment, but she'd wanted him to grow up in a house, with a room of his own, a puppy. She'd been abandoned at age two and placed in foster care.

Never, no matter the circumstances, she never would have walked away from him. He'd never heard her say anything bad about her mother. "Life is a series of choices," she often said. "You have to live with the good and the bad."

She never wanted him to do without because she was a

single parent. Around eleven, when he'd caught on that she wasn't eating to ensure he had enough, he'd started to say he wasn't hungry. He wasn't eating until she did. They'd both be full or hungry.

She'd cried, berating herself that she wasn't taking good care of him. It was the only time he'd ever yelled at her, the only time she'd let him. He'd told her if he had to choose a mother, he'd choose her every time.

She'd kept him, always been there for him. No other person loved him that way. As troublesome as he was, he doubted if anyone could. He was in the principal's office at least once a month. When pushed or bullied, Dillon responded with his fists.

She never scolded him or threatened him. Just cleaned him up and tried to make him realize fighting was never the answer to a problem. That he was to use the intelligence God gave him and figure out another way to solve the situation. He knew what it was to be loved, and she was the reason. Other kids might have both parents, but he bet none were loved or cared for more.

She'd cried some more, but she'd never again mentioned that she wasn't taking good care of him.

"Yeah. Although I might thank Abe on one hand, that doesn't mean I have to reorganize my life for him," Dillon finally answered as he stopped at a signal light.

"Without your help, Samantha will be lost. She probably hasn't had to fight for anything in her life," Marlene said. "You heard Evan mention her trust fund. Money has never been an issue for her. From what I saw this morning, she doesn't have it in her to stand up to Evan. Worse, he knows it, and will walk all over her and relish doing so."

Dillon's mouth tightened. When he worked at Collins for those ten months, Evan treated Dillon as if he were dirt under his feet. Samantha's father, William, had been a good man and had welcomed Dillon. "You should have let me punch him."

"He's not worth the aggravation or the risk of going to jail."

Dillon grinned. "It's not like I haven't been there before."

"But never charged," she quickly pointed out. "Otherwise you wouldn't have gotten the scholarship to MIT."

He turned into the hundred-and-fifty-foot driveway of his mother's single-story house dead center of a cul-de-sac and set in the middle of two lots. That admission letter to MIT had changed his life in more ways than one. "As mean and as bad as the sheriff and his deputies tried to be, they let me slide and called you every time they pulled me over or took me in because of who they thought my father was."

"And you took full advantage of it."

"I was testing my limits." Laughing, he opened his door and got out to open hers. They started up the stone path leading to the wide front door.

He'd wanted to surprise her with the house, but the builder had convinced him that wasn't a good idea. Women had certain ideas about their home. Dillon was glad he'd listened. The two-story red brick had turned into a one-story yellow stucco with sweeping flower beds in front, stone walkways, and generous use of one-way glass.

He followed her inside through the airy foyer with twin tables flanked by cane-backed chairs. The house was as warm and as inviting as she'd intended.

He hadn't been sure about her choice of a dove-gray palette for the home's interior, but it had turned out perfect. There were splashes of yellow and red and green in flowers, pillows, and artwork. The effect was cool and serene.

The baby grand, her pride and joy, sat just off the living room. He'd had it delivered the day she'd moved in. She'd hugged him so tightly he couldn't breathe, but both had been grinning. She didn't read music, but she played beautifully. Next to the piano was a radial arrangement of four wing chairs surrounding a round table. With the light shining through, she liked to sit there and knit.

Across the hall from the living room was the sunken dining room, where mirrored walls increased the brightness. Antique orchid pots with the heavy white petals of the flowers on three-foot stems and candlesticks sat on the table with seating for eight. The floor was sand-washed pine.

Through the wall of glass in the living room, he saw the flower-filled backyard, the infinity pool, the grouping of cast-iron seating, and the big elm trees in the back away from the pool, where a chaise longue waited for her to read and relax on. Off to the side was the newest addition, an outdoor kitchen complete with a dishwasher and refrigerator.

If he could be proud of one thing, it was giving his mother a better life, just as she had given him. "I need to get back."

"I'll miss you." She sat on the arm of the upholstered gray sofa. "We can go by the garage before you leave."

"Just to say hello," Dillon told her. "I never have to worry. Even if you do repairs and let women pay on installment."

"Women need help now and again, and when they come to your garage, they know they won't be taken advantage of."

"Our garage," he corrected.

He'd opened Montgomery Garage after his mother was taken advantage of by an unscrupulous mechanic. Giving the pushy man a piece of his mind wasn't enough. His attitude clearly was, "What are you going to do about it?" It had pissed Dillon off.

Despite never wanting anything to do with Elms Fork, Dillon wasn't going to let anyone take advantage of his mother. Within a month, he had opened a garage and shifted some of his workers from his other locations until he could hire and train additional workers.

Dillon had taken great pleasure in passing out flyers at the beauty shop and grocery stores and running a full-page ad in the newspaper—vetted by his lawyer—of what the inept mechanic had done to his mother's car.

He'd offered to check any woman's car free for the next week and, if repairs were needed, give a 10 percent discount. It had been a resounding success. Women still received the 10 percent discount, and his mother managed the garage.

"Thanks for coming."

"I'll always be here when you need me."

"I know." She hugged him briefly, then headed for the kitchen. "I'll fix lunch."

"What do you plan to do with the money?" Dillon grabbed an apple from the bowl of fruit on the round white oak table and took a sizable bite. Through the window over the sink and the bay window in the kitchen nook, light filled the spacious kitchen and glinted off the glass-front cabinets and the crystal pieces inside.

"Once I have the check, I'll give it some thought." Opening the built-in refrigerator, she pulled out a package of chicken breasts and looked at him. "What do you plan to do with your inheritance?"

He'd certainly walked into that one. "I'll go pack."

. . .

After the reading of the will, Samantha's uncle and his family had been even more hostile toward her. When she couldn't take it any longer, she had retreated to her room and had lain awake most of the night, feeling alone and miserable, wishing there was just one person she could talk to and confide in.

Once she'd thought Mark was that person, but she'd been wrong. She had associates in Houston rather than close friends.

There were too many things running through her mind to sleep. The most disturbing was that her uncle was right. She didn't have the foggiest notion how to run Collins Industry.

At seven-thirty the next morning, she got out of bed, dressed, and went downstairs. Hearing her aunt's strident voice in the dining room, Samantha changed direction and went to the garage. She didn't feel up to more hard looks. After starting her car, she headed for Collins, her thoughts turbulent.

True, she'd worked around the company since she was eight—her grandfather wanted all of the family members to have a rudimentary knowledge of the company and the turbo engine—but that's all she had, a rudimentary knowledge.

She needed Dillon Montgomery. But that wasn't likely to happen. She couldn't even blame him. Although his uncle's salary was discussed, there'd been no mention of a salary for Dillon. She had her grandfather's assets, her trust fund. As half owner, he was entitled to be on the payroll. But she'd learned he didn't need the money.

After he'd left, the lawyer had filled her in on Dillon Montgomery, self-made millionaire. Oddly, she hadn't been surprised that he'd done well. He might have had a bad boy's reputation when he was younger, but when he'd worked for

Collins after he'd graduated from MIT, her father had commented that Dillon's mind was razor sharp and mechanically inclined. He was going places in the industry. In a twist of fate, he had done just that while Collins had spiraled downward.

She stopped at the manned booth. A heavyset man in a gray security uniform came out. "Hello, I'm Ms. Collins, Abe Collins's granddaughter."

The man tipped his sweat-rimmed hat. "Yes, ma'am. I'm sorry for your loss. Mr. Collins was a good man."

"Thank you." She swallowed. "Could you please lift the gate?"

"Yes, ma'am. Sure thing." He scrambled back inside the booth. The arm lifted and she drove through. The plant hadn't changed in all the years since she'd been gone. The picnic tables were still under the trees for the employees to use during nice weather, the basketball goal and the baseball diamond off to the left.

Her father had been a wonderful pitcher. She and her mother had cheered him on at the annual game on the Fourth of July. There had been some good times. In her anger, she'd forgotten.

Samantha parked in the spot designated for her grandfather. She felt strange doing so, but there were no other vacant spots. Her uncle's maroon Jaguar, spotless as always, was already there. Her banged-up two-door, dirty gray Honda Civic looked pitiful beside the luxury sedan. Five years old, it showed the dents and scratches of careless drivers parking next to her and her bad judgment in trying to parallel park. At least she had hit a post and not another car.

Sitting there, she realized she was putting off going inside. She wasn't looking forward to another confrontation. She tended to want people to like her, perhaps because—with the exception of her grandfather—her family didn't. Her cousins planned to fly out this morning, so at least she wouldn't have to deal with them anymore.

Finally, she got out of the car and went inside. She didn't recognize any of the people she met in the entrance or as she moved through the hallway of the offices. She nodded, thinking she might need to call a meeting or something to introduce herself. She hesitated doing that. For one, if she did, they'd know her uncle was passed over for the position.

No matter what he thought of her, she didn't want him embarrassed. But, frankly, she didn't see another way.

She paused in front of her grandfather's door. There was a discreet sign that read, PRESIDENT. Her grandfather wasn't pretentious or showy. He'd built the three-story house because he'd wanted room for his two sons and their children.

His sons and their families had lived with him, but it had never been a happy household. Looking back now, she remembered that, even then, her uncle had been jealous of her father. Unfortunately, the wives and children weren't close either.

Samantha wasn't sure why there was friction between her mother and aunt, but her older cousins seemed to dislike her on general principle. They had rebuffed every attempt she'd made for them to go out together and become friends. They'd always had other plans. She'd finally gotten the message and stopped trying.

Her grandfather must have known and silently grieved for his family.

Her fingers ran lightly over the letters, and she blinked back tears. Her grandfather said he had regrets, but so had she. She'd wasted so much time being angry and missed knowing him better. One thing she'd learned in the past two weeks was that you couldn't go back; you could only move forward.

Opening the door, she came to an abrupt stop. Behind her grandfather's desk sat her uncle. He wore one of his expensive dark gray business suits. When he saw her, his facial expression morphed into annoyance.

She spoke first. "Good morning, Uncle Evan."

"Good morning." He glanced at the metal clock on the desk. "It's seven minutes past eight."

"I'm sorry."

"Sorry is just an excuse." He pushed a file to one side. "Was there something you wanted?"

She frowned. "I thought this was Grandfather's office."

"It was. It's mine now. That farce of a will didn't say anything about office space."

Her grandfather's office was larger, more comfortable, than Evan's. And it would probably make people think he ran the company. "Of course. Is there a time you and I could go over the plant's operations?"

Laughing, he folded his arms across his broad chest and leaned back in his chair. "You want me to help you after what Daddy did to me?"

"You stand to gain as much as I do. You're a Collins," she reasoned.

"Daddy seemed to have forgotten that fact." His mouth flattened into a narrow line. "You're on your own."

She'd suspected as much, but it was still difficult to hear and accept. "I know it's a shock, but the company needs you."

He rose and came around the desk. "Daddy always loved William best. I had to live with knowing I was second. He denied me his love, and now he's doing it again. The company should have been mine. He put me in an untenable position. Once this gets out, I won't be able to hold my head up."

She understood pride. "Maybe we don't have to make an official announcement," she suggested.

"You mean that?"

She had a question of her own. "Are you going to help us?"

"Dillon can go straight to hell."

The reference was too close to her own thoughts of going there. "We're not just talking about Dillon. If the plant closes, it will put people you've known for years out of work. The results will be felt by the town because of the decreased revenues. It will be a domino effect that will leave very few people in the town unaffected."

"Daddy should have thought of that when he put you and Dillon over me," he said angrily.

She loved her grandfather but hated the position he'd put her in. Her uncle and Dillon were both stubborn, and they disliked each other intensely. She was caught in the middle, trying to be a peacemaker. She hated conflict and did her best to avoid it.

How was she going to get them to see common ground . . . if Dillon ever came back? "Dillon is considering not accepting his inheritance," she finally said.

"What?" Her uncle's eyes widened with greed.

"He's not interested," she said, shoving her hands into the pockets of her slacks. He could at least have visited the plant.

Evan studied her. "He tell Boswell that?"

She realized what her uncle was hoping and really didn't want him to go off again, but she knew there was no way out of it. "Yes, but according to Granddad's will, neither one of us can sell or give away our interest in the company for five years."

His mouth tightened. "So, we're stuck with Daddy's bastard."

She bristled. "You shouldn't call him that."

"I'll call him anything I damn well please." Evan went behind his desk and took a seat.

"Uncle Evan, I need your help."

His dark head lifted. "Agree to sign over your half in five years and I might consider it."

She could understand pride, but this was greed. "If you don't help me, there might not be anything left in five years."

"I'm willing to take that chance." He picked up the folder. "You know where to find me."

Dismissed, she left the office, closing the door softly behind her, having no idea what to do. The company had loyal employees who had been there since the beginning. They had no inkling that the company was in danger of closing. Trouble was, she was clueless on how to prevent it from happening.

She only knew she had to try.

The first thing she had to do was move from Houston to Elms Fork, another task she wasn't looking forward to.

At one that afternoon, Samantha pulled into a parking space at the *Houston Sentinel* newspaper. The usual three-hour drive had turned into four because of the heavy traffic just inside Houston's city limits. She would miss many things about Houston; the traffic and the humidity weren't two of them.

After grabbing her handbag and a corrugated box she'd picked up at Collins, Samantha quickly headed for the air-conditioned building. Inside, she checked through security and headed for her office on the third floor, going over the things she needed to take care of before leaving for good. One task in particular she wasn't looking forward to was saying good-bye to Mark Washington.

Stepping into the elevator, Samantha nodded to a couple of employees she'd seen around the building. On the short climb to her floor, her thoughts wandered back to Mark. They'd dated for three months. If it wasn't fireworks, she was comfortable with him and they got along well . . . until he'd been promoted to senior sportswriter seven months ago.

Suddenly he was gone more than he was in Houston. He loved the excitement of covering top sports events across the country, and she hated it. She wanted him there with her. She wasn't like her mother, quietly supporting her husband and taking care of the family while her man was gone more often than he was home.

Once she got over her annoyance, she realized she didn't mind the separation because she missed him; she minded because his job was more important than she was. It had been a startling revelation, one she hadn't been happy with. She hadn't thought she was that needy or that selfish. She was also a coward.

She'd used the old line about "our lives are going in two different directions" as the reason for breaking up with Mark instead of telling him the truth. She didn't love him deeply enough to accept his schedule and be happy for him.

Two steps off the elevator, Samantha came face-to-face with her boss, Isabel Knox, the features editor. In her early sixties, Isabel's auburn hair had turned gray. She had a moody disposition and a penchant for wearing strong colors that often clashed with her pale complexion—today she had on a lime-green suit.

Her walls were filled with awards for her skills as a savvy newspaper reporter.

"Samantha, I'm so sorry to hear about your grandfather." Isabel enveloped Samantha in a brief, awkward hug. "If there is anything we can do, please don't hesitate to let us know."

"Thank you." Isabel wasn't a people person, but she was a great editor. "Actually, I came back to resign."

"Resign?" Up went Isabel's pencil-thin eyebrows.

"Can we talk in my office?" Samantha asked.

"Mine is closer." Isabel entered her office, stepped aside for Samantha, and closed the door after her. "Now, what's going on? You're one of my best reporters."

Samantha was taken aback. Isabel was miserly with praise but quick to rip an article or a reporter apart. "I am?"

Isabel waved a slim hand. "You're still here, aren't you?"

True, but it would have been nice to know she was doing a good job. Since newspaper reporting wasn't her first or second choice, she'd always worked doubly hard to do her best. She had pictured herself working for a high-fashion magazine in New York. She hadn't even gotten a response to her résumé.

"Why are you resigning?" Isabel asked, getting back to the point. "It doesn't have anything to do with you and Mark breaking up, does it?"

There were no secrets at the newspaper. "No. My grandfather left me part ownership of Collins Industry, a company he founded and was president of."

"What kind of company?"

"We make turbochargers."

Now Isabel was the one taken aback. "What do you know about turbochargers—or cars, for that matter?"

Add one more name to the growing list of people who

thought she wasn't qualified to run Collins. "What I don't know I can learn. I'm sorry, but unfortunately I can't give you a two-week notice. Today I need to find a Realtor to sell my condo and hire a moving service. If possible, I plan to leave in the morning."

"Can't someone else run this company? You have the piece with the mayor's homeless program coming up."

"Family comes first," Samantha said simply. The newspaper could easily assign someone else. That wasn't the case with Collins. She was it. She'd let her grandfather down by staying away; she wouldn't do it again. "He—he asked me just before he passed to run the company. There's no way I can walk away."

"I suppose." Isabel blew out a frustrated breath and folded her arms. "If you find you miss reporting, the door is always open."

Samantha nodded. "That means a lot. Thank you and goodbye." After leaving her boss's office, she went to hers, which was located at the end of the hall. There wasn't much to pack. She'd never been one for a lot of knickknacks.

Placing the box on the desk she always kept neat, she glanced around. She'd moved from a cubicle to a real office the same week she and Mark started dating. At the time, she'd thought it was a good sign. Shaking away the memory, she removed the awards for journalism and community service from the wall behind her desk. Next came the aloe vera plant that thrived despite her neglect.

Picking up the picture of her parents, she stared at their smiling faces and wondered if they would be proud of the person she'd become. She wasn't sure, and that bothered her. When she'd lost them, she'd turned her back on her family and the family business. She'd let grief and anger rule her every decision.

It had taken the loss of her grandfather for her to take a long hard look at her life. She didn't like what she saw.

Her door opened. She glanced over her shoulder. Mark Washington stood in the doorway, as if hesitant of his reception. His instincts were spot on. She wasn't in the mood for this, but she was afraid he wasn't going to give her a choice.

In his mid-thirties, the cuffs of his blue oxford shirt rolled over his wrists, he was tall and slender rather than muscular. Women at the newspaper thought he was handsome. Her traitorous mind speculated on what they'd think of Dillon.

"Why didn't you call and tell me you were coming home?"

No condolences, no "I'm glad to see you," just accusations. Mark was also pragmatic. Once she hadn't minded. "I've had a lot on my mind."

He cursed under his breath, then quickly crossed the room to take her into his arms. "I'm sorry to hear about your grandfather. I missed you so much. Missed us being together."

Samantha briefly closed her eyes, searching for the spark of excitement at being held by a man she thought she loved, and felt . . . nothing. Dillon made her tingle with just a look.

Pushing out of his arms Samantha went behind her desk before speaking. "I'm resigning to run my grandfather's company."

"What?" He rounded the desk to stand beside her. "You've got to be kidding me."

She tossed a cup full of pens into the corrugated box. "Thanks for the vote of confidence."

He took her arms, turned her toward him. "Don't be angry. You told me time and time again how much you disliked your grandfather's company, complained that it overshadowed your parents' lives and ruined yours."

He was right. "Seeing Grandfather, talking with him during his last hours, made me realize a lot about myself, my parents, and the company. I was angry with everyone when my
parents were killed, and I transferred that anger to the town,
the company, my grandfather. I was wrong. My father loved
Collins. I won't turn my back on the company."

"All right." He nodded slowly. "I can probably drive down
in a couple of weeks—"

"No." She stepped away. "I'm sorry, Mark. It's over between
us. You're a great friend—"

"We were more than friends," he interrupted.

"Once." Her smile was sad. "I'd like for us to always be
friends."

His mouth narrowed into a thin line. "This is not what I
wanted between us."

"It's the way it has to be. Good-bye, Mark."

He went to the door. "I won't say good-bye. You know how
to find me."

Samantha sighed as the door shut a little too firmly. Another man she'd ticked off. She reached for her tape recorder
and continued to clean out her desk and office.

Both her uncle and Mark expected her to change her mind
and give in. They were in for a long wait.

Three

· · · · · · · · · · · · · · ·

Some things you ignored. A red light on the dashboard of your car wasn't one of them.

Wednesday afternoon, a mile inside Elms Fork city limits, Samantha gripped the steering wheel and called her automobile service. In a matter of minutes, she was creeping toward Montgomery Garage with her caution lights on. Well aware of how long she might have to wait for a tow truck, she'd decided to chance damaging the car.

Out of nowhere, she remembered Isabel's and Mark's comments about her not knowing anything about cars. She gritted her teeth and flicked on her signal to turn into the garage.

She counted nine bays. All were full, and more cars were in the parking lot. Samantha backed into the first available parking spot, proud that she'd considered giving them enough space when they looked under the hood or had to push the car into one of the bays.

Getting out of the car, she sniffed. She was only marginally less nervous that she didn't smell smoke.

"Samantha?"

Samantha jerked around to see Dillon's mother coming toward her. She wore chocolate slacks, a cream-colored blouse, and chocolate walking shoes. The mother was as striking as the son, with hair just as thick. Hers was straight and framed a face with high cheekbones and warm black eyes.

"Hello, Ms. Montgomery."

"Marlene, please." She extended her hand. "Your emergency car service said you were on your way."

Samantha took the hand, surprised to feel the slight calluses. "The red light came on." She shifted uncomfortably, stuck one hand into the pocket of her jeans. "I'm a bit late with my oil change."

Marlene smiled. "That's probably not the cause of the light. Let's take a look." She popped the hood. Smoke billowed.

Samantha automatically caught Marlene's arm, pulled her away from the car. "Be careful. You could get hurt or ruin your clothes."

Smiling in reassurance, Marlene gently brushed Samantha's hand aside. "Believe me, after all these years, I know how to get grease stains out." She bent over the engine, then straightened a few seconds later. "Busted water hose. It will be a couple of hours before we can get to you. The cost will be sixty-five dollars and take about thirty minutes. We can take you home or you can wait."

Samantha simply stared. "You know that quickly?"

Marlene's smile wavered. "If you'd like another mechanic to look at it, I can pull one for a minute."

Samantha was shaking her head before Marlene finished. "I'm not doubting you, I just wanted to know how you knew so quickly."

Marlene pointed to the split hose. "Simple visual. It wasn't that difficult."

"It would have been to me." Sighing, Samantha curved her arms around her handbag. "I'd like for you to fix the car and I'll accept a ride home. Have you always known about cars? I only know how to put gas in mine."

"I didn't when I first started, but I was determined to learn," Marlene confessed with narrowed eyes. "Dillon didn't have the time or the inclination to run the business here, and since I was the cause of him opening the garage, I felt obligated to learn and help."

A frown darted across Samantha's brow. "How is that?"

"Long story short, an unscrupulous mechanic cheated me out of fifteen hundred dollars and then got smart about it," she said. "In a month I was running a garage geared toward accommodating women, and in three months the mechanic was out of business."

"Good for you. I've been taken advantage of," Samantha said. "I'm glad you had Dillon."

"He's the best son a mother could ask for. Let's go inside and sign the work release form." Marlene started toward the office. "I called Collins yesterday and couldn't get you."

"You did?"

Marlene opened the half-glass door of the white stone building. "The operator rang your grandfather's office. I spoke with Evan."

Samantha stepped inside the large office with healthy plants and an aquarium. Through an open door she saw a waiting room with a TV and a small bookcase. "I can imagine he wasn't helpful."

"He said you were in Houston and hung up." Marlene

went around the counter and handed Samantha a service con-
tract on a clipboard. "I'm glad you didn't stay."

Samantha bit her lower lip. "You're probably the only one.
Uncle Evan doesn't have any faith in me. Neither did my co-
workers in Houston when I told them."

"Do you have faith in yourself?"

Samantha glanced upward. She opened her mouth, then
closed it. "It comes and goes," she said truthfully.

"Then you'll fail," Marlene said, her expression sad. "The
world will always have an opinion of you, but what counts is
what you think of yourself. It won't be easy running Collins.
If you go in with self-doubts, they'll overwhelm you."

"It isn't easy when no one believes in you." Samantha
handed back the completed form.

"Abe had faith in you. He was a shrewd man. He wouldn't
have made you a partner if he had doubts." Marlene took the
form, placed it in a plastic folder, and hung it on a hook with
several others. "I also have faith in you."

"You do?" Pleasure spread through Samantha.

"Like Abe, you care about the employees and the company.
That counts for a lot." Marlene came back around the counter.
"You came back when you could have stayed in Houston. That
took courage."

"I've put my condo on the market. A moving company
will deliver my things on Friday, but I'm not sure where to put
them."

"Why not the guest cottage behind the main house? Your
grandmother planned to decorate it, but she never did. There
might be some things in there, but probably not much."

Samantha thought of the rumors of Abe fathering Dillon.
"He loved her very much."

"Yes, he did. That kind of love is rare and precious." Marlene pulled a key from her pocket. "I can take you home."

"Thank you." Samantha didn't say anything else until they were in the van. "Is Dillon coming back?"

Marlene started the motor before answering. "I haven't asked and he hasn't said."

Samantha leaned her head back against the seat. "Maybe I should call him." She straightened. "If you don't mind giving me his number."

"Not a good idea." Marlene pulled out of the parking lot into the street. "Dillon doesn't like to be pushed. He has to make up his own mind about Collins."

"But what if he doesn't want to help?"

Marlene stopped for a signal light. "Then you'll have to learn the business on your own."

That was exactly what Samantha was afraid of.

Marlene had been truthful with Samantha when she'd said Dillon couldn't be pushed. Even as a toddler, he'd been independent and wanted to do things his way. She'd fretted that his feet would be crooked because he liked dressing himself and, more often than not, he put his shoes on the wrong foot. But he could be led. She'd learned the gentle art from trial and error, tears, and sleepless nights.

The phone on her nightstand rang. She didn't need caller ID to know it was Dillon. He was the only person who would call her after ten.

"Hi, Dillon. Home or still at the garage?" She closed the book she had been reading in bed and removed her eyeglasses.

"The garage. Pulling the motor out of a Ferrari. The wife was frantic when the tow truck hauled it in. It's her husband's pride and joy."

"Something tells me she wasn't supposed to drive it?"

He chuckled. "They've only been married a year."

"She won't make it to two if she goes behind his back."

"I think she's learned her lesson. I've never seen a woman more hysterical or make more promises to me, her absent husband, and God, before. How was your day?"

Marlene smiled and leaned back more fully against the padded gray silk headboard that matched the draperies. Showtime. "Busy as usual. We worked on Samantha's car. She's one lucky woman. Are you going to give the woman with the Ferrari the usual ten percent discount?"

"Hardly. Why was she lucky?"

"Her water hose burst a few blocks from the garage instead of on the way back from Houston. She's moving back to run Collins."

"What she knows about cars you could probably put on the head of a pin."

"Probably as much as I did, but thanks to you and your patience, I'm as good as any of my crew. It makes a difference when someone has faith in you."

Silence. He probably had a hard frown on his face, but he was also thinking. Dillon might have a bad-boy reputation, but he liked helping people. He mentored potential dropouts with the local school districts. What young boys didn't like cars?

"Thanks for calling. You better get back to work on the Ferrari. Good night. Love you."

"Night, Mama. Love you too."

Marlene hung up the phone. She'd give Dillon a week tops. He wasn't the type of man to walk away from his obligation or let a woman fail if he could prevent it.

However, he wouldn't make it easy for Samantha. But that might be a good thing. She needed to toughen up. Marlene just hoped she'd eventually learn to stand up for herself. If not, Samantha would never be the woman she could be proud of.

In less than a week Dillon was back in Elms Fork.

His mother hadn't said anything more about him helping Samantha, but her silence was making him feel that he'd shirked his responsibility by leaving. That was her way. She never yelled, no matter his provocation, and he'd given her plenty of opportunities—speeding tickets, getting drunk, fooling around with older women—he'd been a hell-raiser. And there had been plenty of people ready to help him earn his reputation for being wild.

He'd come down in his truck, with his motorcycle in the bed. Even though he'd only gotten a few scratches in the past, his mother still didn't like him riding it, and never from Dallas, forty miles away. He figured he'd worried her enough growing up, but he liked to tease her that he hadn't given her any gray hairs.

He slowed going up the rise, aware that when he started down the incline, he'd see Collins Industry on the right. He usually stared straight ahead. This time he looked at the complex. No matter how he tried to go around it, Abe Collins had helped his mother when no one else had.

She'd grown up in foster care and aged out at eighteen. She'd put herself through secretarial school and gotten a job as

Abe's secretary. She could read Abe's "chicken scratch" handwriting, type over one hundred words a minute, and take
Abe's rapid-fire dictation.

She hadn't been afraid of hard work. She'd wanted to make
something of herself, and despite getting pregnant with him
when she was twenty-two, she'd succeeded.

Abe had told Dillon, soon after he'd graduated from MIT
and gone to work at Collins, that next to his own wife, Edith,
Marlene was one of the most loyal and loving women he'd
known. She'd protect those she loved, and God help those who
wronged them.

The old man really had loved his mother, and if for that
reason alone, Dillon flicked on his signal, slowed, and turned
onto the paved driveway of Collins Industry. Not even seeing
one of his school bullies again deterred him.

"You want something, Dillon?"

Dillon stared at Sonny Sparks. His belly hung over his belt,
and his pimpled face was just as homely as Dillon remembered.
He'd barely made it through high school. "I have an appointment with Ms. Collins."

Sonny sneered. "She didn't say anything about you coming."

Dillon scratched his nose, silently reminding Sonny that
his was crooked because he'd provoked Dillon one time too
many when they were in the eighth grade. They both knew
Dillon would happily do it again.

"I'll check." Sonny retreated to the safety of the booth.

Dillon waited. Apparently, Samantha hadn't bothered to tell
anyone that he was half owner. He couldn't blame her, especially since he had walked away. He wasn't worried about her
cheating him, from what he'd been able to find out. He never
went blind into anything—the company was barely making

payroll. One of those reasons was Evan's ten-thousand-dollar biweekly salary plus expenses—and he always had a lot of them.

Dillon might not be able to do anything about the salary, but the expense account came to an end today. He realized as the thought went through his head that he was going to give it a try. For how long, heaven only knew.

The arm of the gate swung upward. Dillon pulled through.

Samantha was surprised to learn Dillon was at the main entrance. She had begun to think he wasn't coming back. She'd driven by his garage a couple of times, tempted to go in and speak with his mother again to try to find out, but she'd always been too chicken. She didn't want her suspicions confirmed that Dillon had turned his back on her and the company.

The door opened after the briefest knock. Dillon stepped inside, looking sinful in faded blue jeans, crisp white shirt, and baseball cap with MONTGOMERY GARAGE on the bill. She desperately needed his help to turn the company around, but she wasn't about to beg him. He'd do it because he wanted to and for no other reason.

"Good afternoon, Dillon."

"Why are you in Evan's office instead of the old man's office?"

He could have at least spoken politely after being gone for so long. "It doesn't matter where I work as long as the job gets done."

He cocked his head to one side and braced wide-palmed hands on his narrow waist. "What have you done in the past week to get the job done?"

Samantha blinked, bit her lower lip. She didn't have an answer.

Dillon grunted. "Let's go."

He didn't give her a chance to answer. But if there was a chance he was going to help, he could be as high-handed as he wanted.

Dillon ignored the stares as he and Samantha walked onto the production floor. Some of the people actually stopped working. He recognized some of the faces. A few he'd had run-ins with, like Sparks at the gate, others he recognized from school. He didn't see how a person could live his whole life in one place.

"Can I help you, Ms. Collins?"

Dillon turned to see a man in his mid-forties he didn't recognize rushing toward them. The monogram on his long-sleeved shirt read, PLANT MANAGER. Dillon recalled he'd been with Abe when he collapsed.

Samantha looked up at Dillon for guidance. It shouldn't matter that even though he knew he must have ticked her off, she was still willing to defer to him. She'd do whatever it took to save Collins.

Dillon extended his hand. "Dillon Montgomery."

Frowning, the man extended his. "Frank Crowley, the plant manager."

"Ms. Collins and I would like to tour the plant and get an overview of productivity and projections," Dillon requested.

Crowley's questioning gaze swung to Samantha.

"Please," she said sweetly, and smiled. "I know you're busy, but we'd really appreciate it."

The plant manager's expression went from puzzled to rapt in seconds. "Anything, Ms. Collins. All you have to do is ask."

Dillon had the strange urge to shake Crowley and tell him to back off when he kept staring at Samantha. "Now would be a good time," he said tightly.

The man jerked, flushed. "This way."

Dillon glanced at Samantha before following. Of course she was frowning at him, but she hadn't minded old Frank eating her up with his eyes. Dillon's problem was that he wanted to do some nibbling of his own.

During the tour, Samantha stuck to Dillon's heels like a burr. He'd lost count of the number of times she had bumped into him or brushed against him. Each time she did, his brain and blood headed south. It was all he could do to concentrate on what Crowley was saying.

He'd turned to glare at her once, only to find her busy scribbling on the pad she carried. She was trying, he'd give her that, but she was also wreaking havoc on him. Perhaps Abe was getting back at Dillon after all.

Samantha learned a lot during the tour and thought it had gone well despite Dillon's abruptness with the plant manager and all the speculative looks from the employees. Some actually stopped working—until Mr. Crowley stared them down. Dillon didn't seem to notice.

Since she had been on the floor before and they hadn't paid much attention to her, she knew they were looking at Dillon. All the stares annoyed her.

He was just a man. Granted, a prime specimen with hard muscles and a sexy mouth, but still just a man. The reasons for the frank looks were probably varied. It could be the rumor that Dillon was her grandfather's illegitimate son or speculation over whether he'd done all the crazy things gossip said he had. Then, too, he'd probably had a run-in with a few of the men, dated more than a few of the women. It could have been because he was wealthy or someone had remembered he used to work there. The list was a long one.

Samantha had tried to keep up with Dillon's long-legged stride, take notes, and pretend she knew what she was looking at. She'd kept bumping into him, and each time her body would heat. He affected her as no man ever had.

Once they were finished and she had thanked the plant manager, she wanted to ask Dillon what he thought, to keep her mind off his tempting body and on the business at hand. But he didn't look as if he were in the mood for talking. The man's eyes could speak volumes. Then, too, discussing the company in the hallway wasn't a good idea.

They were almost back to her office when Evan stepped out of her grandfather's—Evan's new office. He stiffened.

Samantha groaned inwardly and shot a look at Dillon. He had that hard expression on his face that didn't bode well for her uncle. She didn't even think of trying to interfere. She needed Dillon, and they both knew it.

"I want you to move out of Abe's office by eight in the morning," Dillon said without preamble. "Sam and I will be taking over the larger space."

"You can't do that," Evan snapped.

"Wanna bet?" Dillon stepped into her uncle's space. "We can do this easy or hard. Makes no difference to me." Not giving her irate uncle a chance to say anything further, Dillon stepped around him and went into her office.

She didn't like the way Evan was glaring at her. He'd find an opportunity to make Samantha pay. "I'm sorry," she mumbled, and hurried after Dillon.

Inside her office, she said, "That wasn't the way to handle things. There is no reason to make an enemy out of Uncle Evan."

Dillon's dark brows lifted. "He's already our enemy, and if you think otherwise, you're living in la-la-land."

Her chin lifted. "There's no reason to be condescending."

"You haven't seen anything yet." He crossed to the door. "You better get used to it, if you want my help. I've found that the straightforward approach is best. If you have problems with that, keep it to yourself."

"Now, look here. You can't talk to me that way."

"I just did. Take the rose-colored blinders off, Sam. This is the real world, where the weak get stepped on." He opened the door. "I'll see you in the morning at eight sharp."

Dillon closed the door, then headed for the parking lot. He might have an explosive situation on his hands—if he let it happen.

He wouldn't. In his careless youth, he might have laughed at the risks and taken the plunge. Older, and he hoped wiser, he considered the odds and the morning after. He never wanted dawn to break and find himself conflicted.

He'd intentionally called Samantha "Sam" because he'd noticed once again how beautiful she was, how lost she'd looked. It was all he could do not to reach out and pull her into his arms, reassure her that everything was going to be all right. Who would have thought he'd be attracted to the vulnerable, lost type?

He'd seen that look on her face twice before. When her

parents were killed in that plane crash, he'd heard she'd been inconsolable. Who could blame her? Before then, he hadn't considered death. He'd seen her a couple of weeks later in town with her cousins. Shelby, as usual, tried to come on to him. Samantha's gaze had locked with his. He'd never seen such grief and misery. Her eyes had looked lost, and he'd felt bad for her. He'd offered his condolences.

The next time was the night of her prom, the day Abe fired him. She'd offered her body and backed it up with a kiss that rang all of his bells. He hadn't seen her again until the day of Abe's funeral.

He might have looked out for her then, but he wasn't some black knight on a white charger. Wrong woman. Wrong time.

If she wanted a blazing hot affair, he was her man, but he had a feeling she'd want much more. Plus, his mother liked her. Sam might want to be tied down to Collins for five years, but once it was back to making a profit, he was out of there and back to his carefree life.

Samantha counted to ten and then counted again. She would have liked to kick Dillon in his prime butt. He couldn't even be bothered to say her name. If she didn't need him—

The door to her office burst open. Evan's gaze searched the room. "Where's Dillon?"

Samantha almost rolled her eyes. His bravado didn't fool her. He could have easily taken Dillon on in the hallway earlier or at the reading of the will. He'd backed down each time.

Her uncle might try to intimidate her—but not Dillon. He was half afraid of Dillon. So was she, but for an entirely different reason.

"He left, but he's coming back in the morning. It's probably best you move back to this office this afternoon," she told him.

"I see you've made your choice. I thought you might come to your senses," he practically snarled. "Neither you nor Dillon knows how to run this company."

Fear crept over her. She had only one answer. "Grandfather had faith in us."

"He was senile, and you and that no-good Dillon are taking advantage of it. You'll run Collins into the ground," her uncle ranted.

She wouldn't let him see her fear that he was right. "I'm sorry you feel that way."

"Sorry you feel that way," he mimicked. "You're going to be chewed up and spit out. The bad thing is that you're going to take this company and me down with you."

"Dillon—"

"Was fired because of his big mouth and little sense. He could give a rat's ass about Collins. He certainly doesn't need the money. Just because Daddy had remorse he didn't marry his mistress is no reason to pull the company down."

Samantha flinched. Her stomach dipped. "We don't know he is Grandfather's son."

Evan rolled his eyes. "Get your head out of the clouds. Why else would he will a multimillion-dollar company to him?"

Samantha didn't have a comeback. She'd asked herself the same thing. She'd just always hoped the rumors were untrue. She didn't want to be attracted to her half uncle or burn in hell because she couldn't control her wayward thoughts. Her stomach clenched again.

Evan's eyes narrowed. "Don't tell me you're stupid enough to be attracted to him?"

"I'm not," she blurted, then rushed on to say, "He can help Collins. If anyone knows motors and cars, it's Dillon."

"Knowing cars and running a company with two hundred employees are miles apart—but you're going to find that out." Evan went to the door. "I'm going home while I have one to go to."

Samantha sank heavily into her seat. She hadn't thought it would be this difficult.

Cleary, neither Dillon nor her uncle had any faith in her ability. Both thought she was a pushover. The sad thing was, she wasn't sure they were wrong.

Four

· · · · · · · · · · · · · ·

Samantha didn't want to go home, but unfortunately there was no place else to go. She'd put her furniture in the guest cottage, but the electricity wouldn't be turned on until next week. The plant closed at five. At a quarter to six, hers was the last car to leave. She waved to the attendant at the gate as she drove past. He gave her a curt nod. The poor man was probably anxious to get home and was annoyed at her for keeping him so late. Feeling melancholy, she pulled onto the highway.

Sadly, she'd broken ties with everyone in Elms Fork when she'd left for college. She didn't "friend" her classmates online or return for the tenth anniversary of her graduation. She'd blamed everyone connected with Collins Industry for her parents' death. The town and the people living there were an unwanted reminder.

Driving through the town on the bricked streets that still annoyed her no matter how historic, she noted that Elms Fork had changed very little over the years. The shell of the iron factory was a reminder that not all businesses had survived. The same went for the glass factory. Oil derricks dotted the landscape, but they no longer pumped oil.

The one constant in the past forty-one years was Collins Industry. From the taxes it paid to its charitable donations, the company had an indelible impact on the town and, as she'd told her uncle, its failure would touch many of the people living there.

And he didn't care.

She saw the top of her grandfather's house peeking over a strand of trees before she turned onto the long driveway. No matter what the will said, she'd always think of it as his. In the back, she parked in one of the seven bays. She sighed on seeing her uncle's and aunt's Jaguars. Her aunt's was red.

Her granddaddy's black truck sat next to her grandmother's big Mercedes. The cover had grayed over the years. She had to remember to order a cover for her grandfather's truck. Samantha supposed she now owned both. Just as he'd kept his wife's car, Samantha planned to keep his truck. However, she wasn't ready to drive either.

She had no idea what had happened to her parents' cars. She'd cried each time she saw them. One morning they were gone. Now, she wished she had been stronger.

Leaving the garage, she followed the bricked path to the back door. Regrets, she was learning, was something everyone had. The best you could probably do was move forward and try not to make more. When she opened the door, the aroma of food greeted her. Her stomach rumbled. She had skipped lunch because she hadn't been hungry. Worry could do that to you.

After washing up in the utility room, she started for the main dining room. She'd ignore her aunt and uncle as they did her and just eat.

Entering the dining room, she saw her uncle and aunt seated at a table that sat twelve. As usual, he was at the head and she at the foot. Her parents would have been sitting as close as possible. Sometimes she thought her aunt and uncle tolerated each other more than they loved each other.

They didn't wait for her to eat, and if she happened to be there, they made it uncomfortable being in the same room with them. Her aunt ignored her or shot her annoyed looks. Not a pleasant situation. Tonight she was too hungry to care.

Louise, the cook who had been in the employ of her grandfather for as long as Samantha could remember, was serving them. Samantha had gone to school with Louise's youngest daughter, Aretha. A few days after she arrived, Louise had proudly showed Samantha the picture of Aretha with her husband and their three children. They lived in Chicago.

Then and now, Samantha pushed aside the spurt of jealousy. She wanted children and a husband who was there each night to help tuck them in bed. At thirty with no prospects, she was unlikely to get either.

Louise turned from serving her aunt and went stock-still, bewilderment flittering across her face. "Samantha."

"Hi, everyone. Whatever you cooked, Louise, it smells delicious."

Louise's gaze jumped from her to her aunt, then back to her. *Not good,* Samantha thought.

"I didn't think you were dining with us, Samantha. I had Louise prepare only enough for Evan and myself. You know how I detest wasting food." Her aunt picked up her wineglass. "I'm sure the cook can prepare you a sandwich."

"I'm sorry, Samantha," Louise rushed on to say, her hands gripping the gold-trimmed serving dish. "I can thaw out another pork chop. It won't be stuffed, but I can smother it for you and fix some rice."

She'd choke before she'd let her aunt and uncle know how embarrassed she felt. "Thank you, Louise, but that won't be necessary. I just came to let you know I have plans for dinner." Smiling, Samantha left the dining room and went back to the garage. Her uncle had a satisfied smirk on his face. He'd done that on purpose. She wouldn't give him the satisfaction of creating a scene. She certainly wasn't going to put Louise in the middle.

In her car, she headed back to the grocery store. She'd never been much for dining alone, and two nights at the Golden Cow buffet was enough. If she kept that up, she wouldn't be able to fit into her pants.

In the crowded parking lot, she squeezed her car between a truck and a Suburban, almost guaranteeing another dent. She slung the strap of her handbag over her shoulder, grabbed a shopping cart, and headed inside for the meat aisle. She'd learned how to cook out of self-preservation so she wouldn't starve. After eating, her uncle and aunt always retired to their suite of rooms. Louise wouldn't tell on Samantha. They'd never know.

Deep in thought, Samantha started around the corner of an aisle. It just ticked her off that— Her basket rammed that of another shopper. "I'm sor— Ms. Montgomery."

"Hello, Samantha," she said, laughing. "I've done that plenty of times. No harm done. I see you're just getting started."

Samantha felt her face heat. "I thought I might like to grill."

"I'm heading in that direction as well." Marlene reached over to the shelf and picked up a can of black pepper. "Have you gotten settled in at the plant?"

Samantha considered lying. "No, but I'm not giving up."

"Good." Marlene patted her arm. "You can do it."

"Dillon doesn't think so," she blurted. Her eyes widened at her admission.

"Then you'll just have to change his mind." His mother stopped in front of the meat case. "Porterhouse, rib eye, or T-bone?"

"All sound great." Her stomach chose that moment to beg for food.

"Hi, Marlene," a tall man with a white apron behind the counter greeted her. "What can I get you today?"

She pointed to the porterhouse steaks. "Three steaks—two about a half pound each—and a third one the largest you have."

The man chuckled and selected the steaks. "Dillon's back in town."

"Yes," she said, smiling back. "I was at the garage when he called. I know he'll be hungry when he gets home."

Samantha frowned. "He left the plant two hours ago."

Marlene accepted the meat and thanked the butcher as he moved to help another customer. "He said he was going riding on the Black Devil."

"The Black Devil?"

Marlene's brows bunched with concern. "His motorcycle. I intensely dislike him riding it, but he enjoys it so I try not to worry." She turned to Samantha. "You could help. How about coming home and having dinner with us?"

Samantha actually backed up a step. "No, I couldn't."

"You'd be doing me a huge favor, and we could get better acquainted. Abe meant a great deal to me and was there for me when I needed him the most; I'd like to be there for you."

The rumor of Dillon's paternity flickered at the corner of

Samantha's mind, but she pushed it away. It was none of her business. They both had been free adults. At least her grandfather hadn't walked away as some men would have.

Besides, if she went home, there was always the outside chance that her aunt and uncle might come back downstairs. She'd had more than enough of their condescension. And maybe, in a social setting, she and Dillon would learn to get along better and work together. It was well-known he loved and respected his mother. At least he wouldn't be overly rude.

"I accept. I'll go get a steak."

Marlene smiled. "Why do you think I got three?"

Dillon turned the corner of the street his mother lived on and throttled down. There were only a handful of homes on the quiet cul-de-sac. Her neighbors were around her age and settled, with children grown and gone. He was the only one who drove a motorcycle, so when he let it all out she'd get a couple of phone calls. In his youth he would have gotten back on his bike and let it roar again.

Dillon almost smiled as he hit the driveway. He'd been a handful in those days. At times he still was. So why was he letting Samantha Collins drive him crazy?

The smile abruptly died. There had never been a time when he'd needed to let the bike go full-throttle more than now. Somehow he had to come up with an answer.

Seeing a dirty gray Honda Civic in the circular driveway, he was tempted to turn around and leave. He didn't particularly feel like company. At least he knew his mother wasn't matchmaking. She knew his ironclad rule on dating women in Elms Fork.

He scowled. Then why was he lusting after Samantha?

He kicked the rest stand of the motorcycle then threw his long leg over the bike and removed his helmet. Another concession to his mother. He'd much rather have the wind blowing in his face. He thought better that way. He needed to come up with a plan to help Collins and stop thinking about how good it would feel to have Sam's warm breath teasing his neck and other parts of his body.

That kind of thought would get him nowhere but hot and bothered with no way to ease the ache in his body. He had a good mind. His teachers, even when he was goofing off in school, had always been quick to point that fact out. He'd just used it for devilment instead of good.

All he had to do was figure out why he couldn't keep her out of his mind and he'd be well on his way to shutting her out. It could be that it was because he hadn't been with a woman in several months. Running four garages and consulting with the vintage racing circuit took a lot of his time. And although there were women at those events more than ready to show him a good time, that wasn't his way.

He might have the reputation of a stud, but he was careful whom he took to bed. When he did, he made sure she enjoyed herself as much as he did and that they were both protected. He relished the hot rush of pleasure, the incredible feel of a woman's soft, yielding body against his.

But the woman always knew he wasn't sticking around, that both were free to move on. True, he was always the first to hit the door, but he never left the woman feeling used.

At least he hoped not.

Blowing out a breath, he went to his truck and placed the helmet inside. A few steps farther, he smelled the unmistakable aroma of steaks grilling. Instead of going inside, he took the stone pathway to the backyard. Opening the gate, he passed the bed of blooming blue hydrangeas that came to his waist.

When he didn't see his mother at the outdoor kitchen, he headed to the refrigerator to get a drink. He had the beer bottle tilted to his mouth when he heard laughter. He froze. His skin prickled. Slowly he pivoted, knowing as he did that he'd see Sam.

"Hi, Dillon," his mother greeted him. "Perfect timing. Look who kept me company so I wouldn't worry about you riding your bike."

Samantha didn't like the way Dillon slowly lowered the bottle and stared at her. Maybe this wasn't a good idea after all. She'd have to try to bluff it out. "Hello, Dillon. You have a nice ride?"

"Apparently not good enough," he muttered, and lowered the bottle more.

Out of the corner of her eye, Samantha saw Marlene shake her head once. Dillon looked skyward, then took a sip of beer.

"Samantha, why don't you get the vegetables off the grill and Dillon can grab the steaks," Marlene said. "I'll finish setting the table."

Samantha wanted to call her back, but she was already gone. She stared at Dillon. He stared back.

"I won't bite."

"Are you sure?" she asked without thinking.

"Let's just say the jury is still out on that one." Placing the bottle on the wooden work counter, he lifted the top of the grill. Smoke billowed out and with it the mouthwatering aromas. "The corn is not going to get itself off the grill."

Calling herself crazy, she stepped beside him and picked up the platter and tongs. Her stomach chose that moment to growl. Embarrassment tinted her cheeks.

"When was the last time you ate?"

She supposed it was too much to ask that he ignore her stomach. "I grabbed a bite this morning, but didn't feel like eating lunch."

"Louise quit?" He placed the steaks on the platter.

She finished getting the vegetables. He couldn't think any worse of her. "Aunt Janice didn't think I was eating with them."

His mouth tightened. "The house is half yours and that means you can give orders just as well as she can."

"I don't like confrontation," she repeated, already knowing what was coming.

"Then people are going to—"

"Walk all over me," she finished. "My uncle already told me."

"It turns my stomach to agree with him, but he's right," Dillon said. "People respect authority and will push you to the wall if you let them. You're half owner of Collins Industry, act like it."

Samantha bristled. "Coming from you, that's rich. You walked out on me."

Something flickered in his eyes. "I'm back now."

"Are you staying?"

He reached for her platter. "Depends. Let's eat."

. . .

Dillon wished his mother had let him hit Evan. To think any man would be heartless enough to withhold food! Evan could have overruled his wife. He hadn't. He was trying to make it as difficult as possible for Samantha to stay. Despite living with two hostile people, she was sticking. It was no cakewalk living with people who obviously didn't like you. She was also facing up to him.

He'd seen the apprehension on her face when he first saw her, but she'd stayed. She wanted to honor her grandfather's wish. He'd give her points for loyalty and tenacity.

Sam had on the white blouse and black slacks she'd worn to work. His body still reacted to hers, wanted hers. Not good. He'd gone riding on his bike to get her out of his head and here she was, sitting at his mother's table, delicately putting away everything placed before her.

His mother noticed as well. She kept the conversation going with him, occasionally speaking to Samantha, mostly leaving her to eat.

Dillon was aware he'd been a bit terse and figured he could relent just a bit. They weren't enemies. It wasn't her fault he could imagine her needy and naked beneath him.

"Dillon."

Caught, he jerked his gaze to his mother. His mother had an uncanny way of reading him. He worked hard to keep his expression neutral and not guilty. "Yes, ma'am."

"Your steak all right?" Marlene asked, her brows drawn.

He couldn't tell—never could—what his mother was thinking. "Yes."

"Then why aren't you eating?" she asked.

He glanced down at his plate. He'd taken only a few bites. He'd been so angry at Evan and so focused on watching Sam to ensure she ate that he hadn't eaten his own meal. He picked up his knife and fork. "Just thinking."

"You have more willpower than I do." Samantha smiled at his mother. "This is delicious. I'm glad you talked me into having dinner with you."

"So am I." Marlene smiled warmly at Samantha. "You're welcome anytime. I love cooking, but I don't cook much unless Dillon is home."

"Things are busy this time of year." He forked in a bite of salad.

Sam placed her knife on her plate. Only a few scraps of meat remained. "I need your help."

Why did her brown eyes have to pull at him? "Evan sure isn't going to give it to you."

Sam briefly tucked her head. Dillon didn't need his mother's look of censure to feel as though he'd kicked a defenseless animal.

"No, he made that clear," Sam said so softly that he had to strain to hear her.

"Few people know as much as about turbochargers as Dillon," his mother put in.

His mother bragging on him wasn't anything new. Putting him on the spot—something she'd never done before—was. He was afraid her reason was Samantha. His mother liked her and therefore would do everything in her power to help her, including giving Dillon a nudge or two.

"For Collins Industry to be successful again, more than turbo knowledge is needed," he finally said.

"Like what?" Sam turned to him, as eager as a puppy. He'd like to pet her, but not on the head.

"Like I told Abe, we need to improve the turbocharger."

"How?"

"With a new inner cooling system," he said. He'd given it a lot of thought while riding—when he wasn't thinking about Sam. "I've been thinking of an improvement for quite some time now."

"Go on." She leaned closer.

The soft fragrance of her perfume, the softer swell of her breasts against the silky blouse she wore, pulled at him. He leaned back to regain control. What was the matter with him? He didn't lust after women with his mother sitting across the table. Come to think of it, his mother had never met any of the women he'd dated.

"Cooling is the main problem when an engine runs. It cools off the incoming air, which makes the air denser, thus more oxygen to the engine, which makes it more efficient and faster," Dillon explained. "There are a lot on the market, but I think I have a way to make it more effective. We do that and we're back on top."

She smiled and it was like warmth after a cold winter's day. "What?" he said.

"You said 'we.'" She held up her hand when he opened his mouth. "I realize you might have meant it figuratively, but it was nice to hear." She sobered. "I'd appreciate any help you can give me, and I understand that Collins isn't your main concern."

Her acceptance should have given him the leeway he wanted, but somehow it didn't. It annoyed him that she didn't expect more loyalty from people.

"There's peach cobbler and ice cream for dessert." Marlene stood, reaching for Samantha's plate.

"I got this." Samantha picked up hers and Dillon's. "Let me help. This was the best meal I've had in a long time."

"Have you told Louise you own half of Collins mansion?" Dillon asked.

Samantha flicked a glance at his mother, who looked at them and then continued to the kitchen. "No."

Dillon muttered something that she was glad she couldn't understand.

He came to his feet. "How do you expect to run Collins when you can't run your house?"

"By taking one day at a time and doing the best I can," she answered, her voice trembling. "I didn't ask for this anymore than you did. Collins is more than a name, it's people, it's a dream Granddad founded, that my father worked tirelessly to grow. Excuse me."

Samantha went to the kitchen and placed the plates on the counter by the sink. "I think I'll skip the dessert and go home."

Marlene picked up a tray with three bowls of peach cobbler topped with vanilla ice cream and three cups of coffee. "I love Dillon. He's outspoken and doesn't mince words. But he's also a genius with motors and as loyal as they come."

"And opinionated."

Marlene smiled. "That too. But Abe thought he was the man needed to turn Collins around. Somehow you have to find common ground and work together."

Samantha crossed her arms. "I think Dillon lost the memo."

"Then you, Samantha, have to help him find it." Marlene started out of the kitchen with the desserts and coffee. "Come on before this ice cream melts."

Samantha unfolded her arms and followed. It was easy to see that Dillon had learned his forcefulness from his mother.

Dillon was still standing when Sam reentered the dining room. She didn't look at him. His mother said one distinct word when she returned: "Behave."

It wasn't necessary. He'd heard the trembling in Sam's voice. It had sliced through him. She'd just lost the only relative who cared about her, and he was being an ass because he couldn't keep from thinking about stripping them both naked.

"The ice cream is melting," he said, hoping she didn't take it as a reprimand. "You haven't lived until you've tasted Mama's peach cobbler."

She took the seat he held and picked up her spoon.

Breathing a sigh of relief, he took his seat and searched his mind for a safe topic. He usually didn't have to worry about such stuff. Most women talked enough for three people.

"Dillon, Samantha was telling me earlier she worked as a features reporter at a Houston newspaper."

Thank heaven for smart mothers. "Yeah. That sounds interesting."

She finally dipped her spoon into the ice cream. "Most of the time it was, but there were also those times it was boring."

"It's the same with the garage," Marlene said. "But that evens out the time when you have customers that test your patience."

"Don't remind me. A certain socialite didn't like my story on her supposed charity when she was actually spending the money on herself." Samantha grinned. "But I had facts and figures to back me up, so she had to slink away in disgrace."

"Good for you." His mother saluted Sam with her coffee cup.

"There are too many crooks out there ready to con unsuspecting people," she said. "Unfortunately, it's getting worse."

"You want to make a difference," Dillon said.

She turned to him. "It might sound Pollyanna, but I'd like to."

"It appears you did."

"Abe was proud of you with good reason," Marlene told her.

"When we get ready to do press releases about the new turbochargers, your background will be a big help."

"Then you're in?" she asked.

He shouldn't be affected by the plea in her eyes, the sincerity in her beautiful face. "I'm in."

Samantha drove home from the dinner with Dillon and Marlene feeling more relaxed than she had since she'd lost her grandfather. She finally had more hope than doubts that Collins would survive, that she wouldn't let her grandfather or her father down.

The dinner had also brought back pleasant memories of her and her mother in the kitchen, preparing dinner, laughing and talking. Her father often worked late on weekdays, but they always had a big breakfast together on Saturday and spent Sunday together.

Samantha pulled into the driveway of the mansion and stopped. The lights blazed on the upper floor, but otherwise the house was surrounded by darkness. Even the landscape lights were turned off.

It was mean-spirited of her uncle to turn off the lights, but to her, it showed how petty and unhappy he was. Thinking back, she recalled that on weekends when she had been growing up, his family slept late while hers was up and enjoying one another. On Sundays, it had been the same thing. Even though she had lost her parents, she had been loved and had memories to cherish. Sadly, she didn't think her uncle's family had any. She felt sorry for them.

Dillon would call her crazy for thinking that way. But she had wasted years being angry when she should have been grateful. Marlene would understand. Samantha liked his mother, admired her for her strength and tenacity. It hadn't been easy for her or for Dillon.

They admired courage. Since Samantha wanted them to admire her, she had better put a steel rod in her backbone.

After putting the car in drive, she drove around back, parked in the garage, got out, went inside and flicked on the light in the kitchen. She didn't stop until she stood in front of the control panel for the lighting. As she'd known, the dial had been switched from automatic to off. After resetting the timer, she hit the stairs.

In front of her uncle and aunt's bedroom door, Samantha rapped sharply. She knocked again when long seconds passed and no one had answered.

The door jerked open. Clearly irritated, her aunt stared down her nose at Samantha. "What do you want?"

"I reset the timer of the landscape lights to automatic. I don't intend to reset it again." Samantha's voice was just as abrupt as her aunt's. "Good night."

Ignoring the anger in her aunt's face, Samantha headed for the stairs, a smile on her face.

Five

. . . .

Dillon had a strong talk with his libido that night, so the next morning, when he walked into Abe's old office to find Samantha sitting behind her grandfather's desk looking beautiful and outrageously tempting, he almost regretted that Evan wasn't there so he could tear him a new one. He needed to vent some pent-up emotions, and not the way his body wanted.

"Good morning, Dillon," she greeted cheerfully.

"Good morning." He stopped in front of her desk. He had no intention of being swayed by the entreaty or thankfulness in her face and voice. This was business.

"The first thing is to see where the bleeding is—and that means a look at the financial records."

Nodding, she jotted something on the notepad he was beginning to think was attached to her. She really was clueless. How could Abe have put her in such a position? He knew she didn't have the experience or the toughness.

She has you. He could clearly hear his mother say those three irritating words.

Although he hadn't said anything further, Sam sat patiently waiting for him to go on. She had faith in him. He wasn't sure how he felt about that.

"I've asked Roman Santiago, one of the best C.P.A.s in the state, to come in and look over the accounts." Dillon took a seat in front of the desk. "I want it kept quiet. I don't want the employees worried or some other company getting wind that Collins might be vulnerable and mounting a take-over."

"They'll know when he looks at the books," she said with a frown.

"If they want to keep their jobs, they'll keep quiet," Dillon told her. "I'll speak to them personally. In the meantime, he'll look at who's buying and who we've lost as clients."

Sam made another notation. "What can I do?"

"Look cute."

Sam's head jerked up. Annoyance flared in her incredible brown eyes.

Dillon was just as annoyed. The words had just slipped out.

"I can do more than that," she huffed.

Since he'd stuck his foot in his mouth, and hoping she wouldn't think he was attracted to her, he said, "You can help me look over the orders."

She stood and went to the file cabinet. "Granddad was old-fashioned. As you see, no computer for him." She pulled out two stuffed folders. "I've been through his files. He kept records of all sales." She handed him a folder.

"This might take a while."

"Then we better get started." Samantha pulled up a chair to the front of the desk, took a seat, and opened the folder.

"What are you doing?"

"Going over the records." She never paused.

"You're not that obtuse."

Finally she lifted her head and gave him her attention. "You'll be doing the lion's share of work, so you should have the desk and comfortable chair."

He grunted. So she didn't use her femininity as most of the women he knew did. "Take the chair. I'll go check with maintenance to see if there is another desk and chair."

"Dillon."

He swung back around, caught by the sound of his name on her lips and something else. "Yes?"

She bit her lower lip. "I haven't told anyone we're partners."

He'd thought as much. "Do you plan to?"

"I sort of told Uncle Evan that I might not."

"I didn't." He opened the door to leave, then swung back around. She'd probably feel bad for Evan, and he'd probably make her life at work and the mansion even more uncomfortable. "So they think Evan is in charge?"

"Yes," she said, then rushed on, "It's not an excuse, but you weren't here and I needed his help."

"And he's taken full advantage." Dillon put his hands on his hips. "No one is going to take orders from me if they don't know I'm a full partner. I'm not going through Evan every time I need something."

She rose from her chair. "I've been thinking. Maybe if there is an announcement that we're consultants and that our orders are to be carried out without question, that might work."

"The order would have to come through Evan."

"I realize that." She gestured toward the PA system in the corner. "Uncle Evan could make the announcement now."

"He'd chew off his arm first." Dillon's arms came to his sides.

"The way I see it, he has no choice," she said with a bite in her voice.

Dillon's brow lifted. "There might be hope for you yet." Grinning, he opened the office door. "Let's go make your uncle's day."

Samantha didn't like the grin on Dillon's face. There was entirely too much glee in those haunting black eyes of his. She just hoped her uncle didn't provoke Dillon. She stopped in front of her uncle's door and knocked. "Uncle Evan."

There was no answer. She knocked again. "Maybe he's in the plant."

"Not likely," Dillon said, stepping around her. He opened the door.

Samantha entered behind him, closing the door after her. Evan snatched down the newspaper he'd been reading and came to his feet. "How dare you come in here without permission!"

"I dare because I'm half owner," Dillon shot back. "If I were you, I'd be more worried about maintaining my job. You don't get a free ride."

"My father's will said I'm to have a job at my full salary," Evan said, regaining some of his calm.

"But it didn't say you couldn't be fired for nonproductivity or insubordination. Of course, you can fight your firing, but then your check would be frozen." Dillon smiled coldly. "Either way, you lose."

Samantha's gaze snapped between the two men. Dillon had deliberately provoked her uncle, but her uncle had been rude not to answer the door. It was left to her to try to defuse the situation. Again.

"Uncle Evan, Dillon and I have no desire to embarrass you by announcing that we're in charge, but in order to do our job we need the employees to take orders from us without questions." Samantha dropped the other shoe. "You'll have to make the announcement to the employees."

"I won't do it."

"Fine." Dillon turned to the door. "I'd much rather tell them we're full partners."

"Wait!" Evan cried out.

Dillon glanced over his shoulder. "Make it quick."

"I'll do it," Evan said grudgingly.

"You know where the PA system is." Dillon opened the door and stepped back.

Evan made the announcement, but he worded it in such a way that everyone believed his workload was so heavy, he'd asked Samantha and Dillon to help out. It still got to Dillon that Evan treated Samantha as if she didn't matter. Dillon would have much rather told the employees the truth, but he knew Evan would somehow make Sam pay. She was too softhearted.

"All right. You've been glaring at me for the past five minutes." Sam put the folder aside. She was sitting across from him at the small desk. "You think I'm a cream puff."

"Evan is a jackass. He needed to be taken down a peg or two," Dillon said, his temper bubbling again.

"Just because he can't be gracious is no reason we can't be."

She picked up her file. "We can't run the plant if we're at each other's throats."

She couldn't be that naïve. "You think Evan is going to hate us any less or stop praying we fall flat on our collective butts because we didn't out him as a fraud?"

She opened her mouth and then closed it. "I'm hoping he'll eventually come around. He lost his father and the company within a week. He deserves to be upset."

"He was a jackass before then and we both know it. He's taking advantage of you." Dillon wanted to shake some sense into Sam, then kiss her breathless.

"Perhaps, but when we turn Collins around, I want to look back and know we did it fairly and with dignity."

Dillon shook his head and stared at her. "An idealist and a dreamer. Lord help me."

"Lord help both of us," she said under her breath.

"I heard that," Dillon said.

She didn't back down. "You aren't the easiest to work with either. You and Uncle Evan both have your faults."

"And I suppose you don't have any?"

"I have the greatest faults of any of us." She bent her head briefly.

Dillon saw her brush a knuckle beneath each eye. *Damn.* She better not cry. "You all right?"

She grabbed a tissue and raked it beneath her nose. Picked up another folder.

"Sam?"

"Fine." She straightened the papers in front of her. "I can't concentrate with you talking."

It was more than that, but he wasn't going to push it. Tears were the oldest trick in the book. They didn't affect him. The

knot in his stomach was probably due to being pissed off at
Evan.

Picking up the files in front of him, he went back to work.
Tomorrow morning when Roman arrived, Dillon wanted to
be able to give him a better picture of the company's finances.
He snuck another look at Sam, still clutching the tissue. She
had enough to contend with without him on her case.

"Roman is driving down in the morning from Dallas and
meeting me at Mama's for breakfast. How about coming over
around eight and eating with us?"

She didn't even look up. "Thank you, but I'll be busy."

He opened his mouth but caught himself just in time before asking her if she had a date. It was no concern of his if she
dated every single man in Elms Fork. "Suit yourself."

Roman Santiago was a man who believed there was a solution
for every problem and in the order of things. His practical approach annoyed some, but he was a man who lived by his own
standards and rules. Figures didn't bore him. They excited and
compelled him like a beautiful woman, thus making him good
at his job as a C.P.A. He was a bloodhound in Italian loafers.

Roman's clients were usually corporate America, but Dillon was a friend, and if he needed Roman's help to look over
the books of this new business he'd inherited, Roman was his
man.

A free agent for the past five years, he accepted only those
jobs that suited him. And at the satisfactory conclusion, he always took at least three weeks off to revitalize before moving
on to the next job. He might love figures, but when his or-

derly world had crashed around him six years ago, he'd realized that if he wasn't careful, he'd burn out and lose sight of what was important in life. His hands flexed on the steering wheel of his Porsche convertible as it hit the city limits of Elms Fork.

Unfortunately, there had been a time when he had been acquainted with both. Before he became a free agent, he'd worked long, grueling hours, leaving his wife to raise their children. He'd thought she was happy with their home in the exclusive gated community, the expense accounts at the best stores, her personal black Centurion American Express card. She wasn't.

He might never have known she was cheating on him if he hadn't been trying to catch the phone in the kitchen and bumped over the wastebasket. Picking things up, he'd seen the receipt for a night's stay at the Fairmont Hotel in downtown Dallas. He'd been out of town on that date. Flipping back to the master calendar, he'd noted their seventeen-year-old daughter, Amy, had been at a sleepover at a girlfriend's. Their son was a sophomore in college.

Roman distinctly recalled staring at the receipt, trying to come up with any reason except the logical one. He'd done what any sane man would have done. He'd hacked into her personal account for the credit card and found other nights, lavish dinners at restaurants, receipts for men's clothes that weren't in his closet. As strange as it seemed six years later, his prevailing thought had been that he'd assumed she had more class and self-respect than to pay some sleaze masquerading as a man to have an affair with her.

He'd sat at the breakfast table, staring at the screen of his laptop in shock. Late the night before, he'd returned from a business trip for the company he worked for. She'd been asleep, with her back to him. Bone weary, he'd undressed, slipped into bed, and turned out the light.

That had said a lot about the both of them and their marriage.

He'd tucked the receipt into his pocket, called a lawyer and a private detective. He'd acquired a lot of assets. He wasn't about to let her get the lion's share. Some might have called him cold and pragmatic; what he was was royally pissed.

She didn't work, had a housekeeper, a cook. He regularly put money in her checking account. And she had used that money to pay some creep to use her. When she'd come down for breakfast, she'd kissed him good morning as usual. It had been all he could do not to accuse her.

He'd told her he had to go back out of town for a few days. Her eyes had lit up. That night, she'd met her lover. A week later, she was served with divorce papers, the accounts frozen.

She'd been filled with rage, then cried and asked for forgiveness. He wasn't the forgiving type. Wrong him once, and it was over.

They'd told the children together that it was a mutual agreement. Later, he'd learned that they had known and had been afraid to tell him. She'd hurt him, but she'd also put the children in an unimaginable position. He could never forgive her for that. He'd treated her fairly and given her a settlement. It was much smaller than she'd wanted, but more than she'd deserved.

These days he took time to enjoy life, and the softness of a woman now and then. But now, all thoughts about women would have to wait. He never mixed business with pleasure. He liked being focused.

Glancing at the navigation screen, he flicked on his signal and turned toward what looked like the business section of town. It was quaint, sleepy looking. Not his usual scene.

When he checked his navigation system again, he saw he'd reached his destination and turned into the driveway of a beautiful ranch house surrounded by several sweeping flower gardens. Dillon had wanted them to meet at his mother's home to discuss his assignment.

Pulling up to the house, Roman saw a beautifully shaped woman appear in the midst of the flowers with a bunch of gladiolas in a wicker basket in one hand, a pair of shears in the other. The early morning sun was at her back. He'd never seen anything more enchanting.

He leaned forward to get a better look, for a moment unsure if he had imagined her. The stunning image remained. She was real.

And breathtaking.

It was the only word he could think of. She wore some type of light sky-blue summer dress that caressed her shapely curves and made his body clench. Thick, blackish-brown hair billowed around a sculptured face with sharp cheekbones. Like him, she must have had some Native American ancestry.

"Can I help you?"

She had a voice as gentle as the petals of a magnolia blossom. He'd grown up in the Bronx and had always been fascinated with accents. Hers was southern, charming, and meant to whisper naughty words in a man's ear.

Her small chin lifted as if she could discern his thoughts. He certainly hoped not. He didn't want Dillon's mother's friend annoyed at him.

"Good morning." Smiling, he emerged from the Porsche

and extended his hand. "I wasn't expecting to see you rise out of the flowers. It was quite a sight."

The woman coolly looked at his hand, then back at him. He was being judged. He hoped like hell he didn't come up short. "I'm Roman Santiago. I'm here to meet Dillon."

The frown on her lovely face cleared only marginally. After placing the shears in the basket of flowers, she held out her hand. "Good morning, Mr. Santiago. Dillon is expecting you."

He barely felt the warmth of her hand before it was gone. The calluses surprised him as much as the woman and his unexpected response to her.

"Please come inside." Turning away, she started toward the house.

Roman admired the erect posture, the slight sway of her shapely hips, and was glad he'd lifted his gaze when she turned to look back at him. He smiled innocently and tried to look as if he hadn't been admiring her and thinking things he probably shouldn't.

But at sixty years of age, his once coal-black hair liberally sprinkled with gray, he'd learned to live life to the fullest. Each day was a gift. He'd had too many friends and relatives leave this earth unexpectedly. When his time came, he didn't want to have any regrets.

Facing forward, she opened the door and stepped aside. "Please go in."

So, he hadn't fooled her. She'd known he was scoping her out. Touching the brim of his baseball cap, he went inside. The house was as inviting as the woman. He liked the soothing grays with touches of soft greens and yellows amid bold flashes of red and green. It showed restrained passion.

Immediately, he knew the woman had decorated the house.

Perhaps she was Dillon's mother's younger sister. She still had on her left glove. Roman could only hope he wouldn't want to howl when she removed it and he saw a ring.

"Hey, Roman," Dillon came in from the back of the house, his hand outstretched. "Glad you're here."

"Hey, Dillon." The handshake was strong. "You know I like to drive. It gives me a chance to listen to my CDs and books on tape, and best of all, it's a business expense and it's on your dime."

Dillon laughed and clapped Roman on the back. "It's a good thing you're the best. I see you've met my mother."

Roman's mouth gaped open. "You're kidding, right?" This stunning woman, whose eyes had lit up when Dillon entered the room but had gone to frost when he'd made a teasing comment about the business expense, couldn't be his mother.

Dillon happily threw one long arm around his mother's slim shoulders. "She gets that reaction all the time. I like to say she's aged well."

"I guess somebody doesn't want breakfast," Marlene said sweetly.

"Just kidding, Mama," he said. "Roman Santiago, my mother, Marlene Montgomery."

"My pleasure." He tipped his hat again.

"Mr. Santiago, Dillon said you'd be joining him for breakfast," she said.

"Thank you. If it's not too much trouble," Roman said.

"It's not." Her smile brittle, she spoke to Dillon. "Please show your guest to the kitchen. The table is already set. I'm not finished outside. Good-bye, Mr. Santiago."

Dillon caught her arm before she had gone two steps. "You're not eating with us?"

She palmed his cheek. "I'd only be in the way."

He shook his head. "You know I'm not having that. Remember the house rule."

She wrinkled her nose. "Show your guest to the bathroom. I'll be in the kitchen."

Roman's view of Marlene was cut off when Dillon took his arm. "I'll show you to the bathroom. You're about to taste the best cooking in the state."

What Roman really wanted to taste was Marlene's lips and other parts of her fantastic body. He tucked his head and stepped inside the half bath. Dillon idolized his mother. If he had any idea what Roman was thinking, Roman would be picking his teeth up off the floor.

Roman grabbed a fluffy gray towel and dried his hands. He didn't usually mix business with pleasure, but he was pragmatic enough to know that there were exceptions to every rule.

Life had just taken one of those wonderful, unexpected turns, and he couldn't wait to see where it led.

In Marlene's fifty-seven years, she had met more than her share of handsome, smooth-talking men. They all thought they were God's gift to women. All they had to do was smile, turn on the charm, and the women fell into their bed.

She'd learned that lesson the hard way. No man had interested her in years. She hadn't thought one could.

Unclenching her hand from around the flowers, she placed them on the gray marble counter until she could cut the stems and place them in water. For now, she had Dillon's guest to entertain.

"Something smells good."

The rough timbre of his voice annoyed her as much as it unsettled her. She wanted Roman Santiago out of her life.

"Like I told you, there's none better than Mama's cooking. Have a seat."

Dillon's voice calmed her as much as his guest unnerved her. But she wasn't some naïve girl from the country any longer. Removing the sausage-and-egg casserole from the warming oven, she placed it on the table.

"Is there anything I can do to help?"

"Thanks, Roman, but Mama and I have it."

Out of the corner of her eye, she saw Dillon fill three glasses with orange juice. Afterward he placed a cup beneath the automatic coffee machine, an extravagant expense, but one he had insisted on.

She looked at him—handsome, intelligent, and compassionate. And thank God, nothing like the man he was the spitting image of.

"Are you all right?"

Her gaze flew to Roman.

"Yeah. Sure." Dillon placed another cup under the spout. "I'm an old hand at this."

"I was asking your mother."

Dillon swung to her, concern in his face. "Mama?"

"Fine." She busied herself getting the jam, jellies, and syrup. "Just thinking." He wouldn't make her lie to Dillon. They'd always been honest with each other.

"Here you go, Roman. Black, straight, just like you like it." Dillon placed Roman's cup on the table, then his and hers. "Mama and I like ours with lots of cream and sugar."

"I might have to try it one day," Roman commented.

Marlene took her seat. He might have been talking about

the coffee, but she didn't think so. "I'll say grace." Bowing her head, she thanked God out loud for His blessings. Silently, she asked Him to remove temptation from her path and keep her strong.

Looking up, she stared into the hot black eyes of Roman Santiago. She felt the pull, sensed the danger. She served both men, then herself. She noted that, just like Dillon, Roman didn't take a bite of food until she did.

"Roman, we'll drive over to the plant as soon as we finish breakfast." Dillon dug into his meal. "I'm going to tell everyone, outside the two people in accounting, that you're doing inventory. I don't want anyone getting wind of the audit."

Roman sipped his coffee. "You expect theft?"

"I'm not sure." Dillon frowned in concentration. "Although the plant needs a major overhaul and they've lost a couple of clients, it shouldn't be in the poor financial position it's in."

"If someone had their hand in the till, I'll know."

"How long will that take?" Marlene asked as calmly as she could.

"Depends." He gave her his full attention. "I'm very thorough."

Shivers raced through her.

"And the best." Dillon nodded toward Roman's empty plate. "If you're finished, we can leave?"

Roman took one last sip of coffee and stood. "A meal like this should be savored."

Dillon came to his feet as well. "You're welcome anytime. Isn't that right, Mama?"

She tried to smile and hoped she succeeded. "Of course."

Dillon leaned over and brushed his lips against his mother's cheek. "I might be later than usual. Let's roll, Roman."

She could feel Roman's eyes on hers and refused to look up.

"Thank you again, Mrs. Montgomery, for a wonderful meal."

Drawing on all of her courage, she lifted her head and stared straight at him. No man would ever have power over her again. "It's 'Ms.' Good-bye."

His brow arched in surprise, then Roman turned to leave with Dillon.

Marlene just sat there. She was too unsteady to do anything else.

Dillon wouldn't associate with a man who used women. He certainly wouldn't have an easy friendship or bring him into her home. Therefore, Roman might be a charmer, but he wasn't out for his own selfish pleasure—the way A. J. Reed had been.

It didn't matter. She had no intention of being anything more to Roman Santiago than the mother of a business associate.

She'd been a fool once over a man. Never again, no matter how he made her feel emotions she thought she'd locked away.

Six

· · · · · · · · · · · · · · · ·

Samantha walked through her office door at exactly seven
fifty-two with a full stomach and a heavy heart. She'd
sat through a silent breakfast with her uncle. She had to
consider the unwanted thought that Dillon might be right.
She wasn't sure she could face his disapproval at work and at
home.

At least her aunt hadn't been there. The housekeeper said
that if she didn't have a social engagement, she slept in and
didn't come downstairs until after ten.

Going to the smaller desk, she opened the bottom drawer,
placed her bag inside then went to the file cabinet. She had no
intention of being useless. She wanted to help, learn the business, not just tag along.

After removing several files, she shoved the cabinet closed
with more force than necessary. She returned to her desk. Dillon thought she was worthless. His sarcastic comment about
looking cute still rankled. She'd show him.

Last night, she'd gone on the Internet to research turbo

engines. If she had to, she wanted to be able to run the company by herself. She wasn't waiting or being dependent on either her uncle or Dillon.

Her office door opened and the man who occupied entirely too much of her thoughts entered with another man she didn't recognize. Dillon was dressed in a light blue polo shirt and jeans. He looked gorgeous, and for once he was smiling.

"Morning, Sam."

"Good morning," she said, smiling back at him without thought.

Dillon placed his hand on the man's shoulder. "Samantha Collins, meet Roman Santiago, the best C.P.A. in the country."

"I would have settled for state." Roman grinned and crossed the room to extend his hand. "Pleased to meet you, Ms. Collins."

The handshake was firm, the dark eyes dancing with merriment. "Thank you for coming."

"I like challenges." Roman glanced back at Dillon. "Updating all of the accounts onto the computer certainly qualifies."

"I like keeping my friends happy." Dillon chuckled.

For a moment, Samantha simply stared at Dillon. She's never seen him this playful and . . . nice.

"I'll start scanning in the records for the past six months and work on them first to see if anything pops," Roman said.

"Pops?" Samantha stopped ogling Dillon. "You think there's fraud?"

Roman looked contrite. "I thought she knew, since she's aware of why I'm here."

Samantha rounded the desk and didn't stop until she was in front of Dillon. "I didn't, but I plan to. Talk."

"Should I wait outside?" Roman asked with a hint of laughter in his voice.

"With all the orders we went over, revenues should have been better. We need to figure out why they aren't." He nodded to Roman. "He's the best and can do it quickly and quietly."

"You could have told me," she said.

"I just did."

There was no sense reminding him she was a partner. He didn't see it that way. One day he would. She looked at Roman. "I'll show you to your office. It's small, but has a window."

"Once I start working I tend to block everything out."

"I'll come down at closing," Dillon said. "I'll ask Mama to cook for all of us so we can discuss how the day went."

"I'm fast, but not that fast. Give me a couple of days."

Samantha couldn't believe Dillon would ask his mother on such short notice to prepare dinner for two guests. "It will also give your mother more time to prepare for guests."

"Mama doesn't need much notice, but we'll move it to tomorrow evening at six."

"All right." Roman held up two cases. "Then I better get started."

"Certainly." Samantha started toward the door, but a strong hand on her arm stopped her. She felt her body heat, her skin prickle.

"I'll do it," Dillon told her. "I want people getting used to seeing me and giving orders."

"Transition is difficult for people who've been with the company a long time," Roman commented. "They'll soon get used to you and Ms. Collins being their boss."

Dillon's attention switched to Samantha. "If only that was the case."

Samantha accepted the dig. "Mr. Santiago, the employees think my uncle, my grandfather's oldest son, who works here as V.P., is their boss. I didn't want him embarrassed when people learned that he was passed over. I thought it would foster good-will and make a better working relationship between us."

"You wanna tell him how well the goodwill has worked with your uncle?" Sarcasm dripped from each word Dillon spoke.

Samantha sent Dillon a hard frown, which he ignored.

"No? Then I'll tell Roman." Dillon's amicable expression had vanished the instant Samantha mentioned Evan still being perceived as the boss. "Evan Collins is an arrogant prick who thinks he's better than anyone. He refuses to help the com-pany in any way and tells us we're going to fail every chance he gets and treats Sam as an interloper. Did I leave anything out?"

Her face heated. It was one thing for Dillon to know that her uncle thought she was incompetent and didn't like her, but it was quite another for an outsider to know. "No," she said softly, glancing away.

"Come on, Roman, I'll show you to your office." Dillon went to the door.

Samantha could feel Roman's gaze on her. She refused to meet it.

"Thank you again." She went behind her desk and picked up the folder.

"Was that necessary?" she heard Roman ask.

If Dillon gave an answer, he spoke too softly for her to

hear. A few moments later, she heard the door open and close. When she looked up, she was alone. Just as she'd been since she'd lost her parents.

Dillon didn't need Roman's reprimand to know he'd hurt Sam. He hadn't meant to. He just got angry whenever he thought of how badly Evan treated her. If he got another chance to punch Evan, he was taking it.

Opening the door of their joint office, he saw her hunched over the files. She looked small and vulnerable. And alone. Every battle he'd fought, he'd always known his mother would be there beside him battling just as hard. He couldn't imagine going through life with no one to fight for you.

His careless comment had reminded Sam of just that. He felt like crap.

She'd been thrust into this the same as he'd been. It wasn't her fault her uncle was an ass. What made him want to bow his head was that he wasn't sure he wasn't acting like one as well.

Sitting behind the larger desk, he glanced over. She didn't have a tissue in her hand, nor was she wiping at her eyes. He felt only marginally better that she wasn't crying.

He knew exactly why he was hard on her and pushed her. "You shouldn't let Evan walk all over you."

She lifted her head. Her eyes were clear, and they were angry. "I suppose you're the only one allowed to do that."

He was almost proud of her for not backing down. "I have your best interests at heart."

"You have a strange way of showing it." She went back to the file.

She was even prettier with a sparkle in her eyes. Dillon reached for a file. He was *not* going there. "Find anything yet?"

"Two of our biggest accounts' orders have steadily declined over the past year." She turned toward him.

"Who is the account manager?"

She bit her lower lip. He immediately knew.

"Evan," he snapped.

"Yes."

"Figures." Dillon snorted. "If he spent as much time on business as he did trying to impress people and goofing off, the company would be in better shape."

"There are notations in the file made by Grandfather a couple of months ago, but I can't read his writing," she said.

"Chicken scratch, he called it." Dillon walked over to Sam and leaned over to try to decipher the writing.

Somehow his eyes stopped on the arousing swell of Samantha's breasts, the enticing scent of her perfume.

"Can you make it out?"

Dillon straightened. He would like to make out all right. "Nah. Mama probably could."

"Maybe we could ask her tomorrow night."

Was there a catch in her voice? Had her eyes widened just the tiniest bit?

"Yeah." Dillon took his seat. If she was attracted to him, he was going to have one heck of a time resisting not taking her. "What do you know about turbochargers?"

"Turbochargers are engineered to force more air mass into an engine's intake manifold and combustion chamber. Compression by the turbocharger causes the intake of air to heat, rather than the air being heated by contact with the hot turbocharger itself." She took a short breath. "A turbocharger gets its power from the exhaust stream. The exhaust runs through a turbine, which in turn spins the compressor," she finished in a rush.

Dillon leaned back in his chair. "I'd be impressed if it sounded like you knew what you were talking about instead of spouting facts."

She flushed.

"But it showed you're willing to learn."

She smiled and sat up straighter, making her full breasts jut forward. Dillon was thankful he was sitting. His brain was definitely having a difficult time not thinking of Sam beneath him, hot and hungry for him. "There's modification and specifications to be considered."

"Then teach me," she told him. "I want to be an asset, not a liability. My father gave his life for this company. I won't let it fail without a fight." Her voice trembled with earnest emotions, but no tears fell.

Dillon had to clench his hands to keep from taking her in his arms. He stood and gave her a tissue. "The first thing you have to learn is no tears."

She balled the tissue in her hand. "Because it shows weakness?"

"Maybe in some people, but it just shows you have a soft heart." He stared at her and watched surprise round her eyes. "Once your opponent knows that, you'll be at his mercy. If you feel emotions getting the best of you, excuse yourself or think of a person you detest and tell them to back off."

"You never let anyone walk over you, did you?"

"No." He usually didn't like to remember those days when some kid wanted to get in his face because his mother was single or later because of his rep as a hell-raising badass.

"It must be nice being that strong, yet you listen to and respect your mother."

"She went through a lot for me," he said quietly.

"And you probably still give her a hard time," Samantha said, smiling.

White teeth flashed in his gorgeous face. Samantha almost sighed. She was flirting with hell's fire again. "It keeps her young."

They sat smiling at each other. It was Dillon who broke the contact first. "We need those accounts back."

Samantha picked up a sheet on her desk and walked over to his. She could get used to this easy rapport, even the sparks of lust. "I was going to ask you first, but I thought I should call them and kind of feel them out about why they left Collins."

Dillon took the list. "I'll call."

She reached for the list, inadvertently brushing her breast against his shoulder. She jumped back, her eyes huge.

Dillon cleared his throat and rolled his shoulder when he wanted to take Sam in his arms and kiss her until they both forgot to breathe and go from there. "I—I'll make the call. If they ask you anything beyond the basics, you won't know the answer. Plus, I'm not bragging, but if they've heard of my reputation as an expert on high-performance cars and my work with the vintage car racing circuit, it might help us get through."

Sam reached for the phone on his desk, dialed, and handed him the receiver. "You're on."

Dillon took the phone, glad to see that his hand trembled only the tiniest bit. Sam got to him as no other woman ever had. "Frank Thomas, please. Dillon Montgomery with Collins Industry and Vintage Racing calling. . . .

"I understand," he said moments later. "Please have him call me at 955-555-7777 at his earliest convenience. I have some exciting news to share with him. Thank you. Goodbye." Hanging up, he said to a hovering Sam, "He's out of town on a business trip, but his secretary said she'd relay the message."

"When and if he calls, make lunch or dinner reservations. Somewhere reservations are difficult to obtain so he'll be impressed and more inclined to come," she suggested. "If he's married, invite his wife."

He lifted a brow. She straightened up from leaning against his desk. "I interviewed the president of an oil company in Houston who said social settings were the best place to learn about a person and get them to relax."

"Your uncle must have read the article," he said drolly.

She stiffened.

"If one tear falls, you're not going on the business meeting with me." His eyes narrowed.

Samantha was so stunned that he was allowing her to go on the business meeting, she blinked. "You're taking me?"

"You're my partner, aren't you?"

Nodding, Samantha relaxed. If she was offended every time Dillon said something about her and her uncle, she'd be little else. She had another way to get back at him. "Grandfather's funds haven't been released yet, but I was thinking the Mansion on Turtle Creek would be the perfect place to have dinner. Your treat, of course. I'm sure you have connections to make it happen."

"You think I can't?"

She nudged the phone closer to him. "Can you?"

A challenge. He liked this Sam a lot better than the one who teared up at the drop of a hat. Dillon pulled his phone from the holder at his waist, activated it, and punched in a number. "Hey, Carson. I need reservations for four Friday night and Saturday night at seven at the Mansion. I'll wait for your call."

He grinned at her astonished face. "Some of my friends like their privacy. It's nothing to buy out an upscale restaurant— the Mansion included—for the night." He waited for her to be suitably impressed.

"But we can't hold up reservations for both nights. It might be someone's anniversary or something."

Only Sam. "What did I tell you about your soft heart?" he asked. It was a wonder the world hadn't left footprints on her back. He relented when he saw she was still worried.

"If Thomas calls back by noon tomorrow, we'll give him his choice. If he doesn't, I'm sure Mama wouldn't mind not cooking Friday night. Roman can come to round out the fourth person. We'll release Saturday. Anything else?"

"Yes, call your mother and let her know about dinner tomorrow night." Sam went to her desk and took a seat.

It seemed Sam was a quick learner. He might regret teaching her anything, but he was smiling when he called his mother.

Marlene had denied Dillon few things in his life. She'd done without so he wouldn't have to. She'd used reason when people said she should have used a belt or the back of her hand. She was considering denying him now.

"Roman and Sam are coming over for dinner tomorrow night," Dillon said on the phone. "Nothing fancy. Around six, all right?"

Having a son who thought there wasn't anything you couldn't accomplish had its drawbacks at times. But it wasn't so much the cooking as who one of the guests would be.

Roman Santiago. He disturbed her in ways she didn't want to think about.

"Mama?"

"It's fine, Dillon. You know your friends are always welcome, and if it will help you with Collins, so much the better. Six will be fine," she said with more cheeriness than she felt.

"Everything all right at the garage?"

"Business couldn't be better." One thing Roman wouldn't do was cause Dillon to worry about her. He'd had to do too much of that in his life. "All the bays are full and we have cars waiting."

"Wish Collins was doing as well," he said.

"You and Samantha will figure things out and have the company back in the black in time," she told him. She had every confidence in her son.

"Roman is going to help make that happen."

She could have done without that reference. "You sound very confident in him."

"That's because he used to work for Carson's father."

Carson Rowland had been Dillon's freshman roommate in college. They'd roomed together every year afterward. Carson came from a very wealthy background. His father had two cars in the vintage racing circuit with a combined value of well over a million dollars. Carson and his close-knit family had been Dillon's introduction into legitimate racing and an affluent lifestyle. They'd been as accepting of Dillon as they were of her.

"Used to?" she asked in spite of herself. She shouldn't want to know anything about the man.

"He quit for personal reasons, but I happen to know that Carson's father would hire Roman back at his seven-figure salary in a heartbeat," Dillon said. "Keeping track of the money is key to growth and solvency."

Marlene wanted to push for answers in spite of herself. Had he been ill? "Yes, it is."

"My cell is ringing. Bye, Mama."

"Bye." Marlene hung up the phone, determined that Roman would not disrupt her settled life. No man with a pretty face was going to do that again.

But as long as she breathed, she'd never regret Dillon's birth. He was the best part of her.

She'd been scared when she'd learned she was pregnant and single, but she'd never thought of not keeping her baby. By then she'd learned A. J. was married and that he'd never loved her, only used her. It had been a sobering, heart-wrenching time.

Despite the gossip, the whispers when she walked by, she'd wanted her baby. Abe had stood by her, refusing to fire her as Evan had demanded. His reason was that her pregnancy and status as an unwed mother would tarnish the company's image, especially since she was secretary to the president. She thought it had more to do with her rebuffing Evan's advances.

Abe had ordered Evan from his office. She was staying and he didn't want to hear another word.

Alone in the world, she'd been grateful for Abe's support. He blamed himself for her situation. A. J. Reed had been a business associate of Abe's. It was Abe who learned of the rela tionship and told her A. J. was married. The breakup had been nasty. Without Abe's support, she wasn't sure how she would have faced the world. Then Dillon was born, and once she'd held him in her arms, she'd vowed to be the best mother possible.

Dillon eased the loneliness, made getting up each morning a joy. There wasn't anything she wouldn't do for him. That included dealing with a seducer like Roman.

No man was ever going to use her again.

Seven

· · · · · · · · · · · · · ·

Dillon had barely disconnected the call from Carson letting him know his reservations were confirmed when the phone on his desk rang. "Collins Industry, Dillon Montgomery speaking. How can I help you?"

"Mr. Montgomery, this is Frank Thomas with Tasco Automotive, returning your call."

"Thanks, Mr. Thomas, for calling me back," Dillon greeted him, pointing to the receiver. "I realize how extremely busy you must be."

Sam rushed over and leaned down close to the receiver, jarring his concentration. The woman didn't know how dangerous she was to his peace of mind, and he wasn't about to tell her.

"I must say I was surprised to learn you now work with Collins," Mr. Thomas said. "Evan has always been the account manager."

"Since Abe's passing, there's been some restructuring," Dillon told him casually.

"I'd heard about Abe's passing, and sent my condolences," Frank said. "He was a shrewd man and an honest one."

"Thank you," Dillon said. "His granddaughter and I are working together to contact old clients. I'll be frank. We want your business back."

"We're ordering from another supplier," Frank said. "I called out of respect for Abe, and because I've heard of you. I'm proud to say Tasco has a turbocharger on a car in the heritage vintage racing circuit. I've heard your name mentioned as a genius with motors."

Sam rolled her eyes. Dillon grinned, then said, "I've heard good things about Tasco as well. We'd wondered if it would be possible to meet for dinner Friday night. I took the liberty of making dinner reservations at the Mansion on Turtle Creek for seven."

"You and Evan?" Frank asked.

Dillon couldn't be sure, but he thought he heard a bit of distaste in the man's voice. "No, Abe's granddaughter and myself. I made reservations for four. You're welcome to bring an associate or anyone you wish."

He chuckled. "If I took anyone other than my wife there, she'd have my neck. We've been there a few times and it's always great."

"Abe's granddaughter suggested it," Dillon put in. "We'd like the opportunity to tell you about a new intercooler we're working on."

"You have me intrigued. I'll see you Friday night at seven. Good-bye."

"Good-bye." Dillon hung up the phone. "We're in."

Sam squealed and threw her arms around Dillon's neck. "We did it!"

Dillon felt the softness of her breasts against his chest. His lower body hardened immediately. He inhaled her perfume and wanted to explore every inch of her. "Sam . . ." Her name came out hoarse and ragged.

Samantha stiffened immediately, then jerked upright. Her face hot, she quickly returned to her seat. She might not have that much experience, but she knew desire when she heard it.

She couldn't even think it was her he was reacting to. With her boobs in his face, any man would have reacted the same way. She moistened her lips and tried to get her trembling hands to still. She could be mortified or push on. "Whose car are we taking to Dallas?"

Dillon snorted. "No offense, but I don't think we'd make much of an impression if we showed up in yours."

"It gets me where I want to go and back." She dared look at him. "Can't ask for more than that."

"How about looking good going and coming?" he shot back.

He certainly looked good, but that was the appeal of sin. It looked so good, you forgot about the consequences. She picked up another file. "What do you think Roman would like for lunch?"

"If I remember, he's not picky about food. Why?"

"He said he forgets everything when he's working," she said. "He doesn't look like the brown bag type. I thought I'd pick up lunch for us."

Dillon leaned back carelessly, but he was alert. "Define 'us.'"

"You, me, Roman," she said. Evan wasn't included.

Dillon was surprised she'd included him. But then, Sam had been full of them today. "You order, and I'll go pick it up. You helped score a meeting with Tasco."

"It was a fluke. I just thought of the most exclusive place in Dallas," she said with a careless shrug.

"Regardless, it worked. You did good, Sam."

"Thank you." She smiled back, got caught in his eyes, and had to make herself look away. Dillon was much too tempting. It wasn't going to get any easier working with him. Unfortunately, she didn't have a choice. He could save Collins Industry. For the first time since she'd lost her grandfather, she had hope.

Thursday was one of those nonstop days that were a blessing and a curse to businesses. There were customers waiting when Marlene arrived, and as the day lengthened, more came in to have their car serviced or repaired. Of course, all of them wanted it done immediately. Even with nine bays and some of the best mechanics in the business, that wasn't about to happen.

Early on, she'd insisted on a comfortable lounge with a prominent NO SMOKING sign, a small playroom for children, and a TV that was tuned to the home improvement shows instead of sports or talk shows. There was also a van that could take people to work or home. Those in need of a rental were given a 20 percent discount coupon to the only rental place in town.

Having a car in the shop, whether scheduled or a breakdown, could be stressful. She'd wanted her customers to have one less worry. The multiple service awards from the city's Better Business Bureau as well as automotive organizations showed she had succeeded.

Dillon might have started the business to teach an unscrupulous man a lesson, but it had morphed into something so much more. She was an independent businesswoman, respected in the community. Whispers and pointing fingers no longer followed her everywhere she went. She planned to keep it that way.

"Marlene, you told me to remind you when it was five fifteen."

Marlene looked up from her desk to see Gloria Parker, her secretary and bookkeeper. She was the only other woman employed there. In her mid-sixties, she was a tall, thin woman dressed in a denim skirt and shirt, and boots. She wore her gray hair in a long ponytail. She'd taken to the computer instantly and kept scrupulous records.

"Why the frown?" Gloria asked, coming farther into Marlene's office.

"Just thinking." Marlene reached for her purse, annoyed that, once again, Roman had slipped into her thoughts. "Thanks for the reminder. I'll see you in the morning."

"Don't forget you're going to bring me a plate for lunch."

Marlene smiled. Gloria loved to eat and never gained a pound. Marlene had to exercise. "You'll have it." Going past the older woman, Marlene headed for the parking lot in front of the business. She hurried over to her Volvo SUV and started home. This was a business dinner for Dillon and Samantha. She wouldn't allow Roman to make it anything more.

Roman could usually take or leave women. They certainly didn't occupy his usual orderly thoughts. He respected them, was intimate with them when the mutual mood struck, then promptly forgot them and went on with his life just as they did.

Following Dillon and Samantha around the side of Marlene's house, he wondered if seeing her would give him the same clench in the gut, the instant desire to make her his. After considerable thought, he hoped not. He had a feeling that she would change all he thought he knew about women.

"Hey, Mama, we're here," Dillon greeted.

Marlene turned from standing in front of a large outdoor grill. She was a striking woman wearing a floral sundress that bared her smooth shoulders and made his hands itch to touch them. Roman felt the punch twenty feet away, felt the unwanted desire clutch at him. But there was something else he hadn't felt in years: the need to protect as much as possess.

"Good evening, Ms. Montgomery," Samantha greeted.

"It's Marlene, remember?" She gave Samantha a hug and stepped back. "Welcome again."

Roman was sure his welcome wouldn't be as friendly. "Hello, Ms. Montgomery."

"Hello, Mr. Santiago," Marlene greeted with an enthusiasm that surprised him. She glanced between him and Dillon. "You two must be starved. We're having taco hamburgers."

"My favorite." Dillon opened the grill, then looked back at his mother. "Isn't this too much food?"

"I told the crew I was grilling." She lifted her delicate shoulders.

"You're a softy, like somebody else I know," Dillon quipped.

Samantha arched a brow. "It's a good thing or else she would have said no to working all day and then preparing food for us *and* her crew."

Dillon picked up a tong and tested a sizzling two-inch beef patty. "Mama, Sam and I have this. You go take a seat."

"Thanks," Marlene said. "I thought we'd eat out here. I'll go bring out the other dishes."

"Can I help?" Roman asked, finally noting that she never quite looked at him.

"You're a guest." She gestured to a round patio table already set with colorful napkins and plates. "I'll be right out."

"I think that one is ready to turn," Samantha said.

"Who has the tongs?" Dillon said, but he quickly turned over the sizzling beef patty.

"I think I'll go check and see if your mother needs help," Roman said.

"Thanks," Dillon said, placing the meat on the platter Samantha held.

Roman watched them for a moment longer, wondering if they would keep circling around each other and ignore the sexual attraction or act on it. For himself, he'd decided he was going to act.

The back door led right into the kitchen. Marlene looked up immediately. Her eyes widened, and her lips tightened with annoyance.

"I came to see if I could help."

"You can take the potato salad out." She turned back to chopping what appeared to be cabbage and carrots.

He picked up the potato salad. She was two feet away and as wary as a doe.

"Was there something else?" Her eyes and voice clearly said, "Back off."

"Yes, but it will wait." He left. The woman had a knife in her hand and she was very annoyed with him.

. . .

Dillon was enjoying himself. It might be a business meeting, but he found he liked teasing Sam. She no longer teared up or got that wounded expression. He was still attracted to her, but he could handle it. He bit into his second taco burger, which was pilled four inches high with guacamole, salsa, sour cream, tortilla chips, lettuce, and cheddar.

"Anything so far, Roman?" he asked when he'd swallowed, noting Roman was on his second burger as well, while his mother and Sam weren't even finished with one. Probably because they were talking and the men were eating.

"Getting there." Roman placed his burger on his plate. "With the help of the other two accountants, we're almost finished scanning in all of the invoices."

"I hope they remember to keep the real reason you're there quiet," Dillon said.

"I believe they will. They certainly took to the computer and scanner you had delivered to help me." Roman picked up his fork. "They said they'd wanted one for some time, but Abe had been against it."

"He liked being able to see things at will," Marlene said. "He was also afraid of what would happen if the computer went down."

"Which can happen," Sam put in. "It happened more than once to me before I started backing up files."

"Why didn't you do it originally?" Dillon asked, digging into his coleslaw.

"Overconfident that it wouldn't happen to me, I guess," Sam answered. "Or maybe like Grandfather, I don't like change."

Marlene smiled. "He was set in his ways, but he was a wonderful man."

Roman thought of the rumor he'd overheard. The two assistants had been whispering that Abe was Dillon's father. It was the only reason any of the employees could think of that Dillon was a "consultant." What would they say if they knew he was a full partner?

"Would you like more lemonade?" Marlene asked, a smile on her face, annoyance in her eyes. She'd caught him staring.

He held up his half-full glass. "Please."

Dillon poured since the pitcher was closest to him. "Nobody makes lemonade this good."

"I agree." Roman took a sip, looking over the rim of his glass at Marlene.

"Have you discovered anything to help my son and Samantha?" Marlene asked.

"Not yet, but with the last six months scanned in, I should be able to soon." He turned to Dillon. "I do know that there are a lot of sales receipts, so I'm with you that the company shouldn't be losing money."

Samantha shook her head. "I don't want to think of anyone stealing."

"It happens." Dillon handed his mother a folder. "Mama, can you decipher Abe's writing? Evan was the account manager, but the company stopped buying from Collins."

She peered at it a moment, brought the papers closer.

"You can look at it later," Dillon said.

Her head came up. She sent him a grateful smile. "I'll go get my glasses. They're in the kitchen."

So Marlene didn't like wearing her eyeglasses. Roman

wouldn't have thought her vain. He'd long since given up the fight against wearing his while he worked.

Wearing black-framed glasses, Marlene came back in seconds, took her seat, and picked up the file. "Just words and partial sentences. 'Shoddy. Can't believe this. Evan knows better. Trouble coming.'"

"I wonder how long he knew the company was failing and worried about it?" Samantha said softly. "I should have been here."

Marlene touched her arm. "You're here now. He was confident you and Dillon could turn the company around. I've told you before, so do I."

Samantha's smile trembled and she looked across the table at Dillon. "We're going to meet the client tomorrow night for dinner and try to get him to come back to Collins."

"At the Mansion." Dillon reared back in his chair. "Sam hit it out of the park with that suggestion. It appears the man and his wife like going there. My wallet will also take a hit."

Samantha's eyes rounded in distress. "I was just teasing. It's a business expense. Of course I plan to pay half. I still have my trust fund."

"Mama would disown me if I let you pay." Dillon stood, picking up his empty plate and his mother's. "Tell you what. You can buy lunch tomorrow for us."

"Deal." Sam stood and picked up her plate. "Can I take your plate, Roman?"

"You're a guest. I can do it." Marlene started to rise.

"No, you can't. Grab it, Sam," Dillon ordered. "Sam and I can bring out the dessert and coffee too. Cooking was enough."

Sam picked up Roman's plate. "You're not as clueless and as chauvinistic as I thought."

Dillon grunted and started inside. Laughing, Samantha followed.

Marlene sat across from Roman, looking beautiful and as untouchable as the distant stars overhead. He smelled the fragrance of the flowers, felt the faint wind on his face. "It's beautiful here," he ventured.

"Thank you." She picked up her lemonade, no doubt to end the conversation.

"The meal was the best I've had since you cooked breakfast for me."

"I did it for Dillon." There was enough frost in her voice to ensure that most men shut up and made a quick exit.

"Dillon is a man I'm proud to call a friend as well as a business associate."

"Thank you. That's very kind of you to say so."

Her words were precise, very formal, and they didn't invite conversation. With Dillon and Samantha, she was loving and supportive. Roman braced both arms on the table and leaned forward.

"Forgive me, but I believe in being frank. Have I offended you in some way?"

She lowered the glass. "I just met you."

"And sidestepped the question."

She placed the glass on the table and leaned forward just as he had. "Since you believe in frankness, let me be just as frank. You're a business associate of my son's, and that's all you'll ever be. I'm too old for affairs and wouldn't get married if my life depended on it." She stood and picked up the serving dishes. "Excuse me. I'll see if they need help in the kitchen."

Roman stared after her until she disappeared, then leaned back in his chair and sipped his lemonade. Well, she'd certainly put him in his place. And intrigued him. An intriguing dichotomy.

He didn't want to get married either. Just the thought made him shudder. No woman was going to deceive him again. But he wasn't a monk, and no matter how he fought against it, he'd like to kiss Marlene until he melted that frosty reserve and found the passionate woman he was sure lay beneath.

She was proving once again that she was the exception to the rule of no women while working.

Friday evening, Samantha opened the front door of Collins mansion. Dillon groaned, his body hardened. Sam was doing it again. He really wanted a taste of her. Sam had a body made for a man's pleasure. He'd like nothing more than to pull the little one-shoulder black dress slowly from her body and lick every delectable inch of her.

She gulped. Licked her lips.

He saw the desire in her eyes even in the shadows. She wanted him.

"We, er, better get to it," she said.

Too bad she wasn't talking about undressing and doing wicked, delicious things to each other's naked bodies. He stepped back. "Yeah."

She stepped over the threshold, closed the door and started

down the wide steps. Beside her, Dillon didn't touch her. No sense tempting fate. He'd never been hot and bothered enough to try to make love to a woman in his Ferrari, but tonight he wouldn't bet on it.

"Nice car. I can see why you wanted to drive."

Her voice sounded breathy. She was trying to act normal. He'd give her points for that.

Wordlessly, he opened the door. She sat and her dress rose to midthigh. He wanted nothing more than to drop to his knees and slide it up even farther.

"Please close the door."

His gaze moved slowly from her incredible legs to her bared shoulder to her quivering lips. She knew what he wanted.

"It isn't polite to be late."

He closed the door and went around and got in the low-slung car. The motor rumbled. Tension coiled in him.

He'd like nothing better than to let it all out. The sheriff would never catch him. Since Dillon was the only one in town who owned a Ferrari, he'd know it was him but wouldn't dare call in to the next town. He'd be too proud to admit that Dillon had outrun and outsmarted him. There also remained the lie about Abe being Dillon's father. Abe might be gone, but he was still respected.

"Dillon, we need to go."

He looked at Sam. She looked incredibly beautiful and neat. Not a hair out of place. He'd like to muss her up in a wide bed with silken sheets.

She licked her lips. "Would you like for me to drive?"

The thought was so outrageous, it snapped him out of his lusty haze. "Not even my mother has driven this baby." He put the car in gear and took off.

"But you'd let her if she asked," Sam said with complete assurance.

"You're not my mother." He shifted into second.

"Thank goodness," she whispered, but he heard her.

Tonight was going to test him to the limits, and he'd always been a man to push the limits as far as he could.

Roman pulled off his eyeglasses, shut off the scanner/printer, and powered down his laptop. Standing, he stretched his long arms over his head, twisted his neck. He'd been working steadily since a quick lunch around one. All of the invoices were in, now the real job of tediously working though them could begin.

He glanced at his watch. Six thirty-three. He was probably the last person working. Samantha and Dillon would have been there as well if they weren't heading to Dallas for the business dinner.

He picked up the laptop, headed for the parking lot and found it as empty as he'd expected. He placed the laptop on the front seat, exited the plant, waving as he passed the security checkpoint. The wave wasn't returned.

Waiting for a couple of cars to pass, Roman clicked on his signal to turn left toward Dallas, a long hot shower, and a good meal. The cars passed, but Roman sat there.

He wanted something entirely different.

The strident blast of a truck's horn behind him had him glancing in the rearview mirror. The security guard. Apparently, he knew exactly where he wanted to go.

Roman flicked the signal to the right and headed into Elms Fork.

And Marlene.

Eight

. . . .

The last customer had picked up his car from the garage. The tools were cleaned and stored and the bay doors shut. All but one of the workers had left. It was peaceful and quiet. She liked this time best. With no interruptions, she could catch up on the never-ending paperwork.

Tonight she'd work on the payroll, and once that was finished, she planned to order supplies. She didn't have to go home and cook for Dillon, though she never minded. She relished those days he was home.

She paused, removing her eyeglasses. She'd give anything if he decided to move back to Elms Fork permanently. She'd never ask him, of course. He loved the life he had carved out for himself. With his successful business ventures, he didn't have to worry about money.

They'd come a long way, as the saying went, and the journey wasn't over yet.

A knock sounded on the closed office door. The nights she worked late, one of the mechanics always stayed with her, then followed her home. She'd long since given up trying to con-vince Dillon it wasn't necessary.

"Come in, Billy," she said, a smile forming on her lips. Happily married with a darling two-year-old little girl, he was probably wondering how much longer she expected to work. The door opened. Her smile slid away.

Roman stood in the doorway, his hand on the knob, his startling black eyes staring at her.

Shivers raced through her. He closed the door.

She wasn't afraid. All she had to do was scream, but she already knew that wasn't necessary. Roman wouldn't force a woman. Dillon wouldn't associate with a man like that. The thick, lustrous gray hair mixed with black made him look even more compelling. Instinctively, she knew he was a man who knew how to savor a woman.

She opened her mouth to ask what he wanted, but she al-ready knew the answer. She had to be smart about this. She probably presented a challenge to him. "The garage is closed."

"That's not why I'm here, and we both know it." He didn't stop until he stood directly in front of her desk.

"We had this conversation." Folding her arms, she leaned back in her chair, distancing herself from what she hadn't thought about in years, a man who, despite her best efforts, excited her.

"One-sided, if I remember." He braced both hands on her desk. "I've been married once and don't plan to try it again. We might not like each other well enough to have an affair. I'm asking you to have dinner with me and we'll see where that leads."

She already knew—straight to a bed.

"It's not happening." She placed her hand on the mouse. "Please show yourself out. I have work to do."

"Was he that good or that bad?"

The question had her sharply lifting her head. "My personal life is none of your concern. Now leave."

Straightening, he stared at her. She stared back.

Touching one long finger to the brim of his baseball cap, he turned and left.

The door closed quietly behind him. Marlene let out a breath, then closed her eyes. Hopefully, he wouldn't be back. The man really got to her. It wasn't just the body; it was the way he looked at her, as if she were the only thing that mattered.

Aware that her emotions were too muddled to allow her to get any work done, she powered down the computer, grabbed her purse, and stood. She hadn't thought he'd give up so easily.

After a brief knock, the door opened again. Her heart leaped. "Yes."

The door opened. "You ready, Ms. Montgomery?" Billy asked.

She shouldn't be disappointed on seeing Billy. She liked her life calm and uncomplicated. A man like Roman would muddle it up. "Yes, I was just coming out." She set the alarm, locked the front door, and they walked out together.

Billy would go home to his wife and daughter, and she would go to an empty house. She pushed the melancholy away. She had a good life, a full life. Dillon was coming home tonight.

But eventually he would leave and she'd be alone again.

"Your family is waiting for you," she said, digging in her

bag for her keys. "There's no need to follow me home to-night."

He grinned. "You might be right."

Frowning, Marlene turned to see what Billy was looking at over her shoulder. She couldn't believe what she saw.

Roman with a teddy bear, a box of Godiva chocolates, a yellow balloon, and a summer bouquet of flowers coming to-ward her.

"I'll go wait in the truck."

Roman stopped and held the things out to her. "I figured I'd better bring it the first time. I wasn't sure I'd get another chance."

Marlene wanted to take the unbelievably sweet offerings, but she folded her arms around her purse instead. "Thank you, but the answer is no."

"Why can't it be yes?"

He certainly liked to push. "I've already explained my rea-sons to you. Now, if you'll excuse me . . ."

"I can't do that."

Her eyes narrowed. "What did you say?"

"You know I didn't mean I'd keep you against your will or try to manhandle you," he said in disgust. "Or at least, I hope you do. I'd never lay a finger on a woman no matter the cir-cumstances."

"Then how do you propose to keep me from walking off?" she asked.

He took a step closer. "A kiss might do it."

Like a match to kindling. Her body caught fire, yearned. Her gaze went to his sensual mouth. She bet he knew how to use those mobile lips to woo, to seduce.

"But you might punch me and I'd never get a chance for us

to get to know each other better." He held the offerings closer. "Please. I'm really not a bad guy. Dillon wouldn't have hired me or call me a friend if I were."

True. Only Dillon had ever sent her flowers. Despite everything she'd been trying to tell herself, she was flattered and tempted. There had been few dates since Dillon was born. She hadn't missed men . . . at least until Roman had come into her life.

"Dinner and conversation. I'll follow you to wherever you want. You can leave when you get ready," he offered.

"This won't lead to anything."

"I'd like for us to be friends. Can we start there?" he asked earnestly.

A sensible request. She'd tried to lump Roman with A. J. because for the first time in years, her body had reacted to a man's. That had been wrong of her. She went to Billy's truck. "You won't have to follow me home, and if you mention this, I'll stop bringing food for the crew."

He pulled his two fingers across his lips. He started the truck then backed up and stopped briefly by Roman, before continuing on.

"What did he say?" she asked Roman.

"If I wanted to keep a certain part of my anatomy, I better act like a gentleman."

Her crew was almost as protective of her as Dillon. "You still want to go out?"

"More than ever. You lead, I'll follow."

"You get one chance. Blow it, and there won't be another."

"I figured as much." He held out the offering once again. "My arms are getting tired."

She reached for them, and he pushed them toward her. The

backs of his fingers brushed against her breast. She stepped back, but the damage was done. Her nipples hardened. Need pulsed through her.

"That wasn't intentional," he quickly said. "Why don't I follow you to your car and put them in the passenger's seat."

Marlene nodded and started for her car on trembling legs. She'd been right to avoid Roman. If she'd spoken, he would have known how much the simple touch had fired her blood. She could never allow him to know how much he got to her.

Tonight would be their first and only time to go out together. She would be a fool to go out with him again. Once was enough to last a lifetime.

Thirty miles outside of Elms Fork on Interstate 45, Dillon could breathe without desire clawing at him. He'd even slowed to the speed limit. Sitting beside him, Sam hadn't said one word when the speedometer reached ninety. She'd simply looked at him, then the gauge.

The gesture had been so like his mother's that he'd automatically eased off the gas pedal. Guess Sam, like his mother, knew that he didn't take orders well. It would be laughable that she understood him so well, and he'd reacted to the silent reprimand as if he didn't want her more than his next ragged breath.

"I have to agree that this car looks better than mine."

"We're even, because you look better than I do."

She tossed him a quick look of pleasure. "Thank you. Any idea how we play this tonight?"

"Straightforward." Dillon shifted gears and took the ramp to I-35 to downtown Dallas. "The development of the new

intercooler system should keep him interested enough to want
to take a look once it's designed."

"I'll let you do the talking and I'll entertain his wife," she
said, staring straight ahead.

He thought he heard a bit of condescension in her voice.
"You're on the consultant team. Speak up if you find an opportunity."

She turned toward him. "Really?"

She seemed so pleased that he wasn't about to tell her he
hoped she'd leave it to him. "Like I said, you're on the team
and you *have* made a lot of notes."

"Are you teasing me?" she asked, smiling.

"Wouldn't dare."

"Yes, you would, but that's all right because we're partners.
Like Marlene said, Granddad had faith in us."

Dillon glanced at Sam's shapely legs, then took the Oak
Lawn exit, no longer unsure how he felt about Abe's decision.

Marlene drove to Chili's on the outskirts of town. It was the
only national casual chain restaurant in the city. It benefited
from the interstate passing by and the town's only two hotels
across the street.

She parked between cars close to the entrance, got out and
walked to the double glass doors. She planned to say good-bye
there as well, so he wouldn't need to walk her to her car. This
would be quick: in and out.

Roman stepped into the light spilling from the high beams
of the parking lot and the twin black brass lanterns. Marlene
felt the impact of his eyes. Despite herself, she appreciated the
easy movement of the muscled body, the ground-eating gait.

In a tan shirt and slacks, he exuded confidence and masculinity.

"Sorry to keep you waiting. I had to find a parking spot." He took her arm.

Her skin heated. Tingled. Perhaps she should have kept saying no. With his free hand, he opened the door and ushered her inside.

"Welcome to Chili's," the hostess greeted them, picking up two menus. "Table for two?"

"Yes," Roman answered. "A booth if possible."

"Certainly. This way."

Roman followed with a silent Marlene to a two-seat booth. She quickly took her seat and put her purse on the outside. She wasn't taking any chances.

"Your waiter will be here shortly," the young woman said as she handed them their menus. "Can I get you anything to drink?"

"Marlene?" Roman asked.

Without lifting her head from the menu, she said, "Sweet iced tea."

"The same," Roman said, wondering how long Marlene planned to hide behind the menu.

"I'll get those right out."

As soon as she walked away, he braced his arms on the table. "Regrets already?"

After a moment, the menu lowered. Her beautiful black eyes were wary. "Yes."

Roman would have gladly kicked the butt of the man who made her afraid to trust her emotions or another man. Despite the rumors that Abe was Dillon's father, Roman didn't believe it. Marlene obviously was fond of the man and held no animosity toward him, even though he'd fired Dillon. He wasn't the man who had hurt her. Roman felt strongly that it was Dillon's father.

"You're staring."

"I like looking at beautiful things."

Up went the menu again.

He reached over and pulled it down. "I don't lie. You can trust me."

"Your drinks." The woman placed the glasses on the wooden table. "I'm Cindy. You folks ready to order?"

"Marlene?"

"Spinach salad with house dressing." She handed the waitress her menu.

"You, sir?"

Roman stared at Marlene. So she wanted to eat and run. Not happening. "We'll have the triple dipper appetizer out first, then I'll have the chicken-fried steak with a loaded baked potato, and brownie sundae with two scoops of ice cream for dessert."

"Wow . . ." The woman chuckled, accepting the menu. "A man who knows what he wants."

"I certainly do," Roman said, staring at Marlene.

The waitress's interested gaze bounced between the two, then she walked away smiling.

"Wanting isn't always getting," Marlene said.

"I know, but I'm hoping I can wear you down." He picked up his tea. "I've been on my own for the past five years. When I take a job, I put my social life on hold until I finish. I don't want my concentration splintered. This time I can't do that."

Marlene glanced down at the tea, picked it up, then put it down. "I don't want this."

"I can tell." He took another sip of tea. "I'd ask you why, but I don't think you're ready to tell me yet."

Lips that he wanted to press his own against tightened. "Always ready with the smart answers."

"Hardly. I've made my share of mistakes, but the one thing that I've learned is to take each day and live it to the fullest." He leaned back as the waitress placed the appetizer in front of them. He picked up a cheese stick. "That's why when I finish a job I take at least three weeks off to take it easy, visit my two kids in D.C. where they're working."

Her body stiffened. "How long were you married?"

The question wasn't asked idly. He placed the cheese stick on the small white plate. He didn't like talking about his marriage, but he realized Marlene was backing away from him as fast as she could. He had only one chance.

"Twenty-three years. I thought we were happy. I worked long hours. Old story, so I won't bore you with the details. I learned she was having an affair." He briefly tucked his head. "I filed for divorce and got custody of Amy, who was a senior in high school. Jonathan was a sophomore at Yale at the time."

"That must have been hard on all of you."

"You have no idea."

"No, I wouldn't." She glanced away.

Roman shoved his hand over his head in frustration. "You're wrong. You know what it is to want the best for your child. To make the hard decisions to give it to them. Dillon is the man he is because of you. Being a single parent has to be one of the toughest jobs in the universe. But mine were old enough to take care of themselves, and I had money. Don't ever sell yourself short."

"Your food." The waitress moved the appetizer over. "Not to your liking?"

"I guess not." He was batting his head against a wall. "You can take them away."

He was trying. There had been no divorce for her, only the disgrace that she was pregnant by a married man.

What would Roman think of her if he knew she had been the other woman? She still felt the shame.

"No." Marlene reached for a chip. She had no right to be so self-righteous. "Although the salad looks delicious, I don't think it's going to fill me up."

Roman smiled at her. Her heart jerked. Once. Hard. "Can't have that. This is cold. How about we share my food until the waitress can bring out another appetizer?"

She smiled back. She could handle this. "I'd like that."

At six fifty, Dillon pulled up behind a Lamborghini at the Mansion on Turtle Creek. He'd barely stopped before a valet reached for his door and opened it.

"Welcome to the Mansion."

"Thanks." Dillon stood and rounded the car to take Sam's arm. He hoped his body was up to the test.

Now wasn't the time to remember he hadn't been with a woman in months or how much he'd like to take Sam upstairs to one of the luxury rooms, strip them both, and just enjoy.

"It's as beautiful as I'd imagined." Sam glanced around the courtyard with the hotel on one side and the five-star restaurant on the other. Tiny lights twinkled in the trees.

She was just as beautiful, but he wasn't about to tell her that. He wasn't a man to sway a woman with pretty words. He preferred the more earthy approach. He cupped Sam's elbow, felt the soft skin, and smelled her fragrance. It was going to be a long night.

"Mr. Montgomery."

About to pass a small group of people, he paused as he recognized Frank Thomas from his picture on the company's Web site. That would teach him to keep his mind on business. Dillon extended his hand. "I'm sorry, Mr. Thomas. I didn't see you."

Frank Thomas, dressed in a tailored blue suit, laughed jovially and returned the strong handshake. "You weren't expecting a crowd. Don't worry." He smiled at a group of teenage boys standing to the side of them, their mouths gaping, their eyes huge.

"They're not staying. I was in the kitchen when I told my wife about our dinner engagement." Thomas chuckled and shook his head again. "I thought my son would go insane with glee. He went with me to a vintage race once and was instantly taken with the cars. He's gotten his friends hooked on vintage cars as well. Of course, they've heard of you and wanted to meet you."

Dillon nodded at the eager teenagers staring at the Ferrari and the other luxury cars in the courtyard. "Since they're watching cars, I'd like you to meet Sam—Samantha Collins, Abe's granddaughter and fellow consultant with Collins Industry."

Frank extended his hand and pulled a thin woman in a knee-length navy-blue dress forward. "My wife, Cynthia."

"Hello. I'll thank you now for suggesting dining here," Cynthia said. "I'd dine here every week if I could."

Dillon nodded toward Sam. "Thank Sam."

"I thought we could enjoy ourselves in beauty and luxury while the men talked shop," Sam said.

"You couldn't have picked a better spot." Cynthia looked fondly at her husband. "Talking shop, he sometimes forgets I'm there."

"I doubt that," Dillon said sincerely, then smoothly turned to the five teenagers. "Hi, fellows. Got the bug, have you?"

"That's a 1948 166 MM Barchetta, the definitive 1950s sports car, isn't it?" said the tallest of the teenagers, the one in front.

"You know your cars." Dillon chuckled. "I might not be on the circuit, but I still like driving vintage. Speed is best on the racetrack and not on the highway. I know you fellows all agree."

"Yes, sir," they agreed.

Since Dillon had been a teenage boy with a car and a motorcycle, he didn't believe them for a second. "If there was a race, I'd invite you as my guests, but how would you like to come out to my high-performance garage tomorrow in Frisco? I'm restoring a 1982 BMW and a 1983 Lotus. There's enough room in back for each of you to take a short spin."

They whooped with glee. "Yeah!"

Dillon pulled out his wallet and handed a card to the boy in front. "I'll be there after one."

"Thanks," they chorused.

"All right, Douglas, you and your friends have met Mr. Montgomery. Now, we need to go inside for our dinner reservations," Mrs. Thomas said.

Douglas waved the card. "Man. Thanks again. See you tomorrow."

Mr. Thomas clapped Dillon on the back. "I think my son and his friends have a serious case of hero worship on you."

"But you're the one he'll see each day, the one he's learning how to be a man from," Dillon said.

Thomas nodded slowly. "Abe selected well. You have your feet planted firmly on the ground."

"Dillon also has a lot of innovative ideas that will offer a lot to Tasco," Sam said. "With the inner cooling system he's perfecting, we plan to shake things up."

"I believe you will," Mr. Thomas said.

Dillon took Sam's arm. "Let's go in to dinner and we can talk further."

As always, Marlene didn't get out of her car until she had her front-door key in her hand. She heard Roman's quiet steps behind her, and her nervousness grew as she hurried up the walk. She shouldn't have let him follow her home, but he'd mentioned it as soon as they'd exited the restaurant, then hurried to his car. She was left staring after him.

On the porch she kept her back to him until she had the front door open, had reached inside to turn on the light on the porch and in the entry. She turned for a quick good-bye, her hand already outstretched, and found herself pressed against a wall of muscled warmth.

His mouth didn't ask. He took, pleasured, overwhelming her senses. Her body responded before she could take a breath, molding itself against him, her hand in his thick hair. The hot kiss made a mockery of her attempt to deny her attraction to this man.

Roman lifted his head, his breath uneven against her lips. She wanted his mouth, his knowing hands on her again. She shook her head, pushing against his chest. She'd overestimated her control where he was concerned.

"I want you, but I know it's too soon."

She shook her head. "No," she managed, her voice sounding thready with need.

"Yes. I can drive down tomorrow and we can do whatever you like."

Make love in the sunshine.

She barely kept from groaning. She hadn't thought of being intimate with a man in years. She pushed against his chest. This time he let her go. She missed the heat, the solid warmth, immediately. "This has to stop. I can't go out with you again."

He took her arms in his, dragging her against him again. "I'm not him. I won't hurt you."

Anger replaced desire. "You don't know anything about me. Now let me go."

His fingers tightened for a second, then she was free. "It's not over between us."

"There is no 'us.' I don't want this."

"You can lie to me, but your body can't. This isn't over." Reaching past her, he pushed the front door open farther. "Go inside before I show you."

Her body trembling, Marlene went inside, closing and locking the door after her. His words rang in her ears. *This isn't over.*

Heaven help her. He was right. What was she going to do?

Nine

. . . .

Dinner had turned out better than Dillon expected. Sam had been wonderful. Not only had she kept the conversation going, she'd made sure Thomas's wife didn't feel left out. She was definitely an asset.

He'd have to agree with his mother. Abe had been smart to turn the company over to her.

Dillon would be equally smart to think of her only as his business partner. Unfortunately, that wasn't going to happen. He wasn't used to self-denial. Neither said anything as he walked her to her front door. Silently he took her key, unlocked the door, then handed it back to her. He wanted both hands free.

"Thank you. I thought it went well tonight."

"It's about to get better." Reaching out, he slowly pulled her into his arms. Her sharp intake of breath made his body harden. His head lowered. He brushed his lips across hers, swallowed her sweet breath as it rushed in and out.

He wanted to savor, but he couldn't wait. His mouth molded itself against her, his tongue thrusting inside her mouth to taste and pleasure. She was sweet. And addictive. The more he tasted, the more he wanted to taste.

It stunned him how much he wanted her. But the need had been building since he'd first seen her that night. Or had it started all those years ago?

His hand cupped her hips, bringing her against his rock-hard arousal. She whimpered. He wanted to as well because there was no way they were going to finish this.

Breathing as if he'd run for hours, Dillon crushed her against him and tried to control the need pulsing through him. "I have an appointment at eight in Dallas or I'd be knocking on your door to take you out."

"Dillon. We can't do this."

She sounded as shaky as he felt. He lifted his head and stared down into her troubled face. "We already did."

She licked her lips, and he was helpless to keep from kissing her again. She clung to him.

"See?" he teased. Sam was too serious, but he'd change that. "You were meant to be loved by me."

"No. I'm shameless." She tried to break free. He let her go because she appeared so upset.

"What is it?" He'd never felt protective of a woman he wanted. He did now. Sam had a way of changing things.

"Please don't get mad. I really like Marlene and I'm not judging her, but we—we could be related."

He'd heard the rumors about Abe being his father and never once thought to correct them. Neither had his mother. It hadn't mattered what people thought. He and his mother had never discussed the rumor of his parentage circulating around town because she'd already told him years before, when at age ten he'd asked who his father was.

It hadn't been easy for her to tell him about A. J. Reed. She regretted that his father wasn't a man either could be proud of, but she thanked God for Dillon each day. He'd said he felt the same way about her being his mother. It was never discussed again.

Softhearted Sam would be racked with guilt if he didn't tell her the truth. Palming her face, he stared down at her. "Abe wasn't my father."

He saw the relief rushing through her. She didn't question him further. He hadn't expected her trust in him to make his chest feel tight. "Thank God. I won't burn in hell."

His lips curved into a smile. "No. I intend for you to burn for an entirely different reason." His mouth took hers again in an openly erotic kiss. "We'll talk when I get back." He released her then got into his car and drove away.

Her mood mellow, Samantha opened the door and came face-to-face with her uncle in his silk robe and pajamas. His chest heaved with rage.

"You're a disgrace to this family!" he yelled. "How could you shame the family name by going out with Daddy's bastard?"

Samantha bristled. "Stop calling him that, and what's more, it was a business dinner."

He sneered. "I saw the two of you on the porch."

She refused to tuck her head. "Granddaddy was not Dillon's father."

"You'd believe anything the man says."

"I trust him because he's never lied to me. He wants the company to succeed."

Her uncle threw his hands in the air. "Get your head out of the clouds. If he does—and I say if—it's because he plans to take it over when the time is ripe. He's just stringing you along. Why should he want you otherwise?"

Samantha didn't have an answer. She'd seen the way women at the plant and at dinner tonight looked at Dillon. "I'm going to bed."

"I won't stand by and let you drag the family name through the mud, and ruin the company because you can't control your lust."

Samantha spun around. "I've had enough of your bullying."

His eyes widened. "You watch it."

"No, you watch it." She came back to him.

"Don't you talk to me that way. I'm the head of this family."

"Then why didn't Granddad—" She clamped her teeth together to keep the words from spilling out. Her uncle looked as if he wanted to strangle her.

"Daddy was sick or he would have left me in charge," he shouted. "There is no other explanation. You and that no-good are just taking advantage of it."

Samantha felt sorry for her uncle. Apparently he had no idea how his father felt about his poor performance. Telling him now would only make matters worse. "I don't want to fight, Uncle Evan. Please, can't we just work together?"

"I'd rather light a match to the whole thing."

Shock raced across her face. "You hate me, us, that much?" He said nothing, just glared at her. "I guess there's nothing else to say." She headed up the stairs.

"I'm not finished with you."

Slowly she turned, her fists clenched. "Yes, you are. I've

bent over backwards trying to keep the peace with you and Aunt Janice. But the more I try, the more you take advantage of me. It stops tonight. My life is my own. If you don't like it, you can move."

His mouth gaped.

"The house is half mine. From now on, there's going to be some changes. The cook and staff won't cater to just you or Aunt Janice's dictates, so you better tell her. Another thing, you better start preparing yourself. It isn't fair to Dillon or me to let people think we're consultants."

His mouth tightened. "Dillon. It always comes down to him. He's using you."

"Why do you hate him?"

"That should be obvious."

"No, it's not." She came down a couple of steps. "Grand-dad was a good, honest man who loved his family. He built this house so we could all be together. If either of us had stopped to think, we wouldn't have believed the rumors for a second. He wouldn't have abandoned his son."

"I don't call getting him into MIT abandoning him. Daddy bent over backwards for Marlene. He never wanted anyone to say a word against her, but he didn't mind taking me to task in front of people."

Realization dawned. "It's Marlene you hate."

"I wouldn't waste my breath on that nothing," he sneered. "It just makes me mad that Daddy couldn't see it."

He was lying. Was it jealousy or more? Marlene was a beautiful woman. She was probably breathtaking when she was younger.

"The business dinner tonight was with Frank Thomas. He was certainly impressed with Dillon."

Something flashed across her uncle's face. "How dare you go through my old accounts!"

There was no use pointing out that as part owner she had every right. "I didn't have to. Granddad kept duplicates of all the accounts."

Astonishment and something else flashed across his face.

"You didn't know that, did you?" she asked.

He laughed, but it was hollow. "Of course I did. I had just forgotten."

More lies. She had gotten a good look at her uncle, and she didn't like what she saw. He was nowhere near the man her father or grandfather had been. Worse, his own father had seen his shortcomings. And no matter how much he blamed everyone else, it was her uncle's own fault.

"I'm going to bed. Good night." Her euphoria gone, Samantha went to her room on the second floor. Plopping on the bed, she lay back and put her arm over her eyes. She had to assume that her uncle would never accept her and Dillon over him. He'd make it tough for her at work and at home.

Although she'd seen little of him the last week, after tonight she didn't think that would be the case. She didn't want to have a confrontation every day. Becoming involved with Dillon would only make her uncle worse.

If there was the slightest possibility that she wasn't just the next woman on Dillon's long list, she'd take the chance. She knew she was. Collins certainly wouldn't keep him around. She'd seen the excited way he'd talked about the cars he was restoring, his business, vintage racing.

Collins Industry and she were pit stops, so to speak. She had to be sensible and not let herself care for him any more than she already did.

. . .

Whistling, Dillon entered his mother's house through the back door. It had been a good night all around. He grinned as he opened the built-in refrigerator for a soft drink. He'd finally had a chance to see if Sam tasted as good as he'd remembered. He was happy to say, it was much, much better.

He snapped the light off and headed to his mother's room. She'd still be up, waiting on him. She said she was too old to stop now. The can was halfway to his mouth when he noticed there weren't any lights spilling from her room into the small alcove next to it. She usually left her door open and her flameless candles on in case she had to get up.

His concern deepened on seeing her door closed. "Mama?" He knocked softly. "Mama, are you all right?"

"Dillon, come on in."

Still frowning, he opened the door. She was in the queen-sized sleigh bed she loved with a paperback novel in her hand, her eyeglasses perched on her nose. Her eyes were red. He crossed to her in three long strides. "What is it? Are you sick?"

"I'm fine," she said, but her voice hitched.

"You've been crying?" His heart thumped with fear in his chest.

She held up the book in her hand. "I'm sorry if I frightened you." Scooting over, she patted the bed. "Tell me about the meeting."

Relief rushed through him. She'd never been sick. He'd thought she was invincible. Abe probably thought the same thing. "You're sure?" If anything happened to her . . .

"Positive." She laid the book aside and pushed her eyeglasses up on her nose. "I bet Samantha looked beautiful."

"She did," he said. Then, remembering the hot kiss, he took a long swallow of his cold drink. "She's becoming a great asset to the company. Frank Thomas's wife certainly liked her. She's playful and funny. I'm glad she went with me." He took another swallow. "If only she'd tell Evan to take a flying leap."

"It's more difficult with relatives."

Dillon eased down on the bed. "I used to want a brother or a sister, cousins. But now I'm glad it's just the two of us."

"Being an only child can be hard," she said slowly.

He grinned. "Not for me. I don't think I'd share well." He took another sip. "What's left over from dinner? I'm kind of hungry."

She flushed. "I—I ate out. I can fix you something."

"No, you won't." He stood. "I'm heading out in the morning around six. I have appointments at the high-performance garage at eight. It will be a nonstop Saturday and Sunday. I probably won't come back until late Sunday night or early Monday morning."

"Wake me up when you get up so I can fix your breakfast."

"Not happening. And when you hear me bumbling around, don't get up or I'll be upset with you." Leaning over, he kissed her on the forehead. "You taught me how to take care of myself."

She took his face in her hands. "I'm very proud of you."

He stared into her red eyes, noted the puffy lids, then reached over and picked up the book. "Maybe you shouldn't read any more tonight if it's going to make you this emotional."

"Perhaps you're right." She took the book and placed it on the nightstand. "Good night, Dillon. I'm glad I have you."

To make sure, he put the paperback in the drawer, then reached for the covers. "In you go."

Smiling, she removed her glasses and scooted beneath the down covers. "Tucking me in?"

"You've done it enough for me. Good night, Mama."

"Good night, Dillon. I love you."

"Love you too." He clicked off the light, went to the door, stared at her as his eyes adjusted to the darkness. "You're sure you're all right?"

"With you in my life, how could I not be? And just because traffic will be light on the road in the morning, try to stay within the speed limit."

"I'll try." Smiling, he went to his room.

His mother was just being emotional because of the book she was reading. He undressed and crawled into bed, his thoughts turning to Sam, how she'd felt so right in his arms, the kiss that he never wanted to end.

"Abe, you old devil. I might forgive you yet." In less than a minute he was asleep.

Monday morning, Samantha arrived at work shortly before seven thirty. She wanted to be prepared when Dillon arrived.

She'd rehearsed her speech over and over. Any other relationship between them except a business one would be detrimental to their running Collins Industry. The company had to come first.

When Dillon opened the door shortly before eight, looking hot and mouthwatering in a white polo and black jeans that delineated his muscled chest and strong thighs, it was all she could do not to jump up from her desk and run to meet him, to plaster her lips and body to his. She couldn't. If she could stand up to her uncle, she could stand up to, and hopefully resist, Dillon.

If he touched her, though, she was lost. She had to stop him before he reached her.

"Kissing you was a mistake."

Dillon stopped in midstride. His smile died; his eyes chilled.

"We both got a bit carried away Friday night, but it can't happen again." She gripped the pen in her hand beneath her desk and tried to remember the rest of her rehearsed speech. "Collins Industry has to be our only focus."

"Fine by me," he responded as nonchalantly as if she'd asked about the weather. "Business first is the best all around. I just wanted you to know I'm back. I'm going to work on the intercooler. I worked on it while I was in Dallas and brought it back to finish. I'll pick up Roman's and my lunch today. Later."

Samantha stared at the closed door. She'd done it, but what made her soul ache was that he hadn't seemed to mind one bit. The kiss that had made her whimper with need had meant nothing to him. He'd completely fooled her.

"What the hell happened to Sam? Her kisses had set my blood on fire," Dillon muttered as he headed for the shop. He'd bet her worthless uncle had something to do with it.

Dillon spun around and started for Evan's office, then stopped a few feet from the office door. Sam had to learn to fight for what she wanted. He just hoped that included him.

Changing directions once again, he started for the shop. He was more determined than ever to perfect the intercooler. Once that was done, Sam wouldn't have to worry about Collins, and she'd be back in his arms.

"Dillon, we need to talk."

Dillon glanced from the intercooler he was designing to see Roman. His friend's usual smile was missing. *Another problem,* Dillon thought. As if his day weren't bad enough.

There were too many people in the work area to talk. Sam was in their office. The was only one other place. "Follow me."

Dillon led the way outside. He stopped at the back of his truck, looked around to ensure they were alone. "How bad is it?"

"It's not about the financial records."

Dillon wasn't in the best of moods as it was. "Then why did you drag me out here?"

"Because what I have to say to you is personal."

Dillon frowned, then it hit him. "You want to talk about a woman?"

"A very special woman."

"I didn't think you dated women while you worked."

"I didn't expect this," Roman told him.

"Yeah. So what?" Dillon mused, thinking of Sam. His feelings for her had thrown him for a loop. Now, she wanted him to back off. Not likely.

"You might think differently when I tell you who it is."

Dillon's eyes narrowed and he gave Roman his full attention. "It had better not be Sam."

"Of course not."

"I'm having enough trouble with her. She can make me so mad I could shake her. I bet that uncle of hers is behind—"

"It's your mother. Marlene."

Dillon had been only half listening, his mind on Sam. Slowly he faced Roman. "What did you say?" Now Roman had his full attention.

Roman was not going to back down from the sudden shift in Dillon's posture, the narrowed eyes. "Marlene and I went out Friday night. She doesn't want to see me again, but I'm not giving up."

"You touch her?" Dillon asked, his voice deadly quiet.

"We kissed."

Dillon struck, grabbing Roman by the shirt and pulling him closer to his snarling face. "Touch her again, and suffer the consequences. Pack your stuff and get off my property."

"My leaving isn't going to change anything, and if you hit me, it will upset Marlene," Roman said as calmly as he could, his arms by his sides.

"You're pushing it, Roman." Dillon pulled him inches closer. Good thing Roman wasn't wearing a tie.

"I didn't have to tell you, but your mother is being cautious—" Roman felt his temper start a slow boil. "I guess she has her reasons, but I'm not giving up or going away."

"Damn." Dillon pushed him away and studied the other

man he respected and was proud to call his friend. "She's my mother."

"That's why I let you wrinkle up my shirt and get in my face." Roman jerked his shirt back into place. There was nothing he could do about the wrinkles. "If I did anything to you, she'd come after me and I'd never get her to go out with me again."

"She loves me," Dillon said.

"And has probably always put you first. I'm asking that if you can't approve of my seeing her, don't stand in the way or badmouth me," Roman said.

Dillon shoved his hand over his head, paced away then back, studied Roman. He had known Roman since he was a freshman at MIT. Roman could be methodical in what he wanted.

"Why now? Why my mother?"

"She's beautiful, intelligent, courageous. She interests me as no woman has in years. I want to get to know her better—if she'll let me. She's built her entire life around you. I don't think she's ever had much fun in life," Roman said thoughtfully. "I'd like to change that."

Dillon thought back to Friday night. His mother's emotions hadn't been because of a book. Roman had caused them. She wasn't easily rattled or upset. She must feel something for him.

Dillon didn't have to think long to recall that his mother had dated few men, at least that he knew of. It had always been just the two of them. He wasn't selfish enough to want her to always be by herself. "After today, if she sheds one tear, if you hurt her, I'll be in your face again and I'll do more than wrinkle your shirt."

Roman stuck out his hand. "I'd expect no less. I'd do the same thing to a man who messed with Amy."

Dillon accepted the hand. "Your daughter can take care of herself."

"So can your mother, but we both know there are some snakes out there masquerading as men." The handshake was firm. "I better get back to work. I plan to actually take a lunch break today."

"You're going to see Mama?"

Roman smiled. "Yes."

Dillon watched Roman walk away. He'd never seen that coming. He wasn't sure how he felt about Roman dating his mother, but he'd give him a chance. Instead of going back to work on the prototype, he found himself heading toward the office he shared with Sam.

Five feet away, Dillon heard her uncle shouting. He was inside the office in seconds.

"What's going on?"

Evan turned on Dillon, waving a slim strip of paper in his hand. "What the hell do you think you're doing?"

Dillon crossed his arms, feeling better since he had ruined Evan's day. "Running Collins Industry."

Evan advanced on Dillon, waving the paper in his hand. "I want my money and I want it now. I had to pay for my lunch. My card was declined."

"Imagine that," Dillon said, his smile growing.

"You might think this is funny," Evan snapped. "I certainly do not. My secretary said accounts payable wouldn't reimburse me. I want my credit card reinstated immediately and this taken care of."

Peering closer, Dillon looked at the receipt. "Twenty-eight ninety-seven. Mighty expensive lunch for one person. Sam, how much did lunch for the three of us cost yesterday at Subway?"

"Twenty-one dollars and seventy-five cents," she answered, coming from around the desk. "You wanted chocolate-chip cookies."

"So I did."

Evan sneered. "My taste is more sophisticated."

"Sounds like a personal problem to me," Dillon drawled.

Evan looked at Samantha. "Reinstate my credit card. Now!"

"Not happening." Dillon unfolded his arms. "The company is barely making payroll. Collins Industry is no longer going to pay for you or your wife's clothes, grocery bill, cell phone, cable, or the myriad things you claim as business expenses."

"You can't do that!"

"It's already done. Abe's will said you were to continue with your salary, but it didn't say anything about 'business expenses,' so I suggest you learn to live with your twenty thousand dollars a month salary."

"What?" Samantha rushed to her uncle. "You make that much?"

His chin lifted. "I deserve that and more. I helped make Collins."

"And spent the profits lavishly on you and your wife. It stops today," Dillon told him. "I bet you haven't thought of paying your half of the household expenses."

"That's none of your business," Evan snapped.

"Sam," Dillon said.

"We should share the household expenses, Uncle Evan," Sam said. "It's only fair."

Evan looked at them coldly, venom dripping from each word: "You're going to fail, and when you do I'll be there to see it." The door slammed.

"The company failing means more to him than its continuation, or what it will do to the lives of the two hundred employees," Sam said quietly, then looked at Dillon with determination. "We won't let that happen."

He had that urge to hold her again to reassure her, but he tamped it down. Perhaps she was right. From now on it was going to be strictly business between them, just as she'd wanted. "Once the company is running smoothly, I plan to turn everything over to you."

Her eyes widened in alarm. "You aren't staying?"

"Five years! Are you kidding? My life isn't wrapped around Collins Industry. I have my own businesses to run," he told her. "I'm scheduled to be at a vintage race in Las Vegas this weekend. I'm flying out Friday afternoon."

"I see." She started for her desk, then spun back. "If you've perfected the intercooler by then, could one of the cars be fitted with it?"

He liked the idea. "It could work. But we'd have to get the owner on board."

"When we do, the next step is to get a write-up in a sports article, which will get Collins Industry out there," she said. "You handle getting the car, I'll take care of getting us the press."

"You sound as if the article is a sure thing."

"I am." She looked thoughtful for a moment. "I'd like to go with you."

"Who is he?" Maybe he'd been brushed off for more than business reasons.

"Since you're my business partner, his name is Mark Washington. I seem to recall he mentioned covering vintage racing once or twice. I'll call and see if he plans to cover the event."

"How close are you?"

"I think you've gone from business to personal." Sam went behind her desk. "I'll let you get back to work."

He studied her. She hadn't caved this time or made excuses for her uncle.

"Yes?"

"Nothing." Perhaps it was for the best that they keep it business after all. "See you later, Sam."

Ten

. . . .

Samantha didn't look up until the door closed. Blowing out a breath, she leaned back in her chair. She'd done it now, and there was no way she could back out even if she wanted to.

She eyed the phone on her desk. She'd talked as if getting Mark there were a sure thing. It wasn't. Not by a long shot.

Calling Mark would present problems she wasn't sure she wanted to deal with. He'd expect the call to be about them, not about business. Once he understood the reason for her contacting him, there was no telling how he'd react. She picked up her pen and tapped it on top of her files.

There was every possibility he would blow her off. She just hoped that he'd already planned to cover the event and that he'd consider getting a scoop on a prototype of a new intercooler a professional coup. If he did come, she knew without a doubt that he'd press for them get back together. Not happening. Ever.

The reason had just walked out the door.

With a breath-stealing kiss Friday night, Dillon had killed any chance of her ever wanting Mark again. She tossed the pencil aside and admitted that he'd stood between her and every man she'd dated since their first kiss on her prom night. She could have taken her prom date up on his offer to get a motel room in Dallas or said yes to any of the other boys who had been trying to have sex with her. None of them had interested her.

Dillon again.

One fateful look when she was thirteen was all it had taken for her to be struck by the reckless look in his dark eyes, the gorgeous face, the sleek muscled body in skintight jeans and a white T-shirt.

She'd been at the bakery with her mother when he'd roared up on his bike, with Jenny Sanders hanging onto him. He'd been the epitome of the town's bad boy with good looks, easy charm, a loose woman, and the fastest car or motorbike around. It hadn't mattered to her that he was rumored to be her grandfather's illegitimate son and going straight to hell with his drinking and fast driving. Everyone in the bakery turned to look at her and her mother to gauge their reaction.

Dillon had come into the bakery with a clinging Jenny wearing white short shorts and a tiny red tube top barely covering her large breasts. People in line were more interested in watching Dillon than getting their purchases. He'd stopped in front of the cookies. When the salesperson asked if she could help him, he'd nodded toward her mother. "Mrs. Collins was here first."

Her mother had smiled and thanked him, then added, "Samantha can't make up her mind."

He'd turned those captivating eyes on her and smiled.

Butterflies had taken flight in her stomach. "Chocolate-chip, but I bet your mother can make them better. Mine can."

Stunned, she'd just nodded. He'd smiled back, ordered two dozen chocolate-chip cookies, and then he and Jenny were gone. Even then, aware she shouldn't but unable to help herself, she'd wished she were old enough to be on that bike with him.

She'd gotten her chance to be with him on prom night. It had been her suggestion to go to the bar in the hope that he'd be there. Graduation was coming up, and with each passing day, she missed her parents more. The Jack Daniel's she'd drunk hadn't dulled the unhappiness. She was miserable enough to hope the rumors about sex would. At least the whiskey had given her the courage to proposition Dillon.

Dillon had done what she'd never expected—taken her home. Of course, at the time, she'd felt embarrassed and unwanted. Now, she realized he had been noble. Her father had liked Dillon. He would be pleased that they were working together. Thus far, she had contributed very little.

Now was her chance.

She had to suck it up and make the phone call. Collins Industry needed the publicity. Dillon had come through. She had to do the same.

Samantha snatched up the phone before she lost her courage and dialed the direct number to Mark's desk. If he didn't answer, she'd—

"Mark Washington, *Houston Sentinel.*"

Samantha's hand flexed on the phone. "Hello, Mark. This is a professional call about Collins Industry. Do you have time to talk?" She knew she sounded abrupt, but she didn't want him to say anything he'd regret or be embarrassed about.

"So you haven't changed your mind?"

There was a mixture of surprise and disappointment in his voice. Samantha wished there were another way. "No. You might have heard of my partner, Dillon Montgomery. He's designed a top-mounted intercooler where the aesthetics of the car are not compromised, and which will give the car greater speed."

"Dillon Montgomery is your partner?"

"Yes." Samantha sat up straighter. "Dillon has a great reputation as a top-notch mechanic."

"He also has a reputation for playing fast and loose with women," Mark said, a hint of censure in his voice.

"We're just partners," Samantha said. At least now. "Collins Industry will have the prototype in a vintage racing car this weekend in Las Vegas. If you're coming, we'll give you an exclusive."

"Are you going?"

"Yes." She was all too aware that he hadn't asked for any more information. Not even the car or the name of the team. "We're flying down Friday morning so the car can be fitted with the prototype in time for the practice runs."

"I have an event Friday. Where are you staying? I'll call you when I arrive Saturday."

"I'm not sure," she said slowly. "We haven't finalized arrangements."

There was a long, telling silence. "I'll bet."

Annoyed, Samantha came to her feet. "This is business between me and Dillon, just like between us. Perhaps I should call another newspaper."

"I'm sorry. You don't have to be so defensive," he said quickly.

"And you don't have to be so nasty," she shot back.

"All right. All right. There's no need to get upset. I'll call your cell. What's the number?"

She hesitated. They both knew she'd changed her cell phone number because he'd kept calling. "It's 566-555-2222." She needed him.

"See you Saturday."

"Thank you, Mark. See you Saturday." Samantha hung up the phone. She'd done it, but why did she feel uneasy about the coming weekend?

Roman could be a patient man when necessary, but he could also push when needed. Dealing with Marlene definitely called for the latter. With a bakery box in hand, he entered the main office of the garage. A woman who looked to be in her sixties glanced up from working on a computer at one end of the counter. Roman had hoped Marlene would be there.

Smiling, the woman moved to the middle of the counter. "Good afternoon. How can I help you?"

Roman returned the smile and held up the bakery box. "I'm here to see Marlene. I want to surprise her."

The woman's gaze flicked to the box, then back to him. "You've known Marlene long?"

"Just recently. Dillon and I are old friends, and I'm doing some work for him," Roman told her. "A thank-you for the wonderful meal she cooked the other night."

The woman snorted. "If I hadn't seen her come in, the crew would have eaten all the burgers before I got one. They acted like they hadn't eaten in days."

"Marlene wouldn't have let that happen," he said. "She cares about people."

"And we all care about her," the woman said, studying him intently.

"Dillon most of all, and he knows I'm here," Roman said. He wasn't about to be deterred.

She eyed his wrinkled shirt, then angled her gray head to the side door. "We'll be watching you."

"I wouldn't have it any other way. Thank you." Roman went through the door and down the short hallway. The woman's comments just confirmed his belief that Marlene hadn't dated much.

As beautiful and as vibrant as she was, he would never believe it was because she hadn't been asked. Somewhere a man in her past—perhaps Dillon's father—had hurt her so deeply that she refused to trust again, to open her heart for fear of being misused again.

Roman had his work cut out for him. He wouldn't allow Marlene to push him away. He could take a no, but not after the kiss that had unleashed a hunger in both of them. He knocked.

"Come in."

Opening the door, he saw her sitting behind her desk. Sunlight spilled through the windows on either side of her. She was beautiful in a lemon-yellow blouse, and as weary as ever. Her shoulders tensed; the pleasant smile turned to ice. He'd known it wouldn't be easy.

He closed the door and headed straight for her desk. He lifted the lid on the oversize red velvet cupcake. "I thought you'd like a dessert you didn't have to cook. There's enough for you to share with your crew."

"I told you I don't want this."

"So you said." Placing the box directly in front of her, he braced one hip on the edge of the desk. "I told Dillon we went out and asked his permission to try and persuade you to go out with me again."

"What!" She surged to her feet. "You had no right to go behind my back and discuss me with my son."

He stood. "Can't you see, that's exactly what I didn't want to do. I want to date you openly. It's going to be hard enough to get you to trust me. I didn't need the added aggravation of Dillon out for my blood."

"Why can't you just let it go and move on to the next woman?" she asked, her voice trembling as much as her body.

He heard the fear in her voice and again thought he'd like to punch the man who had made her that way. She deserved so much and was afraid to reach out and take it. He'd teach her.

"I'm not a man who goes from woman to woman. True, I try to relax between jobs, but that doesn't mean I have to have a woman to do so," he told her. "I won't hurt you. I promise. Trust me. Trust this."

His mouth took hers, gently, then with growing ardor. Both were trembling when it was over. "That's why I'm not walking away. You move me, excite me." He brushed his hand over her hair. "I want to do wicked things to you, protect you, make you laugh for no reason. No woman has ever made me feel that way."

"Don't do this," she whispered, blinking rapidly.

Pulling her closer, he gently kissed each eye. "Dillon said if you shed one tear, he'd do more than wrinkle my shirt."

Her gaze dropped to his shirt. She ran her fingertips over the creases. "He's protective of me."

"And he loves you. If he thought I was running a con, I'd be in need of a doctor by now," Roman said. "I'm asking again that you give us a real chance. Don't try to read something negative into my every sentence. Just trust me. Please. I won't hurt you or lie to you. Like I said, I know what that feels like."

"You might not want to go out with me if you really knew me," she whispered. She'd been the other woman.

"I doubt that, but I'm willing to take the chance." He lifted her chin. "How about a movie tonight? Or we can drive into Dallas and go out to dinner."

With the muscled warmth of his body against hers, his beautiful face so close to hers, it was difficult to think straight. "If we go to Dallas, you'll be late driving back and then you'll have to come back in the morning."

"I like your being concerned about me, but I'm used to driving." He grinned. "If it will make you feel better, we can go by my place afterwards. I'll pick up some things and when I drop you off at home, I can get a hotel room in Elms Fork."

Going by his place would be too risky. "A movie here should be fine. I'll fix dinner."

"Nope, we'll go out."

"Dillon—"

"Can fend for himself." Roman kissed her. "Six thirty all right?"

He kissed her and her logical mind shut down. She might be getting in over her head. "I suppose."

He brushed his lips across hers. "Thank you. You won't be sorry."

"If I am, you'll be sorrier."

He laughed, kissed her again, and then was gone. Scared, excited, Marlene plopped into her seat. *Roman, please don't be a lie,* she thought.

Dillon was too restless to work on the prototype. He'd gone outside and called Carson's father, Nathan Rowland, about using the intercooler in his 1948 BMW in Saturday's race. Nathan might respect Dillon's ability, but he was a race car fanatic and as competitive as they came. Carson, his oldest son, owned three luxury car dealerships in the Southwest. He drove the BMW on race day and was even more competitive.

The best Mr. Rowland could offer Dillon was a chance in the qualifying trial in Friday's races. If the intercooler did its job, Dillon was in. If not . . . In exchange for the opportunity, Dillon gave a verbal agreement to be on call exclusively for Rowland Racing Team for the next two months. Dillon hadn't hesitated. Both of them knew that ideas for improvements on cars came quickly; it was imperative to get his on the car as fast as possible and see if it worked.

Dillon disconnected the call, got in his truck to go pick up lunch and ended up at the garage. He saw Roman's convertible Porsche pulling out as he was pulling in. He parked and went inside the main office. "Hi, Gloria. You're looking as sexy and as beautiful as ever."

"My husband thinks so, but it's always nice to hear," she told him.

Dillon chuckled. Gloria was a hoot, and he liked to tease her. "I'm going on back."

She leaned over the counter and whispered, "He just left.

He's a handsome devil, I give you that, but I told him we'd be watching him."

"Thanks." Dillon went to his mother's office and knocked. "Come in."

Her voice sounded shaky. She could be upset or . . . Dillon opened the door. His mother's cheeks were flushed, her hair slightly mussed. Scratch upset.

She held his gaze, but he could tell she was nervous. She'd never asked for anything from him, done without so he didn't have to. She'd worked hard to give him a house with a yard, the puppy he'd wanted, the car at sixteen.

Some would say she'd given him too much. As an adult, he realized she hadn't wanted him to have less or, more important, feel less because he didn't have a father in his life.

Dillon knew Roman was right. One word from Dillon and she wouldn't see Roman again. She'd always put Dillon first. Their bond was strong and unshakable. His gaze fell on the bakery box. He lifted the lid, then switched his attention to hers.

"You going out with him again?"

She bit her lip. "Dinner tonight and then a movie."

He let the lid fall. "I don't guess I have to tell you to be careful. No parking. If you need me, don't think. Just call. Home by ten."

Her smile trembled as he repeated the rules she'd given him growing up. "No." She glanced down, then up, her gaze troubled and a bit unsure. "I'm not sure what I'm doing."

He took her unsteady hands and knelt. "Do you want to go out with him?"

She nodded. "But I don't want to make a mistake again.

We're just dating, but . . . I don't want the town whispering about me when I pass."

Dillon's face hardened. "You can't live your life to please the town. Please yourself."

She almost smiled, freed her hand to cup his cheek. "Yes, Mother."

They both chuckled. She'd been the best and, for the lack of a husband, had borne the brunt of the town whispers. He couldn't change that, but he would help her think of herself for once. And if Roman messed up . . . "He's a good man."

She nodded again. "I won't have time to fix your dinner."

"I'll pick up something. Don't worry." He kissed her on the cheek and pushed to his feet. "Have fun."

"Thank you."

He stopped at the door and looked back at her. "Thank me by pleasing yourself for once. I'll make myself scarce if you two want to come in."

She blushed and tucked her head.

Chuckling, he headed to his truck. He trusted Roman, but it wouldn't hurt to be there when he picked his mother up.

"I'm leaving early today," Dillon announced to Samantha as soon as he came through the office door. "See you tomorrow."

"It's just six. You're supposed to be working on the prototype while I work on the files. We have to be ready Friday." Sam lifted a brow and folded her arms. "You got a hot date?"

"No, but Mama does with Roman."

"What?" She snatched her arms to her sides.

Dillon rubbed the back of his neck. "I trust the guy, but . . ."

"He's a man, and your mother is a beautiful woman," Sam said knowingly.

"Yeah."

Her lips twitched. "I guess the stories about protective big brothers goes double for protective sons, especially those with a reputation like yours."

"I'm not that bad."

She rolled her eyes. "Dillon, you're practically legendary in this county. You probably gave a lot of mothers some hard times. I'd say it's payback time."

His eyes narrowed. "If he gets out of line . . ."

"Marlene can handle him." Sam folded her arms and leaned against the desk. "Give them a break. You'll only make her nervous if you're there."

"You might be right, but I plan to be there just the same." He glanced at his watch, then started for the door. "See you tomorrow."

"Dillon, you can't be serious."

"I'll stay out of the way."

"No, you won't."

"You could come with me so it would seem more casual," he suggested. "We could go grab a bite later."

"As if they need two people staring at them."

"We could be in the back or something."

"You're really worried about her, aren't you?"

He shrugged. "Sometimes your best intentions get pushed to the back in certain situations."

She briefly lowered her head. She probably remembered the kiss. "I'll get my purse, but we're staying on the terrace until they leave and then we're going to grab dinner."

"I'll just say hi to Mama and then we'll go to the back."

. . .

Marlene had changed clothes twice. She didn't like the way she looked in either outfit. Besides that, her hair refused to behave. In her bedroom, she stood in front of her built-in floor-to-ceiling mirror and considered changing for the third time. The times she'd seen Roman, he'd been in dress slacks and a tailored shirt. He was coming straight from work.

Remembering the wrinkled shirt, she glanced skyward. What was she doing? Maybe she shouldn't go.

"Mama," Dillon called, rapping on her bedroom door, "Sam and I are going out back to talk business."

She came out of the bedroom, wringing her hands. "Hello, Sam."

"Hi, Marlene. You look fantastic," Samantha said, catching Dillon's arm. "We're going out back."

The doorbell rang.

Marlene started, glanced at her watch. "That can't be Roman. He's ten minutes early."

"He's anxious," Samantha said with a smile. "When he sees you, he'll be glad he was early."

Marlene ran her hand over the pale peach sundress. "I—I don't know."

The doorbell rang again.

"Dillon, what do you think? Maybe I shouldn't go," Marlene said, biting her lower lip. He had yet to say a word. He just stared at her.

"I think you should." Dillon picked up her handbag from the bed, then went into her closet and came back with a light shawl. "It gets cold in the movies."

The doorbell rang again.

"In a minute he'll be banging on the door." Taking her arm, Dillon led her to the front door and opened it.

"Marlene," Roman said. "I was afraid . . . You look beautiful."

"Have her home at a decent hour. No speeding," Dillon said to Roman, then to this mother, "Do you have money in case he gets out of line and you need to call me?"

She nodded, finally smiled. "Yes."

"You have my cell phone. We're going to Dixie Bell to eat and then the seven-thirty movie." Roman caught Marlene's hand and drew her over the threshold. "Good night."

"Night. Have fun." Dillon closed the door.

"I'm proud of you."

"I've never seen her that scared and unsure of herself." Dillon rubbed a hand over his face.

"A man you care about will do that."

Turning, he folded his arms and stepped away from the door. "Speaking from personal experience?"

"You promised me food." She smiled. "Is the Burger Joint on Beacon Street still open?"

"Last time I drove by."

"Then what are we waiting for?"

"I almost didn't come," Marlene said, no longer clutching her purse. Perhaps it was the soft music on the radio that helped calm her.

"I figured as much when no one answered the door."

Roman cut her a quick glance. "I wasn't sure if Dillon had changed his mind about me."

"It was me." Marlene laughed nervously. "I wasn't sure I looked right, then he came home and you were early."

"Sorry." He stopped at a signal light. "Guess I was anxious to see you, and scared that if you had too much time to think, you'd back out."

"If it hadn't been for Dillon, I might have," she confessed, finding her muscles relaxing more and more. "That's the second time Dillon has acted the parent, repeating my words back at me."

"He probably heard them a lot." Roman pulled into the graveled parking lot of a long wooden building with an eight-foot plastic heifer in front.

"He did. Dillon liked testing me and rules," she said. "Sometimes . . ."

"You wondered if you were doing the right thing," he finished.

"Yes. I look at him now and think how grateful I am for him."

"So am I," Roman said. "He led me to you."

Marlene flushed.

"Have I told you how beautiful you are?"

"Yes. Twice."

"Just checking." He grinned, and she grinned back.

He hopped out of the car, then went around to open her door and helped her out. "Any idea what a decent hour is?"

"When Dillon was in junior high, it was nine."

"I think we're going to miss it." His hand closed around her elbow.

Smiling, thinking he might be right, Marlene continued toward the restaurant. The warmth and excitement of his touch wasn't as scary or unnerving as it once had been.

Out of the corner of her eye, she stole a look at him. Her heart did a hop and a skip. Even in profile, he was an extremely handsome man. His hair might be liberally sprinkled with gray, but his broad shoulders were erect, his muscled build evident in the blue cotton shirt and dark gray slacks.

"Hello, Marlene."

"Hi, Ms. M."

Marlene jerked her head around to see Anna Douglas and her five-year-old daughter, April. For a moment, Marlene couldn't think of a thing to say. She was thrust into the past, when people whispered as she passed. She'd never wanted to have that again.

"Marlene?" Anna and Roman said almost in unison. Her gaze jerked from one to the other. Both wore expressions of concern.

"Are you all right?" Roman took both of her arms, stepping in front of her. "Do I need to take you home?"

She opened her mouth to say yes, but, staring into Roman's dark eyes, she couldn't form the word. If he took her home, she knew she'd never get up the courage to go out again, even with Dillon pushing her. She was going to do what Dillon said, what she'd taught him. She was going to live her life.

"No, that won't be necessary." She smiled to ease the worry in his face. "I must have had a senior moment."

He tsked. "Not likely. You're too beautiful and too vibrant for that to happen. You probably just need to eat."

"I'll let you go, then. Bye, Marlene. Hope you feel better," Anna said, her voice sounding a bit odd.

"I'm not so hungry that I can't introduce one of my best friends." Marlene caught Anna's arm as she started to pass, surprised to find it rigid. The other woman looked up. Marlene saw the hurt slowly fade from her pretty face. Anna had had a bad reputation as an easy party girl before she married when she was five months pregnant.

Some of the people in town refused to let the past remain in the past. She'd had it rough, and still did, since her husband abandoned her and their daughter a year after they were married. She was a good woman who had made mistakes just like every adult. Marlene never wanted her to think that she thought differently.

"Roman, I'd like you to meet Anna Douglas and her beautiful daughter, April. Anna, this is Roman—"

"Santiago," Anna finished with her usual bright smile, extending her slim hand. "Mr. Santiago, you probably don't know the women at the plant are keeping track of sightings of you. We actually have the haves and the have-nots."

Smiling, Roman accepted the hand. "Please to meet you, Mrs. Douglas." He bent down to shake April's hand as well. The friendly child giggled. Straightening, he said, "Probably because I'm the newest employee."

"And . . ." Anna drew out the word. "You might have other attributes worth checking out." She switched her attention to Marlene. "See you next week at the book club meeting. Come on, scamp. Let's go home."

"Bye, Anna, April," Marlene called, watching the two head to a beat-up Ford and get in. The engine caught. The soft rumble of a well-tuned car vibrated across the parking lot.

"There are some horses beneath that hood," Roman said as Anna pulled off with a wave.

Marlene smiled with pleasure. "I tuned it myself."

Roman stopped, picked up her hands, then lifted his gaze to hers. "And they're still soft and lovely. Like I first thought, you're an amazing woman."

"I think I'm finally glad you think so."

"Marlene." He breathed her name, his head lowering, his intent obvious.

It took all of her willpower to step back. "Ah, maybe we should go on in."

He blew out a breath. "You make me want you and forget where I am. A dangerous combination, and one I intend to thoroughly enjoy." He slid his arm around her waist. "Let's go have dinner. Some things shouldn't be rushed."

Eleven

. . . .

Samantha slid into the open-ended booth with her cherry Coke. Dillon hadn't liked it, but she'd paid for her own food. It had been important to establish that this was not a date. But, man, did he look good in jeans and a chambray shirt. She wasn't the only woman who thought so. The woman behind the counter could hardly take her order for looking at Dillon. He'd just grinned. Sam had wanted to kick him.

Finished with his order, Dillon started toward the booth she sat in. Samantha didn't have to look around to know he commanded the attention of every woman in the room—with or without a man. A woman would be crazy to think she could keep the attention of a man who oozed sex appeal the way he did.

Instead of sitting across from her, he bent to slide in beside her. Samantha's eyes widened. It was move or have him sit on top of her.

"You're crowding me."

"Then scoot over." His hip touched hers, and she quickly complied.

Heat and a strange longing to touch him washed over her. "Why didn't you sit on the other side of the booth?" Each side easily accommodated three people.

"It should be obvious." He put his lips on the straw of his Coke.

Samantha couldn't help but think of his mouth on hers, him sucking on her tongue. Desire rocked through her. How could her body betray her this way? "Well, it isn't."

"I can see Tracy when she calls out our orders." Crossing his long legs, he slouched down on the bench.

"You know her?"

His grin was pure devilment. "She told me her name."

Samantha had the urge to kick him again or pour her drink over his head to cool him off. Since she needed cooling, she took a long suck on her straw. She felt his gaze on her and looked over. Hot craving stared back at her.

"Numbers twenty-eight and twenty-nine."

"I—I think she called our numbers," Samantha said, glad she could form a coherent sentence when all she wanted to do was crawl in his lap and take the kiss her body craved.

"Numbers twenty-eight and twenty-nine."

"Maybe you should get them." Dillon took the top off his drink and gulped.

Heat climbed up her neck as the reason dawned for his not wanting to get up. She scooted out of the booth and went to get their food. When she returned, she sat on the other side of the booth. However, as soon as she looked up and their gazes met, she knew she'd miscalculated. It would be worse sitting across from him, looking at what she wanted and couldn't have.

"Did you call Mark?"

"What?" Mentioning Mark was like throwing a bucket of ice water on her.

"The reporter friend." Dillon picked up a French fry. "Is he on board?"

It took Samantha a moment to notice his hand wasn't steady. He was as affected as she was and trying to remind them both they had a business-only relationship. He wasn't going to take advantage of her weakness. For a crazy second, she wished he weren't being noble again.

She unwrapped her hamburger. "He is. He's coming in Saturday."

"To see you or the race?" Dillon asked, not even pretending to eat.

She placed the burger on her tray. "We will not do this. Please. Collins—"

"Has to come first," he finished for her, picking up his burger and taking a bite. "Can you cook?"

"Yes. Why?"

"If things go the way I think they might between Mama and Roman, they'll be going out every night, which means she won't be cooking."

Samantha eyed him suspiciously. "You can't be asking me to cook for you."

He placed his hamburger back on his tray and pushed it away. "It makes sense. You know Mama wouldn't care about you coming over. I could work on the prototype at the plant, then go over the files with you in the evenings."

It sounded reasonable, tempting. And risky. "Sorry. I don't think that's wise."

"Probably not." He crossed his arms and leaned back in his seat.

"You're not eating?"

"It's not what I want."

Samantha felt the pull again and tucked her head to eat her hamburger. She was definitely staying clear of Dillon. He was much too tempting.

Marlene must know half the town, Roman thought. Unlike the other night when they'd gone to eat and were left alone, here people recognized her. Women waved from their tables or as they passed when leaving. If they were near, they stopped for a hug and to give him a critical once-over as she introduced them.

"I'm sorry," she said after the last woman and her husband walked away. "You're hopping up and down so much, you haven't been able to enjoy your meal."

"I don't mind the women. But if a man comes over, we might have a problem."

The small smile slid from her face. "You won't have to worry about that."

"Good, because I'm a possessive kind of guy." He said the words casually as he cut into his chicken-fried steak. He figured he might as well get it out there.

"Because of what happened?" Marlene asked, her fork poised over her broccoli.

His gaze lifted to hers. "No. It's you. Just you. I look at you and feel . . ." He paused, searching for words. "Things I never felt before."

"Oh."

His gaze dropped to her mouth. He hungered for her. When he lifted his eyes to meet hers, he knew she'd see the raw need and he didn't try to mask it. He wanted her to know how much he desired her.

She picked up her glass with an unsteady hand. "Perhaps we should discuss something else."

"Sorry if you're embarrassed, but as I said, I believe in frankness." He took a bite of mashed potatoes. "The guys working with me said this place had the best home cooking in the city. Both recommended the chicken-fried steak. What do you think?"

"That you're a patient man," she said, the smile that warmed him and turned him on returning.

He breathed easier. "Comes with the territory. It can take weeks, months, to investigate an account."

"How are things going?" she asked.

He frowned. "Dillon is right. I can't put my finger on it yet, but I will."

"You're as self-assured as Dillon."

Roman shrugged. "If you don't believe in yourself, you can't expect anyone else to. But I figure you know that already."

She placed her fork and knife on her plate. "Life offers a lot of challenges."

"And rewards," he said, his meaning clear. "Has Dillon told you how we met?"

"He said you worked for Carson's family."

"Carson's father and I graduated from MIT together. Our families have known each other for three generations."

Interest sparkled in her eyes. "Three generations. How wonderful."

"Coffee and your dessert." The waitress placed the cobblers and their coffee on the table and left.

"An understatement. My father and Nathan's father met while working in basic training for the air force." Roman picked up his spoon. "Both came from poor parents. Both were the first to finish college. My younger sister is married to Nathan."

Surprised delight flittered across Marlene's face. "Dillon never mentioned you were related to the Rowlands. I've met Tess. She's a beautiful woman on the inside and out, and unpretentious as they come. She and Nathan have always made Dillon feel welcome when he went to visit them. One weekend here when Dillon and Carson were freshmen was enough for Carson." Marlene smiled. "He enjoyed my cooking, but not the quiet life."

"To think I could have met you long ago."

"Perhaps. Please go on."

In other words, Roman thought, *she would have brushed him off.* "There are five of us children. I'm the oldest. Blessedly, my parents are still alive. All of us live in Dallas since my youngest brother recently relocated from Charleston. He's also the only one still single. Our families were always close. My divorce changed that for my children." His hand clenched on the spoon. He sat back in his chair.

"I can forgive my ex for cheating, but not for disrupting the lives of my children. They live in D.C., apart from both of us because their mother makes them feel guilty if they show a preference for me."

Her hand covered his. "I'm sorry."

He'd barely felt the warmth before her hand moved. "You're lucky Dillon is around."

"We almost grew up together."

"It's still difficult to believe that you're his mother." Roman smiled. "I guess you know he talks about you. He's proud of you."

"There were times—" Shaking her head, she picked up her spoon but didn't eat. "It wasn't always easy."

"Yet, you did it, just like you run the garage. Like I said, you're a remarkable woman, Marlene. It's going to be a pleasure getting to know you better."

"So this isn't our first and last date?" she asked with a bit of a twinkle in her eyes.

"Not by a long shot." He leaned across the table. "This is just the beginning."

The movie had been a romantic suspense and one she had wanted to see. She liked both the male and female leads. The movie should have kept her attention. It hadn't.

Marlene kept thinking about when he'd take her home and the good-night kiss. The torrid love scene between the leads had only made her more aware of the man sitting beside her, his male scent, the strong arm around her shoulders . . .

Now, walking to her door, she couldn't stop shivering. She could no longer deny the reason. Anticipation, not fear.

Thankfully, the first try unlocked the door. Reaching inside, she switched on the light, wondering if she should invite him in. Dillon had said he'd make himself scarce, but . . . She turned and found herself where she had wanted to be all night,

wrapped in Roman's strong arms. She sighed with the right-
ness of it. His hand slid into her hair, angling her head up.

"I can't wait any longer." His mouth brushed against hers,
warming her lips, heating her body. It seemed an eternity before his lips settled firmly against hers, his tongue gliding inside her mouth. She was incredibly aware of his lean body
pressed against hers. She felt cherished. She'd never felt that
way with a man. Her knees trembled. Her hold tightened as
she sank more deeply against him.

He tore his mouth away, his breathing harsh, then pulled
her to him. "You . . ."

Trembling, Marlene just held on as her heart tried to settle.
"I might be too old for this," she mumbled, then stiffened as
she realized she'd said the words aloud. Mortified, she shut her
eyes. She might have joked about a senior moment earlier, but
she hadn't just had a kiss that made her ache and burn.

She heard a muffled sound and realized it was laughter.
Seconds later, her laughter joined Roman's.

"I'm older and I say we're definitely not too old." He
straightened, brushed her hair away from her face. "You're so
beautiful."

"Would you like to come in?" she asked. She was going to
reach out for what she wanted.

"I'd like nothing better, but I don't think I'm that strong.
How about a game of putt-putt tomorrow night?" he asked.

Marlene unhappily accepted that he was right. She'd prefer
Dillon not catch her on the sofa. "I've never played."

His thumb played with her ear, sending shivers in its wake.
"It will be my pleasure to teach you. Six thirty all right?"

She'd miss cooking dinner for Dillon again. "Yes."

"That's my girl." Roman took her in his arms again and made her world tilt, her body burn.

When she could think clearly again, she said, "I wish you didn't have to drive back tonight."

"Don't worry. I'm used to night driving," he told her, his arms around her waist. "Listening to my tapes, I'll be home before I know it."

"All right. Why don't you come by for breakfast in the morning?" she asked.

"I don't want you going to the trouble of having to get up earlier because of me," he told her.

"I'd already planned to cook Dillon a good breakfast to make up for not cooking for him tonight, and it now looks like tomorrow night." Few people besides Dillon had ever worried about her.

"Then I'll see you at seven-thirty." He kissed her again then gently pushed her inside. "Night."

"Night," Marlene breathed the word. A smile on her face, she turned and saw the light on in the kitchen. She glanced at her watch. Ten fifty-three. Heat flushed her face. It wasn't unusual for Dillon to make raids on the kitchen even after a full meal.

She could go to her room or . . . Tossing her handbag on the sofa as she passed, she went to the kitchen. Dillon, his back to her, was at the stove.

"Hi, Dillon," she greeted him.

"Hi. You have fun?"

He hadn't turned. He'd seen her all right, clinging around Roman like plastic wrap. She tried to remember where Roman's hands were and couldn't, only that they had felt good on her body.

She went to the stove. The sunny-side-up eggs were just beginning to bubble around the edges. Taking his arms, she turned him to her. "Dillon."

He looked at her, then down. "I was on my way to the kitchen. The Burger Joint hamburger was as bad as I remember. The light came on and I . . . I'm sorry."

"Don't be." She turned to grab a metal spatula and turned over the eggs. "I'm your mother. It's difficult to see me as just a woman on a date."

"I guess." He grabbed a plate.

Marlene slid the eggs onto the plate and went to the refrigerator for the loaf of bread. She put four slices in the toaster, then placed strawberry preserves on the table. When the toast was ready, she placed them on his plate.

"Dillon, if you're going to be this embarrassed if you see me kissing Roman, perhaps I shouldn't see him anymore."

He finally looked at her, down at his plate, then back up at her. "I did promise I'd make myself scarce."

"Yes, you did, but this is your home as well."

He glanced around the stainless-steel kitchen with custom cabinetry. "We've come a long way, haven't we?"

"And we did it together, and by being honest with and loving each other."

"I don't guess you'll scar me at my age," he said lightly, and picked up his fork.

"No more than your wild antics while you were growing up scared me."

Chuckling, he dug into his eggs. "Thanks for the food."

"That's what mothers are for." Leaning down, she touched her head to his. "I'll see you in the morning."

"Mama?"

Stopping at the door, she looked back over her shoulder. "Yes."

"I love you. I'm glad you're going out with Roman. He's a good man."

"Thank you, Dillon. I think he is too." Smiling, Marlene continued out of the room.

Dillon didn't wake up in the best of moods. Sexual deprivation would do that to you. *And he wasn't likely to be satisfied anytime soon,* he thought as he stepped from the shower. He didn't believe in using women. Sam was the only woman he wanted, and she had put up a huge NO TRESPASSING sign.

He could probably work on changing her mind this weekend while they were in Vegas. But he didn't want to seduce her. He wanted her willing and eager in his bed, and just as eager and wild after the dawn came. He didn't want regrets and recrimination.

Dressed, he left his bedroom on the other side of the house. He smelled breakfast, heard male laughter. Roman. Dillon admitted what he hadn't wanted to last night. He'd been embarrassed seeing his mother kissing Roman, but he'd also been a bit jealous that he was having so much trouble with Sam.

He stood in the doorway a few seconds before they saw him: his mother, wearing a pretty pink dress instead of her usual slacks, making French toast; Roman, standing close, drinking coffee.

"Good morning."

Both turned with easy smiles to greet him. "Good morning, Dillon."

Three was definitely a crowd. He crossed to his mother,

kissed her then grabbed his keys off the hook. "I'm not hungry. See you both later."

His mother dropped the bread into the egg mixture and came to him. "You feel all right?"

"Sure. Guess I'm still full from eating last night," he said.

"Since when?" she asked. "You can eat two hours after a huge meal."

He touched her shoulder. He didn't want her worried about him. "Probably thinking about the designs for the intercooler. I'm putting it in Carson's BMW this weekend. See you." He went out the back door, but the door opened behind him before he reached his truck.

"Dillon." Roman caught up with him. "Marlene is in the kitchen with her head down. She got up early to cook you breakfast because she didn't cook for you last night. There's an enchilada casserole in the refrigerator because we were going out tonight. If it's me, I'll leave. I won't come between you. She loves you more than anything."

Muttering, Dillon shoved his hand over his hair. "It's not you. It's . . ." He eyed Roman. "Honk when you pull up next time." Then he brushed past Roman and went back inside.

As Roman had said, Marlene sat at the kitchen table with her head down. Dillon could have kicked his own butt. He knelt and took her unsteady hands. "I forgot the house rules. Hungry or full."

"If—"

"It's not you," he repeated. He'd never discussed his women with his mother. Never had a problem with one that he couldn't solve on his own.

"Should I leave?" Roman asked.

Dillon saw the longing in his mother's eyes. Yet she didn't

say one word for him to stay. She'd let the man she cared for walk away. She'd always put Dillon first. He could do no less, even if he had to bare his soul. "Sam and I are having a bit of personal problems. I guess I'm not taking it very well."

Happiness crossed his mother's face. "Oh, Dillon. I never thought this day would happen."

"Whoa. It's just a passing thing."

"Hmmm."

He didn't like the sound of that. "I mean it. We both have different goals in life."

Her hands palmed his face. "There has never been an obstacle or challenge in your life that you haven't met head-on and conquered. Different isn't always bad." She glanced over at Roman, then pushed against Dillon's shoulders so she could stand. "I'll finish the French toast. Please get the juice. Roman, help yourself to more coffee. We can eat in a minute and Dillon can tell us about the race this weekend."

Dillon rose and went to the glass-front cabinets for the juice glasses. Thank goodness he hadn't ruined his mother's day with Roman because Sam had shut him down.

His mother had brought up a good point. Sam was different from the other women he'd dated. She challenged him, resisted him so naturally when he'd tried to make her submit. The old Sam might have given in, the new emerging Sam was learning to stand her ground and push back. Oddly, he preferred the new Sam, but that didn't mean he'd let her or any woman get the better of him. "Where're you two headed tonight?"

"Putt-putt," his mother said, laughing. She smiled at Roman. "I'll probably embarrass us."

"Not a chance." Roman sipped his coffee and watched

Marlene with an intensity that was almost tangible. "But even if we have a terrible score, we'll have fun and be together."

Dillon was sure that if he weren't there, they'd be in each other's arms. To make up for his bad behavior, he'd eat and then leave so they could have a few minutes alone. He had work to do. First, he needed to get his mind exclusively on finishing the intercooler. Second, he had to try to forget how good Sam felt in his arms.

Samantha got what she wanted. Dillon stayed away from her the rest of the week at work.

Where she was, he wasn't. And if they did happen to be in the same place, he quickly excused himself. Knowing he was working against the clock to finish the intercooler before Friday didn't make her feel any better.

Wednesday, he'd come to their office—which he never used anymore—to disclose their travel plans to leave Friday morning and return early Monday morning. Practice was Friday, qualifying runs against the clock Saturday, with the actual race on Sunday at noon.

"You can come down on Sunday morning," he'd suggested in front of her desk. "I can talk to Mark, explain the intercooler, introduce him to the Rowland Racing Team, and make sure he has a good time."

He'd made the statement in a businesslike manner. There'd been no hint of jealousy. Clearly, he'd relegated her to the past and moved on. It had hurt, but she hadn't let it show. She'd sign over her half of Collins mansion to her uncle before she'd let him know. Just because they didn't have a personal relationship didn't mean that they couldn't have a harmonious working one.

"I'd rather go with you on Friday," she'd said just as formally. "I want to learn as much as possible about vintage cars, especially if there is a market there for the intercooler. I'll make hotel reservations."

"Already made." He'd gone to the door. "I requested separate floors."

So he planned to be with another woman. "Thank you."

She'd gone back to work before the door closed, wishing there were some way to turn off her feelings for a man who obviously no longer cared. There wasn't. He was it for her.

Her door opened moments later. Her uncle came in, grinning. He'd have a fit if she entered his office without permission. "Did you forget to knock?"

He paused as if he hadn't expected the reprimand, then his smile returned as he continued to the seat in front of her desk. "Things aren't going so well between you and Dillon, I've noticed."

"Was there something you wanted, Uncle Evan?"

Lines raced across his forehead as he studied her. She held his gaze. She wasn't the same woman, eager to please and keep everyone happy. Being stronger hadn't come without a price, however.

"Sign papers that at the end of the five-year period your half of Collins is mine, and I'll help you," he told her, his hands laced together over his trim stomach in a tan tailored suit. She didn't think she'd ever seen him wearing the same suit or tie.

Samantha arched a brow. "How?"

"I have my ways," he came back, his smile growing.

Samantha doubted that. He might arrive at work on time, but he still went home promptly at five. In between that time, she'd never seen any indication that he did anything productive behind his closed door. "Have you talked to any accounts or tried to acquire any lately?"

Disbelief widened his eyes as he shot to his feet. "Are you checking up on me?"

She asked a question of her own. "How can you help the company when you aren't doing anything since we lost Granddad to help the bottom line?"

"I helped make this company!" he shouted. "I'm not doing anything more until Dillon is gone and you come to your senses. He can't help this company."

Samantha picked up her pen. "Then this conversation is over. Please let yourself out."

"You're going to lose."

"No, we won't." Tossing the pen aside, she came to her feet and moved around the desk. "Dillon designed an intercooler that will be fitted on a car for the Rowland Racing Team in the vintage racing this weekend in Vegas. When the car wins, the entire auto industry will take note."

"If," he sneered.

"You better hope it does."

"Why would I do that?" he asked, his sneer growing.

"Because," she said sweetly, "if Collins Industry has to make adjustments to keep going, guess whose paycheck will get cut first?"

Horror and then anger chased across his face.

"Good-bye, Uncle." Samantha went behind her desk. "I know you wish us well this weekend."

"You—"

"Was there something you wanted me to tell Dillon?"

He strode from the room and slammed the door after him. Leaning back in her chair, Samantha smiled.

Early Thursday morning, Dillon positioned the intercooler in his BMW. It was the same model Carson would be driving. He tightened the bolts, then straightened. It was ready to test.

"I'm not sure about you racing on the FM roads," Marlene said from beside him, worry in her voice.

"He knows what he's doing, Marlene," Roman said, his arm around her waist.

Dillon had finally gotten used to seeing them that way. The happiness on his mother's face, the way it lit up when Roman walked in the room, helped because he reacted the same way when he saw her. Last night, they had watched a movie at the house. "The real racing has twists and turns. It's the closest I'm going to get without actually being on the highway."

"But the race is regulated. Don't you dare push the car over ninety."

Cars in the vintage circuit didn't reach the 220 mph of NASCAR, but they did reach 180 mph. He had to test the intercooler to see if it gave the car the power boost he hoped for. "It's barely seven. The FM roads should be relatively empty."

She bit her lip. "I never liked you racing."

"There's no other way, Mama."

She hugged him and stepped back. "Go test the thing before it gets much later."

He nodded to Roman then got behind the wheel, started

the car, then backed out of the bay. He'd had one of his men bring the car down on a flatbed yesterday. He still had a thing about other people driving his car. His mind flashed to Sam asking if he wanted her to drive. He shut it down and pulled onto the street. Two minutes later, he hit the farm-to-market road. There wasn't a car in sight.

He didn't hesitate. "Let's see what you can do."

In three seconds, he'd hit 90. Five seconds later, he was flirting with 160. Then the car hit 180 with a burst of speed, the horses of the turbo roaring.

Dillon grinned devilishly. The intercooler worked, keeping the motor cool and upping the power. It would allow Carson to kick butt and put Collins Industry out there. But even as the thought came, Dillon accepted that once that happened, he was leaving.

His grin faded. So did the thrill he'd experienced earlier. He attributed it to leaving his mother and took the bridge over the highway to return to Elms Fork.

Twelve

. . . .

Friday morning, Samantha and Dillon flew first class to Las Vegas. They sat side by side but barely acknowledged each other during the long flight. She was too aware of him and more than ready for the plane to land when they did. Once they had their luggage and the intercooler, a car took them to the Bellagio Hotel.

"Here's your key," Dillon said, his first words since he'd picked her up at her home that morning.

"Thank you." She gripped the card in her hand.

"I'm meeting Carson in an hour. Do you want to go with me or rest and order room service?"

So he'd noticed that she hadn't eaten on the flight. Neither had he. "Go with you."

For a moment his lips tightened. "Meet me here in thirty minutes."

Samantha watched him walk away. Despite the beautiful hotel and the very real possibility that they were going to pull

Collins back from ruin, she felt tears sting her eyes. Dillon didn't want her near him.

Resisting Sam was more difficult than Dillon had thought. Her soft fragrance had taunted and beckoned on the long flight. If that weren't enough, sometimes she stared at him as if she wanted to crawl into his lap and kiss him until his brain short-circuited. The brush of her thigh against his had been sheer torture. He wanted her, hot and naked.

Seeing her waiting for him only heightened his need. She looked lost and lonely. He'd like nothing better than to take her into his arms, reassure her. But touching her wasn't a good idea. He wanted her too badly. "I have a car."

He walked off, expecting her to follow. It wasn't until he was several steps away that he sensed she wasn't behind him. He glanced over his shoulder until the crowd parted enough for him to see her. She hadn't moved. He didn't have time to deal with this. He stared. She stared back.

She was challenging him again. Well, this time she'd lose. He started for the entrance. So what if his steps were slow. There was no sense in rubbing his victory in her face. Outside the busy hotel, he saw the four-wheel-drive Jeep he'd rented. The keys had been delivered to his room, the papers signed. All he had to do was get in and drive away.

He couldn't get his feet to move. Damn.

He started back inside. She still stood in the same spot, but now tears sparkled in her eyes. A fist clutched his heart.

Seeing him, she turned away. He saw her arm go up, then she faced him. He realized she had wiped away her tears.

Never let your opponent know you cried. So that's what they had become. Opponents. His fault.

"You haven't even spoken to me. Said my name once. I don't want us to be enemies."

He didn't either. Staying away from her, ignoring her, had been his way of keeping his desire for her under control. Now, with hundreds of people surrounding them, the faint sounds of the gaming machines, his hunger strained to be freed and satiated. He longed to take them both back upstairs and love her until they were both spent. Perhaps then he'd stop thinking about her.

"Dillon."

His name wobbled over berry-colored lips that he craved to press his against, bite, suck. She just wasn't reacting to the way he was looking at her, but she wanted him as much. She simply controlled herself better, which annoyed the hell out of him. Before Sam, he'd prided himself on his restraint.

His breath shuddered out. "Let's go, Sam. Carson is waiting."

"Thank you for not leaving me."

He grunted. She smiled.

Man, he'd like to taste her. All over. Starting with the nipples pressing against her white knit top. If she knew, she'd be mortified. "Come on."

He started from the lobby with her on his heels.

Samantha caught the excitement at the racetrack the moment she got out of the Jeep. There were trailers with awnings over cars, while other cars were in garages. The crowd was energized, laughing, talking.

"This seems like fun."

"It is, but the teams take their racing seriously. Carson should be this way."

Samantha followed, trying to keep up while taking in the sights and sounds. The cars were amazing. She wouldn't have known their make except for the name or symbols. Vintage meant just that, older-model cars in top condition and restored to their former glory. She whistled. "They must cost a mint."

"They do and are meticulously cared for."

Dillon turned into a garage where there were two cars and several people hovering over each. "Hey, Carson. Ready to take the checkered flag?"

A tall man straightened, his gorgeous olive-hued face breaking into a devilish smile. He stuck out his hand and he and Dillon gave each other a one-armed hug. "You know it."

"This will do it." Dillon picked up the case he had put on the ground before greeting Carson. He held it out to his friend.

Carson took the case, then looked at her. "Your partner?"

"Samantha Collins, meet Carson Rowland."

The case in one hand, he extended the other to grasp hers gently. "Ms. Collins, glad to meet you."

She smiled back. "Thank you, Mr. Rowland."

He grinned lazily. "My pleasure."

He was probably almost as dangerous to a woman's peace of mind as Dillon, and that was saying a lot. "Thank you for allowing Collins Industry the chance to test the intercooler on your car."

"Not without a price," Dillon snapped, glaring at the both of them.

Samantha frowned up at him. "What's the matter now?"

Laughing, Carson leaned over and then whispered loudly, "Guess he hasn't had his fiber in a few days."

Samantha laughed before she could stop herself.

"Very funny," Dillon muttered.

"I thought so." Carson faced Dillon, his eyes serious. "Especially since we know each other so well."

Dillon's arms slowly dropped to his sides. He glanced skyward.

Carson clasped him on the shoulder. "Better you than me. Now, let's get this on so I can see what it's got."

Samantha watched the two go to the BMW. Carson opened the case and took out the top-mounted intercooler. She had no idea what had just gone on, but she sensed that whatever it was, the tension between them was now gone.

Not wanting to get in the way, she stayed where she was. It had nothing to do with the nice view of Dillon's backside, the flex and play of muscles as he lowered the intercooler into place. It was enough that Carson's family was giving them a chance.

"Sam, come here."

Surprised delight had her moving toward Dillon, who was bent under the hood. "Yes?"

"I want you to see what we're doing." His gaze dropped to her hands. "No pad. You'll have to remember."

"I will." Once she got her mind off his hands roaming freely over her.

He dove back under the hood. "Good, because like I said, I'm not sticking around once Collins is back on track. I agree with you, you need to learn all you can."

She crashed back to reality. Collins was all that could ever be between them. "So teach me."

. . .

Marlene's hands clenched on her handbag in her lap as Roman pulled into her driveway. All during dinner and then putt-putt, there had been this underlying sexual tension humming between them. Each touch fueled a desire for more.

Before tonight, both knew Dillon was in the house. That had changed with Dillon in Las Vegas. Now, when she and Roman went inside, there was no need to pull back when they wanted to move forward, to search and explore each other at their leisure.

Roman turned off the motor. Silence stretched between them. They'd made a habit of not listening to the radio so they could talk. "I guess there's no need to honk."

"No," Marlene said, trying to answer in the same playful vein as Roman. But as seconds ticked by and he didn't move, she realized his thoughts were much like her own. Otherwise he would have opened her door by now. Tonight they didn't have to stop at just kissing.

Heat flushed her body, tightened her nipples. Embarrassed, she reached for the door handle.

"I'll get it." Roman jumped out of the car.

Marlene kept going. She didn't want to make the same mistake of letting desire lead to heartache. She'd never regretted Dillon's birth; her regret was the way he'd been conceived.

The house key in her hand, she opened the front door. Soft light from the twin lamps in the entryway bathed the terrazzo floor. Just beyond, more light shone in the living room. She always left lights on when she went out if Dillon wasn't there. She hadn't needed Roman to remind her. The thought helped calm her nerves. Roman was always considerate of her. He wouldn't push her. The problem was, she wasn't sure of what she wanted.

She pushed open the door, stepped inside, and glanced back. "Would you like to come in?"

His hands came out of his pockets. She caught a glimpse of an unsure Roman. He'd always been so self-assured; it tipped the scales further in his favor. She didn't think, she just walked into his waiting arms and put her lips to his, where she'd wanted them for the past hour.

Her mind emptied, her body caught fire. Need surged through her. She let herself go and just enjoyed.

Suddenly, she was pushed away. "I don't want us to make love."

Consumed with a pulsating need, she was reaching for him until his words slammed into her. Shame hit her. All she could think of was getting away. Tears blinding her, she stumbled through the door, then shut and locked it behind her.

"Marlene, wait! You don't understand."

Pushing away from the door, she started toward her bedroom. The ringing of the doorbell and the banging followed her. She had been shameless. How could she ever face him again? And she'd have to. He hadn't finished his audit for Dillon.

Her head fell forward. She wouldn't be able to face Dillon when he came home. He'd called, but the call had gone straight to voicemail. He'd promised to try her cell—

Her thoughts stopped abruptly. Her cell phone was in her purse. Fate couldn't be so cruel that she'd dropped it outside.

Slowly, she went back to the front room, listening for the doorbell and looking for her handbag in front of the door. It wasn't there. She crept to the window and checked for Roman's car. The driveway was empty.

She opened the front door and looked for her purse just outside the door on the porch and didn't see it. Perhaps Roman had kicked it off the porch when he—

"Looking for this?"

Marlene's gaze swung to Roman at the end of the porch. He was holding her handbag, a hard frown on his face. He had nothing to be pissed about. She fought the instinct to flee. Her greatest regret was pleading with A. J. to stay even after she'd learned he was married. She'd been so sure he'd loved her, and so wrong.

No man would make her feel less again. "Yes."

Roman approached her with the look of a predator. For a second, she wished she had fled. She used bravado instead. "My handbag, please."

"Don't you dare look at me and think of him," he snapped.

The angry reprimand caught her off guard. One thing she'd never planned to discuss was Dillon's father. "Do I need to call the police?"

He stepped to her, his jaw clenched, his face so close she could see her reflection in his eyes. "I'm trying, Marlene, to be patient with you, but you're not making it easy."

"So take the hint and leave," she snapped.

"If I didn't care about you, I would." He blew out a breath, shoving his hand through his hair in obvious frustration. "This is my fault. I handled things wrong earlier."

She found she wasn't as brave as she thought. She couldn't stand there and carry on a conversation when all she wanted to do was crawl away in shame. She turned for the door. Roman caught her arm.

"Let me go." She hated that her voice trembled, hated that his touch still made her want. She'd learned nothing.

"No, Dillon isn't here to intercede for me, so I better talk fast. All I can think about when we're together is making love to you, but you're not ready," he said. "Your running away from me tonight proves it. If we made love now, you'd start doubting me, comparing me to him even more than you do now."

His hand flexed on her arm. "Stop comparing me to him. Look at me and see me. Have I ever treated you with anything but respect? You're a strong woman except when it comes to us. Trust me, but more importantly, trust yourself."

Marlene listened to his words. He was right. Deep down, she didn't trust herself enough to trust a man. She'd grown up in foster care, dreaming of having a family, being loved. The betrayal had cut deeply. "I'd like to go inside."

"Only if I'm going with you," he said, his hand sliding up her arm and turning her to him. "You're a fighter. Fight for us."

She shook her head. The scars and hurt were too deep. She thought she could move forward. She'd been wrong.

Perhaps if she had had a family to support her, friends to talk with, she might have been able to get over A. J., the betrayal, the shame. But she hadn't. She'd been used, then scorned and pointed at and whispered about by the townspeople. She'd worked hard to gain their respect, for Dillon to be proud of her. She wasn't about to take a chance and throw that away.

"I'm not sure I can."

"I am or I wouldn't be standing here, aching for you, if I didn't feel one day you'll leave the past in the past and learn to trust again," he said softly.

"Roman, please just leave."

"No. I'm not going anyplace. We're going inside and watch something on TV, or even better, maybe you'll play for me." He caught her other arm, turning her toward him. "When Dillon calls, you'll happily tell him how you beat me at putt-putt. Because if he thinks you're upset, race or not, he'll be on the next plane out of Vegas and this time he'll do more than wrinkle my shirt."

Stubborn as they came, and it was all she could do not to sink more fully against the warmth of his toned body. "Where is your car?"

"Beside the house."

"Sneaky."

"You better believe it," he said. His voice became unsteady. "You were crying, and it was my fault. I never wanted you to regret going out with me. I failed, but I'm not giving up."

He deserved as much honesty as she could give him. "I'm glad, but there might come a time when I get scared again."

"Then we'll talk about whatever it is." He pulled her more fully into his arms, his hand rubbing up and down her back, sending ripples of need in its wake. "I was terrified I wouldn't be able to get you to listen."

"I was embarrassed," she whispered, lowering her head.

Gentle fingers lifted her head. "My fault. I should have explained better, but my brain doesn't function at its analytical best when we kiss." His thumb grazed over her lower lip. "I've wanted you from the moment I saw you rising out of the flowers. You took my breath away. You still do."

Her heart knocked against her ribs. If she wasn't careful, it would plop at Roman's feet.

Her cell phone rang. *Dillon.* Roman handed her the purse and she pulled out her phone, opening the door as she accepted the call. She noticed Roman hadn't followed. He wouldn't push unless he had to. She beckoned him inside.

"Dillon."

"Hi, Mama. You beat Roman at putt-putt?"

Marlene's gaze went to Roman, his arms crossed as he leaned against the baby grand, and she found she could return his smile. "I did."

Dillon chuckled. "Way to go."

"How is Samantha?" This time there was no response. Another stubborn man. "I hope you took time to take her out to dinner."

"You know things can get hectic the night before qualifying."

Translation "no," but he didn't want to come out and say so. "Just remember, you know people and the routine, Samantha doesn't. She might get lonely."

"Not likely with the way Carson and some of his crew are acting," Dillon snarled. "You'd think they'd never seen a woman. I'm trying to teach her about motors and vintage racing, and they kept butting in."

Jealousy. She'd begun to lose hope that he'd care enough for a woman to be jealous of her. "Oh, Dillon."

"What?"

"Nothing. Good luck tomorrow for the qualifying runs."

"Thanks, Mama. I better get back, but can I speak to Roman first?"

"Is this about the audit?"

"No, it's about the best mother a guy could ask for."

"That's because you're the best son." She crossed the room

and gave Roman the phone. "I think he wants to discuss wrinkled shirts."

"Hey, Dillon." He caught Marlene's hand when she started to move away.

"Mama sounded happy. Keep it that way."

"Will do," Roman said, staring into Marlene's eyes. "I don't take lightly the trust either of you have placed in me."

"Later. Tell Mama I love her and I'll call her tomorrow after the qualifying runs. Night."

"Night." Roman ended the call and gave the cell phone back to Marlene. "Dillon said to tell you that he loves you and that he'll call you after the qualifying runs tomorrow."

For a second, Marlene wondered what it would feel like for a man to say he loved her and mean it.

Roman's dark eyes narrowed. He pulled her to him, his hand splayed at her waist. Her heart rate accelerated. Her gaze dropped to his tempting mouth. "See me and no other man."

"When we're this close, I don't have a choice."

"Marlene."

He whispered her name, wrapping his arms around her seconds before his mouth closed over hers. With exquisite gentleness, his tongue traced the seam of her mouth. She opened for him, her tongue sweeping lazily against his. Desire began a slow burn. She could feel reason slipping away and need taking its place.

They drew back at the same time, stared at each other. Her arms slid from behind his neck and rested on his chest.

"Maybe we should do something else."

Her eyes widened.

"No. Bad choice of words." He blew out a breath. "I better get out of here."

It was for the best, but her body wasn't very happy with her. "All right."

He didn't move. "What are you doing this weekend?"

"Working on Saturday, cleaning the house, working in the flower garden," she answered. *Missing you.*

"You need another pair of hands in the garden?"

If she was brave, she'd ask for them on her body as well. "You have to be tired of driving back and forth to Dallas."

"Knowing I'll see you when I get here makes it easy."

"All right. The garage closes at one. I'll feed you before putting you to work," she told him.

"You and great food. A man couldn't ask for more."

They both knew he could, but he was willing to wait. Not many men would. "Promise me something."

"Anything."

"That you won't let my fears push you away."

"Never." His hands cupped her face. "I see you and my heart skips a beat. Although you don't need me to, I want to fight your battles, strut when we're out together. There's a need when I see you, a possessiveness I've never felt before. You bring happiness to my life that I didn't have before."

"Roman." His name trembled across her lips, lips she pressed to his, felt them warm beneath hers. No kiss had ever consumed her, made her thoughts swirl, her body yearn.

She heard Roman groan, felt his hand cup her breast, felt her nipples harden. Her mind said to move away. She moved closer and whimpered when he inserted his thigh between her legs when she began to throb. She pressed against him as the ache intensified.

Roman felt reason slipping from his grasp. No woman, no kiss, had ever affected him this way. His body ached as her tongue licked his. He wanted her naked and wanton beneath him, wanted to hear her cries of pleasure as he filled her.

And then what? Intimacy would destroy their fragile relationship, not bring them closer. He knew it as surely as he knew his name. Before they made love, she had to believe without a doubt that he cared, because if she didn't, in the back of her mind she'd always think he wanted her body more than he wanted her, and it would eventually tear them apart.

Lifting his head, he pulled her to him. The incredible feel of her warm body, the slender curves against his, almost had him taking her mouth again.

"I did it again."

"Do you see me complaining?" His hand swept down her back, felt her tremble.

"No," she whispered, her cheek against his chest. "I've never met a man as patient as you."

He kissed her hair, inhaled her sweet fragrance. "I hope that's good." Seconds ticked by without her answering. Beginning to worry, he was about to lift her head when he heard her voice, so soft that he had to strain to understand her.

"Someone abandoned me when I was two. I grew up in a series of foster homes, some good, some bad. I aged out of the system at eighteen, worked to put myself through secretarial school because it was the only training I could afford. I got the first job I applied for because I could read Abe's writing and take his rapid dictation."

She stopped talking. Roman pulled her closer, kissed her on the head. Somehow he knew she was debating whether she should tell him about Dillon's father.

"Three years later I met a business associate of Abe's who

was older, wealthy. I didn't care about the money. I thought I had found a man to love me as I'd always wanted." Her voice trembled, then firmed. "He only wanted one thing. I learned he was married the same day I found out I was pregnant with Dillon. He didn't want either of us."

Rage swept through Roman. He hoped the bastard had a hell on earth.

She pushed against him. He didn't want to let her go. "Please."

He let his arms slowly fall away, but if she thought she was walking away from him, she'd better think again. He cared about her even more. Cared. Hell. He was halfway in love with her and falling fast.

Incredibly sad eyes lifted to his. She looked lost. Alone. "I'm what you probably hate. I was the other woman."

The shame in her shaky voice tore at his heart. His arms ached to hold her, take away the shame, the misery. "It's not your fault he lied to you. You survived all the hell and misery life dumped on you. You didn't just survive, you thrived. Alone, you raised a man any parent would be proud of. You're respected and loved by half the town, and I should know because I've met most of them. Be proud of yourself. Don't let that bastard take any more from you."

"I thought you'd despise me when you learned the truth," she murmured in surprise.

He did hold her then. He couldn't wait another second. "Never. There's no deception in you. What you see is what you get, and one day I'm going to be the lucky man who gets to see it all."

She laughed as he'd intended. They still had a chance.

"I better hit the road. I'll be knocking on your door at one thirty tomorrow." Holding her hand, he went to the door, leaned over, and kissed her on the cheek. "Dream about me."

Then he was gone.

Marlene slowly went back to her bedroom. Roman hadn't branded her the other woman, hadn't thought less of her. She'd seen the outrage in his eyes, the softening, just before he'd pulled her into his arms. He was right, she needed to let the past stay in the past. Easier said than done.

She'd always taught Dillon that you made mistakes, you learned from them, and you moved on. However, this time moving on meant letting Roman into her life even more. Intimacy. Tossing her handbag on the bed, she sat down. She hadn't been intimate with anyone since Dillon's father. Initially she'd been too busy working full-time and taking care of Dillon.

She'd cautiously started dating when Dillon was four and whispers and looks no longer followed her. There had been no sparks with the men, so she'd seen no need to continue dating. She'd assumed her pregnancy had affected her sex drive—which was never very high—and went on with her life, until she'd stared into Roman's captivating black eyes.

He'd changed everything, frightened her so that she'd tried to push him out of her life. He hadn't budged.

Smiling, Marlene stood and began undressing. He was stubborn and patient. He went out of his way to please her. And, Lord help her, she was falling for him. Her smile vanished. She plopped down on the bed with her blouse clutched in her hand. Caring about a man made her vulnerable. Then, too, when the audit was over, Roman would leave. Did she really want a short but extremely hot affair?

She'd told Roman she was too old for an affair. She'd spoken out of fear. She wanted to explore the sensual side of their relationship. If he hadn't halted tonight, they would be in bed by now.

Marlene shivered and accepted the truth. She wanted to be with Roman. She just had to make sure that when he left he didn't take her heart with him.

If she lived to be two hundred, she would never understand Dillon, Samantha mused Saturday morning. Yesterday he'd become increasingly grumpy while teaching her about car motors, turbochargers, and intercoolers. He'd even snapped at a couple of men in Carson's crew for trying to help her. Then around six, he'd sent her back to the hotel alone. This morning, he'd awakened her at seven with an unexpected invitation to go to breakfast. Once they'd finished, they'd returned to the racetrack to check out Carson's car before the inspection by race officials.

She'd shoved her need and her growing love for him to the back of her mind and concentrated on learning all she could. Despite everything, she was grateful that Dillon was willing to help her turn Collins Industry around. Her uncle certainly wasn't going to help.

Her proudest moment was being there for the final check on Saturday. Dillon tested the intercooler, then asked her if she saw a problem. Her gaze went over the entire engine. Everything had to be right for the intercooler to do its job.

"The battery cable is loose."

"Then tighten it," he said matter-of-factly.

Without hesitation she did, then stepped back. "Done."

Dillon reached out to make sure, then nodded. "We're ready for inspection."

They moved aside as Carson's team went over the car again. Once they'd finished, it was the officials' turn. They were methodical and thorough, to ensure the car's specifications followed standards. Finally, the car was given the all-clear for the qualifying run.

Carson, who was mobbed by fans—mostly women—finally joined them in his zipped-front racing uniform. "This is it."

"She's ready." Dillon nodded toward the 1948 BMW. "Sam and I checked."

"A lot is riding on this."

Dillon slapped Carson on the back. "I know. I wouldn't have fitted the car with the intercooler if I hadn't been sure it would work. My reputation is on the line as much as yours."

"You have the honor of having the first Collins intercooler," Samantha added.

Carson shook his thick head of coal-black hair. "Or the disgrace if I come in out of the top ten."

"You won't," Dillon said with confidence. "I tested the baby out myself. You're almost as good a driver as I am. The intercooler will give you the power and speed to finish in the top three."

"*I'm* the better driver, but you know motors and how to get the most power. See you after I cross the finish line." Carson put on his helmet and got inside the car. His crew pushed him onto the track.

"No matter how it goes," Samantha began, following the slow-moving car, "thank you for giving Collins a chance."

"You sound as if he's going to lose."

"No." She dared look into Dillon's strong face; he had carried her through so much. "He'll win." And when he did, she'd lose Dillon.

Her unshakable faith in him made his chest tight. No words from anyone except his mother had affected him more. He kept walking so they could watch Carson's qualifying run, pushing away what he wanted with increasing need—to drag Sam to the nearest bed and make a feast of her. He knew just where he'd start.

"Samantha."

Dillon looked around to see a man of medium height in a gray polo shirt and jeans heading toward them. Immediately, he knew it was Mark Washington.

Thirteen

. . . .

Dillon's gaze swung to Samantha. She hadn't rushed to meet the guy. Neither did she have the look of a woman missing a man. His fists unclenched.

Samantha waited for Mark to reach them. He was trim and good-looking, and he did nothing for her. She hadn't felt the slightest twinge at the sound of his voice when he'd called this morning while she was eating breakfast with Dillon. Dillon's deep voice teased her senses, stroked her, and, yes, ticked her off at times. But he made her feel. Mark didn't. She wondered if he ever had or if she'd just been lonely enough to settle.

Mark hugged her. She accepted the hug, but when his lips moved toward hers, she pushed him away. She ignored the angry frown. She'd told him this was business. "Mark Washington, Dillon Montgomery."

"Mr. Montgomery, I've heard of you, naturally."

The handshake was brief. "I can't say the same of you."

Samantha wanted to swat Dillon. This was too important for him to be impolite. "I'm glad you could make it, Mark.

Carson is about to take his qualifying run with a Collins intercooler installed in his car."

"That's taking a big risk." Mark stepped past her and looked
down the track. "His car has come in the top five in the last
four races."

"With my design, it will allow the engine's hot air to
run into the compressor before it runs into the coils. He'll
come in in the top two," Dillon said. "Carson's best has been
fourth."

"No new intercoolers have come out in the past year for
good reason," Mark said. "They don't work."

"Mine will."

"We'll see," Mark said dismissively.

Ignoring Mark, Dillon turned as the announcer called out
Carson's name and number. Sam couldn't have been interested
in such an uptight jerk.

"Here we go. I understand the '48 BMW has a new intercooler designed by Collins Industry. Rowland is certainly
tearing up the track."

"Go, Carson. Make it roar!"

Dillon looked down at Sam, her small fists clenched, excitement on her face. He'd like to get her excited for an entirely
different reason. Lifting his gaze, he stared into Mark's angry
face. Dillon grinned and turned back to see Carson burning
down the track.

"Man," the announcer said as Carson zoomed across the
finish line, "that's the top speed of the day! Carson Rowland
of Rowland Racing Team in a 1948 BMW is in position to
take the pole. If he does, it will be his first this year."

Dillon folded his arms, turned to Mark, and said, "You
were saying?"

"It could have been a fluke." Mark caught Samantha's arm. "Let's go someplace where we can talk."

She threw a glance at Dillon. "Don't you want to talk to Carson?"

"Later. I'd like to get more background on the story." Mark looked at Dillon. "You don't mind, do you?"

"If I did, you'd be the first to know it."

Samantha didn't watch Dillon walk off. It would have been too tempting to give him a swift kick. Now he was possessive, when he'd ignored her most of the week. "Let's go to the media room."

"They're always crowded." Mark stared down at her. "I have a suite at the Bellagio."

"It's the media room or nothing." Samantha freed her arm. "I called you because I know and respect you as a journalist. I wanted you to get the scoop on the intercooler, but that's the only reason. If you've come for any other purpose, it's not going to happen."

"You just can't throw away all we meant to each other. We were together three months."

"That ended over six months ago." She touched his arm. She knew how it was when your love wasn't returned. It hurt like hell. "I'm sorry. I just don't feel the way you do."

"Because of him?"

Yes, but that was her secret. "We'll talk about turbos and intercoolers or nothing. I'm sure I can find another newspaper."

"Turbos and intercoolers." Taking her arm, he led her toward the media room.

Samantha knew that would be his answer. For Mark, his job always came first. One day she wanted to meet a man who'd put her first. They passed Dillon at the Rowland slot. He didn't even look up.

Roman didn't know what to expect when he pulled up to Marlene's house Saturday afternoon. He was thirteen minutes early. Staring at the house, he tapped his fingers against the dash. It had taken a tremendous amount of trust for her to tell him about her childhood and Dillon's father. She probably didn't even realize it. She was so used to being self-sufficient. He didn't want to take that from her, but he did want her to know he would always be there for her.

His hand brushed over his face. When this assignment was over, he wasn't walking out of her life. She'd once told him she was too old for an affair and she wouldn't get married if her life depended on it. Very soon he hoped to change her mind about one of those statements.

The front door opened and Marlene stepped out wearing a long-sleeved blouse and loose pants. She smiled and waved.

Breathing easier for the first time since he woke up that morning, he got out of the car. He didn't stop walking until his arms were around her slim waist, his lips on hers. He inhaled her soft sigh and lifted his head. "Good afternoon."

"Good afternoon." She stood easily in his arms, her hands splayed on his chest, before stepping away. "Lunch is ready."

Roman followed her inside, his gaze dropping to the easy sway of her hips. Even in loose-fitting clothes, she got to him. She was going to be his. "I guess you're used to me being early."

"Do you see me complaining?"

Hearing her repeat his words from last night, he relaxed even more. "What can I do to help?"

"If you'll grab the tea and the rolls, I'll finish putting the food on the table." She picked up a platter of chicken.

"As usual, this looks good." After placing the bread on the table, he got their tea. "How was work today?" he asked, holding her chair.

"Hectic." Marlene glanced back at him over her shoulder before taking her seat. She was flirting. His heart jumped for joy.

"I'll never lie to you or use you, Marlene."

"I believe you." She said grace when he sat down, then she served them both. "Dillon called. Carson is in position to take the pole."

"Way to go, Carson. I know he and my brother are ecstatic. Tess will be just the same." Roman picked up his fork. "So everything is going well."

Marlene took a sip of her tea. "Very. The intercooler he developed is being credited with Carson's speed. Collins and Dillon have quite the buzz, I understand. When orders start rolling in, Collins will be able to pull itself out of the red."

Roman frowned. "I'm not sure that's the reason for the problems."

"What did you find?" she asked, leaning forward.

"I don't want to say anything until I have all the evidence I need," he said cautiously.

"Someone is stealing?" she persisted.

"Yes." *But not in the way Dillon thought.*

Anger flashed across her face. "Abe might still be here if he hadn't been worried. Find the thief and Dillon will prosecute whoever it is."

Roman wasn't so sure about that. "What's the first order of the day?"

"Mulching the azaleas and roses. You might wish you hadn't volunteered."

He picked up a roll. "As long as I'm with you, I'm happy."

"Tell me that two hours from now," Marlene said, but she was smiling.

Of course, once they were in the nursery of the home improvement store, Marlene saw some pink begonias and a trailing petunia basket she just had to have. Roman hadn't seemed to mind her wandering, stopping to check the merits of a plant, discussing various plants with other customers. Not for the first time, she noticed women looking at him. However, for the first time, she wanted to say he was hers. She didn't berate herself at the thought.

She was fully grown and single.

"I know squat about plants." Beside her, Roman pushed the shopping cart rapidly filling with plants. "Maybe one weekend we could drive up to my house in Dallas and you can tell me what I need to get it in shape."

Intrigued, she scooted over so a customer pushing a flat cart could pass. "What do you have now?"

"Dirt, a bit of mulch, and weeds." He rushed on when her eyes widened, "I have a yardman to keep the grass cut and take care of the flower beds, but I don't think he's doing a good job."

"Then give him a choice, do the work or hit the road." She placed the gallon Gerber daisy back on the table. "It irks me when unscrupulous people take advantage of people."

"Dillon said that's how the garage here started," he said.

"Yes." She continued down the aisle. "Talk to your yard guy. Get him to clean out the flower beds and then I'll help."

"Next Saturday afternoon too soon?" he asked.

Her heart knocked against her ribs. They'd be alone and free to do as they pleased. Plus she wanted to see his house. His confidence in her delighted her. "No."

"Good. I'll pick you up at around one, and after you see the yard, we can go to a nursery." He caught up with her. "Thanks, Marlene."

"I haven't done anything yet." She glanced at him.

"We both know you have," he said quietly, his eyes grateful.

She did trust him, and she wanted him with a growing need. "Let's check out and get to work."

Carson retained the pole position, and because it was his first all season, there was a lot of talk about the Collins intercooler Dillon had designed. By the time Sam and Mark returned an hour later, Dillon had called his mother with the good news. She sounded happy and said she and Roman were working in her yard.

Despite his aggravation with Sam for being off with Washington, Dillon smiled at the image of neat Roman spreading mulch and planting flowers. Since Roman wasn't the yard type—if the bare flower beds in front of his house were any indication—he was there to be with Dillon's mother. Dillon would do his best to stay out of it and not think about them being alone at her house.

He'd much rather think about ruining Washington's pretty face.

On the plus side of Dillon's day, several reporters and two vintage car owners wanted to talk with him about his design. Carson, his eyes full of devilment and still on a high, happily told the owners that Rowland had an exclusive two months with Dillon.

He didn't mind Carson having the exclusive, but Mark Washington set Dillon's teeth on edge. It galled him to give the reporter an exclusive. Dillon made up for it by inviting the reporters to visit Collins Industry and promised to talk to them Monday morning. Washington hadn't liked it, which pleased Dillon even more.

It was almost eight that night when Dillon drove Samantha back to the hotel. "The race starts at twelve. Things will be even more hectic than they were today," Dillon told her as they walked down the long hallway to her room on the floor below his. "Do you want to meet at seven for breakfast?"

Her hands in the pockets of her slacks, Sam hunched her shoulders. "All right."

He frowned. She had been quiet since know-it-all Washington had finally left the garage around five. "Missing Washington?" The question just slipped out.

She stopped in front of her door and stared up at him in puzzlement. "Why would you ask me that?"

"Because you've been unusually quiet and moody since he left," Dillon snapped.

She turned to unlock her door. "I have a lot on my mind."

She was worried. Before he thought, he took her into his arms, his hand sweeping from her waist to the nape of her neck. His thoughts tangled as the warmth of her body, the lush softness of her breasts, nudged him.

He wanted to pick her up and lay her out on the wide bed in her room, kiss her from head to toe, then start all over again, loving her so completely that there'd be no room for any thought except the pleasure they gave each other.

She snuggled against him. She wanted comfort. He wanted her naked and sweaty. He pushed his need away and tried to give her what she needed instead.

"Carson is going to take the checkered flag tomorrow, and when he does, Collins Industry will have so many orders they'll have to have a second shift."

"Thanks to you."

His brows bunched. She still sounded sad. Setting her away from him, he lifted her chin. Was she scared she couldn't handle things by herself? "I won't leave until you feel comfortable in running the company by yourself."

She straightened. "That's very nice of you. Good night."

The door closed in his face. No woman had ever called him nice or closed the door in his face when he was stiff from wanting her. His jaw tight, he headed for the elevator. Sam better learn fast or he was going to be taking a lot of cold showers.

Samantha and Dillon were at the track by eight Sunday morning. The stands were already filling up. Even the little space left for motor coaches was filled. Many were elaborate, with a TV built into the side of the vehicle. Some even had chairs on top to give a better view of the race. The tempting aromas of grilled food wafted through the air.

During breakfast, Samantha had been too nervous to do more than pick at her food. If Carson didn't finish in the top five with all the buzz circulating around the track about the intercooler, she knew that the intercooler would be blamed.

"Carson is as competitive as they come. He doesn't like looking at bumpers."

Samantha thought she was hiding her fear well. Hands deep in the pockets of her slacks, she watched the cars slowly circle the twelve-turn 2.5-mile track. "I want it for Carson, too. He and his family have a lot at stake as well."

"That we do."

Samantha turned to see a handsome older couple. The man was lean, with a devilish smile identical to Carson's. The beautiful olive-hued woman by his side barely came to the middle of his chest. Although they were in casual dress, their clothes obviously had designer labels.

"Mr. and Mrs. Rowland," Dillon greeted them with a wide grin. After shaking the man's hand, he hugged the woman. "I was beginning to think you wouldn't get here for the start of the race."

"Carson would have never forgiven either of us," Mrs. Rowland said. "I've never seen him this excited about a race. He plans on taking the checkered flag today. I wouldn't like to see him disappointed."

Samantha felt a moment of dread.

"We both know race days are unpredictable. A lot can happen between now and the end of the race." Dillon's gaze was as direct as Mr. Rowland's. "The intercooler will give Carson an edge, but whether he'll cross the finish line in front of the thirteen cars in the race today will depend on his driving and a lot of other factors."

"That's why I admire you, Dillon. You never blow smoke."
Mr. Rowland turned to Samantha. "You must be Samantha
Collins. Forgive my bad manners for not introducing our-
selves sooner. This is my wife, Tess."

"I was getting around to it," Dillon interjected.

"Nathan hardly gave you time." Tess laughed and accepted
Samantha's hand, then hugged her. "Hello, Ms. Collins. Please
call me Tess."

"Please call me Samantha." Next she spoke to Mr. Rowland. "Sir, I realize the amount of faith you placed in Dillon,
and his design of the Collins intercooler. I've learned in my
short association with Dillon that he likes to win and he's
proud of his friendship with your family. He wouldn't jeopar-
dize either."

Mr. Rowland glanced at Dillon. "You have yourself a smart
partner."

"It seems," Dillon said slowly.

"The pace car is pulling off. The race is about to start,"
Tess said. "When it's over, let's hope and pray Carson is still
leading the pack."

To call the race nail-biting would be an understatement. The
course tested the skill of the driver and the performance of the
car. Carson lost the lead by the fifth turn. Without thinking,
Samantha reached for Dillon's hand. By the seventh, he had
dropped to third.

"Come on, Carson. Push it!" His mother was on her feet.
"Take back that lead!"

"Come on, son!"

A parent's love. It was more than a race to the Rowlands; they were pulling for their son. Samantha felt the huge responsibility on her shoulders. She wasn't sure she could look them in the eye if Carson finished out of the top five.

"He's making his move," Dillon said.

"Rowland managed to move back to third, now second position, and is pushing hard to regain the lead," the announcer said. "Franklin, who won already this year, is not about to give it up lightly."

"He won't have to give it up, Carson will take it," Dillon said.

Carson did just that by the eleventh turn. Samantha's heart was beating so hard in her chest that she felt light-headed. "You can do it, Carson!" she screamed.

"Rowland is pulling up fast," the announcer said. "This is going to come down to the wire. Both cars are going all out."

"Come on, son!" Mr. Rowland screamed.

"Take it, Carson!" Dillon shouted.

"Here they come. Here they come. They're almost front bumper to front bumper. The flagman is out. It's Rowland by a half-car length!"

"Carson won! We did it!" Sam shouted.

"You doubted?" Dillon said, then laughed, swinging Samantha around and lowering his head to take her mouth. He told himself he intended the kiss to be congratulatory and brief. He lied. The moment their lips touched, his body caught fire, and he remembered the intoxicating taste of her, the feel of her in his arms. He wanted more.

"Carson is putting the car into a victory spin," said Tess with a laugh. "He's been waiting a long time to do that."

Nathan slapped Dillon on the back. "Thanks to you, he got the opportunity. You did it. Come on, let's go down and congratulate Carson."

Dillon reluctantly lifted his head and barely kept from snarling. Later, he promised himself, he was going to have that kiss without any interruptions. He caught Sam's hand, felt it tremble. She was just as affected as he was. Her talk of just business between them was just that, talk.

They passed Mark on their way out of the stands. The other man wasn't happy. Tough. Dillon had no intention of giving the reporter a chance to become involved with Sam again. He'd had his chance and failed. After their kiss, Dillon decided he had no intention of doing the same.

The celebration of Carson's win moved from the racetrack to his parents' spacious suite at the Bellagio. By nine that night, the party showed no sign of winding down. Along with a scrumptious buffet, couples were dancing and everyone was having a good time.

Since their flight back to Dallas wasn't until early the next morning, Samantha was enjoying her second glass of wine. At least, as much as she could with Mark glaring at her. He'd attached himself to her shortly after he'd spoken with Carson and his father.

"I thought there was nothing between you two. You kissed him."

At his accusatory tone, she took another sip of wine. Technically Dillon had kissed her, and what a kiss it was. The memory still heated her body. Telling Mark it was none of his business would only make him grumpier. She couldn't very well tell him the kiss meant nothing, since she could still taste Dillon and wanted to taste him again. She settled on the truth. "I'm not sure what's going on between us."

"Montgomery has a bad reputation with the ladies."

"Yes, he does." That didn't seem to stop her from wanting Dillon. Seeing him coming toward her, the easy grace, her body tingled in anticipation.

"Excuse me, but I think this dance is mine." In typical high-handed fashion, Dillon took the glass from her hand, gave it to a passing waiter, then pulled her into his arms.

Samantha didn't even think of protesting. She was tired of fighting her attraction to him. She decided to enjoy the thump of her heart, the tingling of her skin. The music was slow and soft, Dillon's body hard and muscled, his steps smooth. It was the perfect combination to make any woman forget consequences and just enjoy.

"Enjoying yourself?"

How could she not, in his arms? "Yes."

Lifting his dark head, he stared down at her, his eyes narrowed in concentration. "Then why so quiet? You should be shouting from the rooftops."

Collins would win, but she would lose the man she loved. "Just thinking."

"Hmmm." He pulled her back closer against his enticing length. "Maybe you think too much."

Samantha didn't respond. She knew what he meant—her wanting a business-only relationship. Yet in his arms, all she could think of was getting closer.

The music ended. Dillon was as reluctant to release her as she was to move back.

"You wanna say our good-byes and get out of here?"

Staring up at him, she knew that wasn't all he was asking. "Yes."

Taking her hand, they wound their way through the crowd to find Carson surrounded by three beautiful women. "We have an early flight, so we're cutting out now."

To his credit, Carson didn't roll his eyes at the flimsy excuse to leave. He stuck out his hand to shake Dillon's, then gave him a hearty one-arm hug. "Thanks, man. As soon as you get another intercooler, we want it on the backup car."

"You got it." Dillon glanced at Samantha. "I haven't discussed it with my partner yet, but I'm also thinking of some modifications for the turbochargers we make to fit high-performance cars."

"This partner says when can we get started," Samantha said. The modifications would take time. She felt like doing a jig. Dillon wasn't leaving anytime soon.

"If you don't let Rowland have it first, we're gonna have a problem," Carson said.

Dillon grinned, ignoring Carson's hard frown. "Since you asked so nicely, you got it," he said.

Carson laughed and held out his hand to Sam. "Thanks, Samantha. I'd hug you, but I have plans for tonight and I need to be healthy."

Samantha accepted the brief handshake. She didn't dare look at Dillon. He'd become annoyingly possessive since Mark's arrival.

"We should be thanking Rowland for taking a chance on us. When the new turbo is developed, you'll be the first to hear from us," Dillon said.

"Thanks, and just so you know, in every interview I've mentioned Dillon's design of the intercooler and Collins Industry." Carson glanced between her and Dillon. "Today has been one of my best to date. I can't thank you enough."

"Putting Collins Industry out there is enough." Dillon grinned. "Roman will get a kick out of me telling him about your spin after winning."

Carson chuckled. "That he will. Mom says he's getting back late from Elms Fork. You must be working him hard."

Samantha shot a look at Dillon.

"It keeps him out of trouble," Dillon replied.

"Yeah, because when he finishes he'll be off someplace to relax and find a beautiful woman to pass the time." Carson looked thoughtful. "I hope when I reach sixty, I still have as much juice as he does."

"Yes," Dillon said thoughtfully, his brows bunched.

Samantha knew he was thinking of what his mother and Roman might be doing. He'd called her after Carson's win. From what she'd heard, Roman was with Marlene.

"We'll say good-bye to your parents. Bye." Samantha tugged Dillon away. Lines formed in his forehead. "Your mother is a grown, sensible woman."

Dillon grunted. "Even sensible women can be seduced."

Since Samantha considered herself sensible, and she knew where the night was leading, she didn't say anything as they made their way to Carson's parents. This time Dillon's good-byes were quick. He pulled out his cell phone as soon as the hotel door closed.

Samantha grabbed it. "Leave your mother alone."

"I don't want him to take advantage of her." He reached for the phone.

Samantha put the cell phone behind her. "If you didn't trust Roman, he wouldn't be your friend or work for you."

"He's a man."

"Yes, and your mother likes him. He likes her. So back off."

His eyes closed. "I hear what you're saying, but . . ."

"You need to get your mind on something else," she said.

His eyes snapped open. Unabashed naked hunger stared back at her.

Her breathing changed. "I was thinking of hitting the slot machines or gaming tables downstairs."

"I have a better idea." Catching her hand, they headed down the hall to her room.

Fourteen

· · · · · · · · · · · · · · · ·

Samantha could have protested, reminded him she was a sensible woman, but she pulled the key from her small purse and opened her door. She was barely over the threshold before the door slammed shut and she was in Dillon's arms, his mouth ravishing hers. She returned the compliment. It was as if her body had waited a lifetime for this moment.

She arched against him, wanting more, needing more. He gave it to her with his greedy mouth and knowing hands. Her whimpers and moans drove him on. Clothes were cast aside in heated urgency until she was beneath him.

Fierce dark eyes stared into hers as she lay beneath him. "I promised myself I'd make a feast of you, and I plan to do just that."

True to his word, his lips nibbled and licked their way down and over her body, each touch branding her as his. She'd never wanted this way, hadn't known desire could leave her aching and trembling with need.

She wanted to run her tongue over the corded muscles of his chest, take his nipple in his mouth as he had hers now. The thought had no more formed than she was pushing him away to feast on him. Hearing his guttural moan of pleasure drove her on. She cupped him, ran her hand up and down the hard length of him. He was perfect in every way.

She was killing him, and he was enjoying every second. He was caught between the pleasure of her lips and hands on him and wanting his on her. He couldn't wait any longer.

He rolled her over and he was on top. His eyes drank in her flushed beauty, the swell of her breasts. He quickly sheathed himself, thankful that when they'd hastily undressed he'd slipped the condoms from his pocket and shoved them under the pillow.

His mouth fastened on hers; he brought them together with one thrust. She clamped around him, stroking him. He gritted his teeth against his release, the pleasure so intense.

His eyes closed and he fought for control as she clamped her legs around his, her tongue tangling with his. Her body called to his. He began to thrust hard and fast. She met him stroke for stroke, her face against his neck. He'd never felt more, wanted more.

He breathed her name; she cried out his. They shattered together.

Blissfully happy with Dillon's arms wrapped around her, her back to his front, Samantha snuggled closer, loving the feeling of being surrounded by him. His groin nudged her lightly, an unnecessary reminder of what had happened between them and what they were going to do again. She couldn't wait.

She'd never felt more content. She loved Dillon, had probably started falling for him when she was thirteen. He was all that she desired.

"Together we'll take Collins Industry to new heights." Dillon tensed. Lifting her head, she frowned at him over her shoulder. "What is it?"

"I haven't changed my mind about leaving."

Those seven words shattered her dreams and her heart. Her eyes shut. Pain and regret lanced through her. She scooted away, drawing the sheet with her, well aware that she might distance her body, but her heart was forever his. "Please leave."

He reached for her. She shrugged his hand away.

"Sam, you can't mean that."

"I do. I won't be used until you find my replacement."

His brows furrowed. "What are you talking about?"

If he wanted it spelled out, she was hurting enough to give it to him. "I want what you can't give me—family, home, permanence."

Eyes that earlier had been filled with passion chilled. "I suppose Washington can," Dillon snapped.

"If that was the case, I would have married him when he asked. Good night."

Her easy dismissal of him ticked him off. She sat primly with the sheet clutched to her breasts when minutes ago he'd kissed and licked every inch of her, had been buried deep in her satin heat.

"I asked you to leave."

So she had. With any other woman, he'd be out the door. "Why can't you be happy with how things are?"

Up went her chin. He was learning Sam had a latent stubborn streak. "Because I deserve more."

"Have it your way." Dillon rolled from the bed, looked for his clothes scattered around the bedroom, and began dressing. He wasn't changing for any woman or begging one. He slammed the door on his way out.

Samantha jumped at the angry sound, then lay down and curled into a miserable ball. She'd gambled and lost. She'd mistaken lust for caring. Her fault. Dillon hadn't made any promises. Collins Industry was saved. Her grandfather and her parents would be proud of her.

She just wished that were enough.

Dillon had a horrible night and his morning wasn't much better. It became worse when he decided to act as if nothing had happened and call Sam's room. He'd reserved a car to take them to the airport.

"The guest in that room has already checked out."

Dillon barely kept from slamming down the receiver. Downstairs, he had another surprise: Sam had paid their bills. Dillon was spitting mad and hadn't calmed by the time he saw her waiting in the terminal to board.

He walked directly to her, his booted feet inches from her black flats. Her head was down, so she had to have seen him. He could be stubborn, too.

Ten minutes later, tired of people and their luggage banging against him, he reached out and lowered the e-reader. He was ready to blast her until he saw her lower lip tremble, and tears slid from beneath her sunshades. His anger disappeared. His gut twisted. "Sam."

"First-class passengers for Flight 70721 to DFW can now board."

She slid her e-reader into her overnight case, picked it and her small suitcase up and headed for their gate. Dillon was left staring after her. As he followed slowly, it occurred to him that women didn't fight fair. In any case, hadn't he told her about those tears showing weakness? Sam just didn't listen.

After working his way through the crowd waiting for the next call to board, Dillon boarded the plane. Sam, looking small and vulnerable, was already buckled into her window seat, her head buried in the e-reader.

He stored his luggage and took his seat, his long leg brushing against hers. She jumped, swinging her face toward him. He swore he felt an electric jolt, and it wasn't static. She moistened lips that he hungered for, then turned toward the window.

His hand reached out to touch her trembling shoulder, but instead he straightened and leaned back in his seat. Perhaps it was best that he leave her alone. Despite his intention not to, he'd done it anyway. He'd thought she'd understood that their being together last night—no matter how unforgettable— wasn't forever.

A man with gray hair came down the aisle, and Dillon thought of Roman and his mother. He reached for his phone on his belt. It wasn't there. "Do you have my cell?"

After a few seconds that seemed like forever, Sam reached into her overnight bag at her feet and handed it to him—end to end. She was taking no chances of touching him again. He wasn't keen on the idea either. "Thanks."

He activated the phone, then remembered the two-hour time difference. She'd just be waking up in bed—hopefully alone—and the ringing phone would worry her. Shutting off the phone, Dillon tried to push away the erotic images of him and Sam last night, locked in passion and need, and hoped like hell Roman had gone home last night.

He didn't want tears on his mother's face.

She'd broken her promise to herself; she'd cried in front of Dillon. It was harder than she'd imagined ignoring him now that she'd experienced the arousing touch of his hands, his wicked mouth on hers.

The flight seemed to take forever before the pilot announced the approach to DFW. She wasn't sure she could have lasted much longer. Each time Dillon moved—which seemed like every five minutes—his legs brushed against hers, bringing back memories of the wild night they'd spent together, her weakness for him.

As soon as the plane touched down, she grabbed the case in front of her feet. She'd rent a car. There was no way she was riding with Dillon.

The seat belt light clicked off. People stepped into the aisle to leave or grab luggage. Trying not to look at Dillon, she didn't move to grab hers until he moved down the aisle. Then she jumped up to get her bag. It wasn't there. Her gaze snapped to Dillon. He had her luggage.

He'd left her no choice but to follow him. Watching the easy way he moved, the broad shoulders and lean build, wasn't helping her get over him. She caught up with his long-legged stride. "I want to rent a car."

"People in hell want ice water."

She was so struck by his response, she let him get several

feet ahead of her before she caught up with him again. "Now, see—"

He swung around, his black eyes glittering. "Not happening, and unless you want both of us talking to airport security, you'll save your tantrum for later."

Samantha actually swung her arm back to throw her handbag at him—until she caught a man in uniform watching her. Flushing, she hurried after Dillon.

In his Ferrari, Dillon made the hour-long drive from DFW to Elms Fork in forty-three minutes. His jaw was clenched the entire trip. Sam could drive a man crazy. She was either tempting him to kiss her or shake her. It had taken all of his control not to stare at her long legs in the short skirt. He'd think she'd worn it to punish him if he didn't know she played fair.

He wheeled into the driveway of Collins mansion at seventy miles an hour, reached eighty before easing off the gas, and came to a smooth stop in front. Without a word, he removed her luggage from the trunk and placed it on the porch by the front door.

She opened the door, picked up the luggage, and said a quiet, "Thank you," as she passed.

The door closed quietly, and he wanted to kick something. She had no right to sound so wounded. He shoved his hand over his head and got back in the car.

Six minutes later, he pulled into his mother's driveway and stopped in back by the garage. Her Volvo was still there.

She was usually at work by now, but knowing her, she'd stayed home to fix him a late breakfast and get an update. He just hoped she left Sam out of the conversation, but he knew it wasn't happening. Opening the door, he was greeted by the smell of fresh-baked cinnamon-raisin bread, the sight of his mother smiling at the stove.

"Good morning," she greeted him. "Roman said you and Carson made the AP news. I tried to call you and ask if Sam wanted to come to breakfast, but your phone was off."

He stuck his hands into his pockets. "Sam and I are on the outs again," he admitted, the words spilling out before he could stop them.

"Oh, Dillon." His mother was no longer smiling at him. In fact, he had the distinct impression she was a bit annoyed with him.

"She wants me to stay and I can't." He went to the half bath to wash his hands, then returned to take his seat and say grace.

"Is that the only reason?" she asked.

Dillon was glad he didn't have the coffee in his mouth. "What else could it be?"

"Hmmm."

Dillon felt his face heat. His head down, he piled warm slices of bread, soft-scrambled eggs, pan sausages, and red-skinned potatoes that he didn't want on his plate. He hadn't fooled his mother. Worse, Roman might have left his mother with a smile, but Dillon had left Sam miserable.

Samantha would have liked nothing better than to crawl into her bed, pull the covers over her head, and cry—which would settle nothing. She'd still love Dillon and know he didn't love her.

She showered again, dressed, and went downstairs. She had

no idea if Dillon planned to come in today, but she wasn't hiding from him.

Grinning, the cook held up the Elms Fork newspaper. Collins Industry had made the front page. There was a picture of her, Dillon, Carson, Tess, and Nathan. She looked happy.

"The whole town is buzzing," Louise said. "Mr. Abe and your parents, God rest their souls, must be smiling down from heaven on you."

"Thank you," Samantha said, hoping her voice didn't crack. "I'm going to the plant. I'll probably be late tonight."

"You don't want anything to eat?"

It would stick in her throat. "No, thank you."

"Tonight I'll leave dinner in the refrigerator for you," she said.

Samantha nodded then went to her car and drove to the plant. She made herself get out and discovered Louise had been right. Every person Samantha met congratulated her with handshakes, a hug, or both. People were excited about the company's recognition. More than once she heard, "Abe would be proud."

Tears stung her eyes, but she didn't let them fall. She was not shedding one more tear. Dillon had given her all he could. It wasn't his fault she wanted more.

Dillon arrived at the plant a quarter to twelve. He hadn't come earlier because he didn't want to see tears in Sam's eyes. Once there, he was surprised at the well wishes from many of the people working there. Sparks at the security gate had been his usual snarly self, however.

Dillon wanted to go to the work area and start with the

modification on the turbo, but he found himself in front of the door to the office he and Sam shared. He didn't realize his hand was shaking until he turned the knob and stepped inside.

She glanced up from her desk, dry-eyed and serene. "Hi, Dillon. We're getting a lot of calls for interviews about the intercooler. I put the notes on your desk. One of the largest auto supply houses left a message as well."

She was all business, as if she'd never come apart in his arms, as if he'd never held her as aftershocks rippled through her body.

"Was there something else?"

Dillon had the strongest urge to cross the room and kiss her until he melted the frost. Instead, he went to his desk and picked up the notes in her small, precise handwriting. If she could act as if nothing had happened, so could he.

"Mr. Kingston, this is Dillon Montgomery returning your call. How can I be of service?'"

Shortly before lunch Thursday morning, Samantha considered ignoring the knock on her door. She wasn't sure she could keep pretending everything was all right in her world. Since their return, she and Dillon were ignoring each other, and she was miserable. But she had a company to run.

"Come in."

Evan entered her office, and she wished she had followed her first thought and ignored the knock. For once, he didn't appear so cocky.

"Uncle Evan, I'm busy. I'm doing an interview in ten minutes." She barely kept from sighing. Mark had insisted on doing a follow-up piece. She wasn't so sure he wouldn't pick up that things had gone badly between her and Dillon. He'd jump to the obvious and, unfortunately, correct conclusion.

"Maybe I should stay in case there are any questions," he suggested, taking a seat in front of her desk. "I might have been wrong in my estimation of your ability to run the company. With my help, we can put Collins back on the map. I've already had a couple of calls about purchasing our turbochargers."

"So have I." Tossing the pen on her desk, she leaned back in her chair, working the muscles in her neck. She had been going over orders since eight. "Mark did a good job of getting Collins Industry out there. Nathan and Carson Rowland helped."

Evan's eyes gleamed. "Nathan is a multimillionaire. He comes from old money when oil and land were moneymakers. His family got out before the economy tanked. Racing is his hobby. He has his fingers in more pies than anyone can count. When he says something, people listen."

"You'd never know it. He and his wife are as down-to-earth as they come. So is Carson," she told him.

Her uncle leaned forward, bracing his elbows on his knees, his chin on his folded hand. "We need to cultivate that friendship. Take them out to dinner, the theater."

Samantha got the impression that her uncle wanted to use them. Not in this lifetime. "We'll see."

He frowned at her. "Connection in the business world is paramount to success. Surely you know that. Now that Collins is in the news, we have to capitalize."

He actually sounded excited about Collins. Maybe there was hope for him after all. "Once Roman is finished putting the financial records into the computer, we'll know where we stand financially and can tell more about increasing production."

"Financial records?" Evan jerked upright. "You said he was doing inventory."

Samantha could have smacked herself. She hadn't meant to let that slip. "That's what Dillon wanted people to think."

"I see."

Dillon would have her head. She hadn't been her best since the weekend. "Uncle Evan, please don't tell anyone else."

"No. I won't. I'll let you get ready for your interview." He rushed out of her office.

Her uncle hadn't been gone two minutes before another knock sounded at her door. She took Dillon's chair and leaned back. "Come in."

Mark slowly opened the door. This time he had a photographer with him. Samantha came to her feet. He crossed the room, shook her hand, holding it far longer than he should have as his eyes searched hers.

She pulled her hand free and waved him to a seat. "Thank you for the press. Bloomberg service picked up your articles, and Collins is all over the news."

His nostrils flared as he continued to stare at her. He tossed a glance at the photographer. "Go grab a cup of coffee, and give us five minutes."

"Sure thing." Gently he placed the long-lens camera on the small couch in the room and left.

"I warned you."

Samantha took her seat. Oddly, Dillon's chair was giving her the strength not to back down. "And I told you, it's turbochargers and intercoolers or nothing. What will it be?"

He cursed beneath his breath. "What do you see in him and not in me?"

She could think only of a phrase she'd once heard, that the heart wants what the heart wants. Her foolish heart had chosen at the impressionable age of thirteen. "Have a nice trip back to Houston."

"I love you, Samantha. I wanted to marry you. What has he offered?"

She barely kept from flinching. Dillon offered a hot night of sex and nothing of himself.

"I'm sorry if I spoke out of turn," Mark finally said when she refused to answer him.

"Mark, I'm sorry too. I don't love you the way you deserve to be loved," she said as gently as she could. "You'll find her one day, but it won't be me."

"I guess you can't make it any plainer." He pulled out his tape recorder and placed it on the desk. "As you like."

Nothing was as she liked. She was afraid her life never would be again.

After the interview in her office, she invited Mark to tour the factory. Thanks to Dillon, she now could talk with more authority about how the turbocharger worked and not just spout facts. Judging from Mark's surprised expression, he hadn't expected her to have the command and knowledge she had.

They were almost finished when the cameraman spotted Dillon working. "Mark, you want to get a shot of Montgomery?"

Samantha tensed as much as Mark did. No matter how

hard she tried to still the yearning of her heart, it didn't do any good. She loved the pigheaded, argumentative man and there was nothing she could do about it.

"Dillon is working on a modification of our turbocharger to work on high-performance cars. Rowland Motors have already requested that they provide the test car."

Without speaking, Mark moved toward Dillon, who was working in a small area of the factory. He looked up, eyes narrowed, his cutting gaze going from her to Mark. By the time they reached Dillon, his arms were folded across his chest, his stance combative.

Samantha forged ahead. "Dillon, I just told Mark about your working on modifications of our turbo for high-performance cars."

"I didn't expect to see you again," Dillon said.

"You might be seeing a lot more of me," Mark tossed back.

Her gaze swung to Mark. He was being as baiting as Dillon.

"Lucky us." Unfolding his arms, Dillon went back to work.

Samantha forced a smile. "We can go back to my office, if you don't have any other questions."

"Do you mind if I get a shot, Mr. Montgomery?" the cameraman asked.

"Since I'm working on modifications, I'd rather the competition not see what I'm doing," Dillon continued without turning. "One with Ms. Collins and a turbocharger just off the assembly line might be better."

"We already have that shot," Mark said with satisfaction.

Dillon looked up, his face hard. "Then I won't keep you."

"This way, gentlemen. Thank you, Dillon," Samantha said, her smile stiff. Finally, Mark stopped trying to outglare Dillon and followed her back to the office.

Fifteen

. . . .

Dillon clenched the wrench in his hand. *Seeing more of him.* Sam couldn't possibly be thinking of taking that loudmouth Washington back. Could she? He tried to continue working and couldn't. He tossed the wrench on the workbench and headed for Sam's office.

He rounded the corner and saw Washington reach out his arms. He couldn't see Sam and was actually glad he couldn't see her hugging another man. He didn't know if he should warn him off or ask Sam what the hell she was doing. *She was his!*

The thought slammed into Dillon's brain. He tried to get around it but couldn't. He didn't want to be tied down to any woman. He'd always felt protective of Sam. Intimacy had made him feel more so, that's all. Sure that he had explained his strange possessiveness to his satisfaction, he went back to work.

Minutes after arriving, he glanced up to see Mark walking toward him. The reporter was really begging for a bloody nose.

"If you don't want Samantha, leave her the hell alone," Mark clipped out, then turned and walked away.

Dillon's first thought was to go after Mark and tell him to mind his own business. Just as quickly, he remembered Sam trembling on the flight back. He'd hurt her. He hadn't meant to do that. She had so much to deal with already, and he had only added more.

Dillon tossed the wrench aside again and started for his truck. He needed to think things through. He ended up at Roman's office door. He and his mother had been out every night, and she always came home smiling. For the first time in his life, Dillon felt like a failure. He'd always kept his own counsel, but this time he needed help.

Opening the door, he saw Roman working at his desk. Luckily the other two people in the office with him weren't there. They were probably at lunch. Roman wouldn't stop except to stretch or if Dillon or Sam brought lunch. Dillon wondered if Sam was eating and taking care of herself. When he messed up, he did it royally.

"Are you coming in or did you just want to see if I'm working?" Roman asked, continuing to type on the computer keyboard.

"In, I guess." Dillon closed the door, shoved his hands into the pockets of his jeans.

Roman's hands paused, and his gaze snapped up to Dillon's. "Marlene okay?"

"Mama's fine."

Roman nodded and went back to entering data. "It can't be the company. You're getting good press, thanks to the intercooler and Carson talking it up."

"Speaking of, he said his mother thought you were working hard since you spent so much time here."

"If I told her I was dating instead of just going through the motions, she and the rest of the family would blow up my phone. No, thank you." Roman shook his head. "It's bad enough that everywhere we go people come over to visit. I know some of them by name now."

Dillon studied Roman. "You don't seem bothered."

"That your mother is so well liked that the women of the town want to ensure I'm not up to no good? Hardly. Even some of the men have looked me dead in the eye and told me what a good woman she is. Then there are those men who obviously missed their chance and wish I'd drop dead." He looked thoughtful. "I don't think your mother really knows how well liked and respected she is."

"You make her happy."

"She does the same for me." Roman leaned back in his chair. "I would have considered myself a happy man before, but now things just feel so much better." He shrugged, laughed. "I can't explain it, but that's not why you came. If it's about the accounts, I'm almost through. I had to track down some invoices and a company three years back. Once I'm finished, I'll have an answer for you and a name."

"It's not about either of those."

"Ah. That leaves Samantha."

Dillon's hands came out of his pockets. "Why did you say that?"

Roman stopped typing. "Besides being there when you mentioned her to Marlene, I've seen the two of you circling each other even more since your return from Vegas. Marlene likes her."

Dillon hunched his shoulders. He knew that. His mother

wouldn't be happy with him if she found out he'd hurt Sam. His hands returned to his pockets. "Sam's different from other women."

"Meaning she wants a commitment?"

"When Collins is back on its feet financially, I'm outta here," Dillon told him.

"Life offers choices. Make the wrong one and pay for the rest of your life," Roman told him. "You have to decide what's most important to you, your freedom or making Samantha yours."

Dillon wasn't sure he had an answer, and he asked a question of his own. "What are your intentions toward my mother?"

"Honorable." Roman moved his mouse. "Don't bother with lunch for me today. I'm working straight through. Marlene is leaving early and we're grilling, then planting the rest of the flowers we picked up Saturday before it gets dark."

Lines radiated across Dillon's forehead. "Mama never leaves work early unless she has a medical appointment or has to do something for me."

Roman grinned. "She is today."

Dillon simply stared, then headed for the door. What was Roman doing right that he was doing so wrong? "I'll make myself scarce."

"Marlene would be concerned if you're not there. Don't worry, she said you hate yard work, but would do it if she asked. She won't."

"I'd do anything for her."

"So would I," Roman said, his dark eyes intense.

There it was, the difference. Roman was clearly committed to doing whatever it took to please his mother. Dillon wanted to please Sam—only on his terms.

"See you later," Dillon said, closing the office door. He'd never been this conflicted in his life. He'd always known what came next. Even when Abe fired him, he'd had an idea of what he wanted to do.

His cell phone rang. Almost thankful, he reached for it. "Hello."

"Hi, Dillon, it's Nathan."

"Hello, Mr. Rowland. Thanks again for letting me fit your car with the intercooler. The press has been great for Collins Industry."

"I should be thanking you." Nathan laughed. "Carson is still walking on air. No matter how old your children get, you want them to be happy."

"Mama always said the same thing," Dillon told him.

"Marlene is a smart woman. I called to ask a favor, if you have the time."

"Name it." He needed a distraction. Besides, Nathan had been there for him.

"My home builder and friend, Zachary Holman, has a close friend, Cade Mathis, with a Lamborghini that he's having some problems with. I told him you were the best. Could you meet him at the Dallas garage and check it out?"

Dillon had had these special requests before and knew some people—especially men—wanted only one person working on their car. Any other time, he might have passed. "If he can make it, I can be there in an hour."

"He'll make it," Nathan said. "Dr. Mathis is a noted neurosurgeon, one of the best in the country, I understand, but he said he was available anytime today or whenever you could get free."

"Good."

"Thanks, Dillon. I knew I could count on you."

"Bye, Mr. Rowland." Dillon disconnected the call. Too bad Sam couldn't say the same thing.

Samantha stared at the papers on her desk more than she worked on them. Her head was propped in the palm of her hand when the door opened and Dillon walked in. Her pride dictated she straighten and act busy. She didn't. She was tired of pretending.

"You all right?"

"Don't I look all right?"

He hesitated, which was unusual for Dillon. He had enough one-liners for a comedian. "I need to drive up to Dallas to check the car of a new client."

His business came first. But then, so did Collins for her. "I'll pick up Roman's lunch."

"He's skipping lunch today. He's taking off early to work with Mama in her flower garden."

Marlene's romance was clicking along, while Samantha's had tanked. Her fault for expecting too much. "I'll see you tomorrow."

He didn't move. "You gonna go get something to eat?"

"Probably," she answered. She'd been nibbling at food and eating junk since Sunday. Last night it was a dozen chocolate-chip cookies from the bakery, the same bakery where she'd first met Dillon.

"Take care of yourself, Sam."

She glanced up, but he was gone. So, he cared about her. It wasn't enough. She wanted his love and was destined never to have it.

. . .

Dillon had his mother on the phone before he reached his car. "Sam's not eating. Can you invite her over to eat with you and Roman this afternoon? I have to drive up to the high-performance garage to meet a new client."

"She's not the only one not eating."

After activating the automatic lock on his car, he slid inside. "I probably won't be back until night."

"Be stubborn, but tonight I'm grilling chicken breasts, and when you get back I'm going to watch you eat every bite." The line went dead.

Dillon almost smiled. His mother wasn't to be messed with. He should have remembered. She was handling dating Roman just fine. He was the one floundering, and if he didn't get his act together and put Sam out of his mind for good, he was going to sink like a rock.

Samantha absently picked up the ringing phone. "Collins Industry."

"Hello, Samantha, it's Marlene. You got a second?"

"Always." She liked Marlene. Her crashing with Dillon wouldn't ruin their budding friendship.

"I want to invite you over for dinner tonight. Roman is coming as well," Marlene said. "I'm grilling. You'll hurt my feelings if you don't come."

Suspicion entered her mind. Who wanted a third person when a date was coming over? "Did Dillon ask you to call me?"

"He did, but I really want you to come over and just relax.

Abe would have wanted me to look after you, but I'm asking because I truly like you and hope we can be real friends."

Samantha massaged her forehead. Real friends meant she might run into Dillon when he came back to visit.

"I cooked an Italian cream cake for dessert. Your favorite."

"How did you know that?"

"I baked one for Abe last year and he told me."

Samantha's eyes misted. "I wish we could have had more time."

"You were there when it counted. You made your peace with each other. Sometimes that doesn't happen, and you have to live with the regrets."

Samantha wasn't sure if Marlene was talking in generalities about Samantha and Abe or about Samantha and Dillon. She'd made the wrong decision so many times in the past. Was she right to ask Dillon for what he couldn't give her?

"Is five all right?" Marlene said into the lengthening silence. "For once, you can leave before Evan."

The idea had instant appeal. Tonight, she didn't want to be alone with her thoughts. "You talked me into it. I'll see you at five."

"Wonderful. Bring an appetite. Bye."

Samantha went back to work, yet somehow she didn't feel as melancholy as she had before Dillon's visit and Marlene's subsequent phone call. He didn't have to call his mother. He cared. Perhaps not in the way she'd hoped, but he did care. She just had to convince herself that it was enough.

Dillon drove to Dallas with the pop station blaring, and at just over the speed limit. His thoughts were too scattered to speed.

By the time he pulled into the parking lot of his high-performance garage, it was an hour later and he had no idea how to settle the problems with him and Sam. All he was certain of was that he wanted her more than ever, wanted her more than any woman before her.

Climbing out of the low-slung car, he spotted the black Lamborghini immediately. Sleek and mean, with enough horses to hit 120 in five seconds. He'd worked on other million-dollar cars, but to him the Lamborghini was in a class by itself.

The front door of the office opened and two men came out. Both had broad shoulders, were over six feet, and moved with the loose-limbed grace of athletes. One was dressed in steel-toed shoes, well-worn jeans, and a chambray shirt. The other wore one of those tailored suits that cost five figures, the kind Nathan preferred. They walked easily beside each other, as if old friends.

"Mr. Montgomery?" asked the one in the expensive suit.

"Dillon, please." He stuck out his hand.

"Cade Mathis, and this is Zachary Holman." The handshakes were firm. "Thank you for coming on short notice."

"I had the time, and I owe Nathan," Dillon said, then twisted his head to one side as the men studied him openly. "Did I grow another head?"

"Sorry. I guess I'm in awe of meeting you," Cade said. "You made quite the splash with headlines over the weekend."

Dillon waved the words aside. "I put on my pants the same as you do."

The men shared a smile. Zachary explained, "A mutual friend of ours said the same thing when my wife met his fiancée. Only it was panty hose."

"Your wife is . . . ?"

"Madison Reed. She's the one who brought your accomplishment to my attention. I called Nathan and asked for the introduction for Cade."

"I've heard of her. She's one of the few live programs my mother allows on the TV at our garage in Elms Fork."

"Please thank your mother," Zachary said. "I'll be sure and tell Madison."

"Was there a reason you wanted to see me so quickly?" Dillon asked.

Zachary slapped Cade on the back. "Cade recently became engaged and needs to enjoy that toy of his before he has to park it. I drive a truck with a booster cab."

"He has two adorable children," Cade explained. "And I won't mind parking it one bit." He nodded toward Dillon's Ferrari. "Nice."

"Thanks. I was admiring yours." Dillon walked over and unlatched the hood.

"Looks good, but it's sluggish." Cade peered under the hood with the other men. "Traffic is too crazy for me not to be able to accelerate."

"Not to mention embarrassing." Dillon laughed, and the men laughed with him. They were easy to talk with and friendly. Lots of his clients were stuck-up. "Start her up."

Cade got inside, started the motor, then rolled down the window. "Rev the motor a couple of times," Dillon instructed.

The car rumbled, but it wasn't smooth. Dillon flicked his wrist, indicating to cut the engine. "I think it's spark plugs, but I won't be sure until I put it through a full analysis. You can make an appointment and bring it in next week, if that's all right."

"Will you be working on it or one of your trained mechanics?"

"I will." Dillon slammed the hood. "Don't worry. We'll take care of your car."

"If I didn't trust you, I wouldn't be here." Cade stared at the car for a moment. "Another reason I want it at peak performance is that my fiancée has been hinting that she wants to drive it."

"Madison was the same way about my truck after we became engaged." Zachary chuckled. "What is it about driving your man's car?"

"My guess would be that they want to know that everything we own is now theirs, even our prized automobiles." Cade turned to Dillon. "What do you think?"

"Probably, and that's why I've never handed over my keys," Dillon said. "Nobody drives my cars but me."

"You're obviously single and not 'seriously dating,' as they say these days," Zachary said.

Dillon shrugged. "I'm too busy for anything serious."

"I sometimes have twelve-hour days, but when I go home there's Madison and our two kids. They make the long day, all the problems associated with building homes, fall away."

"The same with Sabrina, my fiancée," Cade explained. "She pushed her way into my life, but I'd be lost without her." He briefly clasped Dillon on the shoulder. "One day I hope you know what it feels like to have a woman who loves you waiting at the end of a long, hard day. You won't even mind her driving your car."

Dillon wasn't sure about Sam driving his car, but he did want her in his life. For how long, he wasn't sure.

Charlie, Dillon's office manager, stuck his head out the door. "Dillon, phone."

"Is it Mama?"

"No, it's the woman who messed up the Ferrari."

Dillon rolled his eyes. "Surely she didn't try to drive the car again and screw up the gears."

Charlie nodded. "She's hysterical."

"Tell her I'll be there in a minute." Dillon turned to Cade and Zachary. "Unlike the women in your lives, the customer on the phone would rather sneak and drive her husband's car when he's out of town."

"That's a marriage headed for disaster," Zachary said. "You can't build anything solid without trust, and that works both ways."

"My mother said the same thing," Dillon told them.

"Smart woman. We'll let you go." Cade stuck out his hand again. "Thanks."

"Anytime."

"Since Sabrina has never driven a stick, that might be sooner than you imagine," Zachary kidded.

"Just so she's safe. I can replace the car, but not Sabrina." Cade turned to the car, then looked back. "We're going to dinner later with another couple. Would you like to join us? You can bring a date, of course."

Dillon immediately thought of Sam. She needed more friends. "I'll take a rain check. Good-bye."

"I'll see you when I bring the car back in." The car rumbled to life. "Thanks again." Cade pulled out of the parking space and hit the streets.

"Dillon. Please," Charlie said, his face and voice frantic.

"Coming." Dillon started toward the office, his thoughts on what Zachary had said about not being able to build anything without trust. He and Sam might trust each other, but they saw things differently and were headed in different directions. Yet even knowing all that, he still wanted her.

"Dillon looked even more like A. J. Reed in person than he did in the pictures Madison showed us," Zachary said. "It's a good thing she saw the interview in the newspaper."

"He might be the spitting image of A. J., but thank goodness he's the opposite in personality." Cade checked the mirror and took the ramp to the freeway. "He didn't have a BS meter that was off the charts. I liked him."

"Same here." Zachary turned in his seat to stare at Cade. "He might be our brother."

Our brother. The two words resonated through Cade. They had different mothers, but the same arrogant man for their father, A. J. Reed. Cade had discovered his brother, Zachary, only six weeks ago. The thought of finding another brother was scary and exciting at the same time. "According to the report from the private investigator I hired, it's rumored in his hometown that he was the son of Abe Collins. Collins died recently, and now Dillon works for the company as a consultant."

"We have to assume that he might not know who his father is. He didn't react when I mentioned Madison's professional last name."

"A. J. Reed didn't stick around after the woman became pregnant," Cade said, the words coated with bitterness. "His mother raised Dillon alone."

"Looks like we'll have to contact her first. Neither one of us wants to cause her any embarrassment or discomfort," Zachary said.

"No. A. J. put our mothers through enough misery to last a lifetime." Cade shifted gears and passed a slow-moving car. "We'll see how my meeting with him goes when I bring back the car, then we'll take it from there. Agreed?"

"Agreed."

Sixteen

. . . .

S amantha pulled up behind Roman's car in Marlene's driveway and got out. It was barely five. Looked like he was anxious to see Marlene again. She was glad some-one's romance was going well. She opened the gate to the backyard, rounded the corner of the house, and came to an abrupt stop.

Roman and Marlene were standing just outside the back door, his arm around her waist, hers looped around his neck, their mouths inches apart. Obviously Marlene was no longer unsure about dating Roman. Good for her. Roman was a great guy.

Samantha turned to leave. Three was definitely a crowd.

"Hi, Samantha," Marlene said, her voice a bit breathless.

"Hi, Samantha," Roman said, his strained.

Samantha turned to see Marlene in front of the grill. Next to her Roman held a platter of skewered vegetables.

"Hi," Samantha greeted, slowly approaching. She didn't want to embarrass them. "Smells good."

"We should eat in about ten minutes." Marlene closed the lid of the grill, her gaze sweeping over Samantha. "Wine or raspberry lemonade?"

"Wine, definitely."

"I'll get it." Roman touched Marlene's shoulder as he passed.

"We didn't mean to embarrass you," Marlene said when Roman closed the back door.

"You didn't." Samantha smiled. "I'm happy for you."

"It took me a while, but so am I." Marlene waved Samantha to a seat at the round glass-topped table.

"Here you go." Roman came back with a glass of wine for Samantha and raspberry lemonade for Marlene. "I'll start taking things to the flower bed."

"Thanks, Roman."

"Good practice for Saturday." He dipped a kiss on her head, then headed around the side of the house toward the garage.

"If I might ask, what's happening on Saturday?" Samantha sipped her wine.

"I'm helping Roman landscape his house," Marlene told her. "From the pictures he showed me yesterday, it's badly needed."

Samantha glanced around the backyard with its colorful flower beds of azaleas, geraniums, and daisies. "You certainly have the talent. Your home and yard are spectacular."

"Thanks to Dillon." Marlene picked up her glass. "He had this house built for me, indulged me with the extensive flower beds although he can't stand yard work. I couldn't ask for a better son."

"Without him, there is no way I would have made it this

far," Samantha said. "We certainly wouldn't have gotten the press or be in the process for a new design."

"But you wanted more," Marlene said softly.

Samantha opened her mouth to deny it, then slumped back in her seat. "He's giving all he can."

"Knowing that doesn't help ease the loneliness your heart feels."

"No, it doesn't," Samantha admitted.

"I came to Elms Fork because I thought it sounded quaint, and I'd always heard that small towns were almost like a big family where everyone worked together to help everyone." Marlene's slim fingers circled her glass. "It wasn't that way for us. Perhaps it would have been different if I had grown up here. Dillon's memories of Elms Fork aren't all good. If I wasn't here, he never would have returned once he left for college."

"Just like I wouldn't have returned if Granddad hadn't gotten sick," Samantha murmured.

Marlene's smile was sad. "You both needed a reason to return permanently to the place that holds so many unhappy memories. You found yours. Given time, Dillon will find his."

"What if he doesn't?" Samantha asked, aware that she sounded desperate.

"Then, just as I did you'll have to decide which is more important, accepting what he can give you or walking away. For me, I already have enough regrets." Marlene came to her feet. "I better check the food."

"I'm not as brave as you are."

Marlene opened the top of the grill. Hickory smells and smoke wafted upward as she removed the chicken breasts and vegetables. "I'll admit, when you first came here, perhaps. But you're not the same woman anymore. You stood up to Evan and Dillon. Don't sell yourself short."

True, Samantha thought, *but risking heartbreak was an entirely different matter.*

Roman rounded the corner of the house. "Just in time to help." Marlene's gaze dropped to his hands. He chuckled. "I washed them at the sink in the garage."

"Please take a seat." Marlene picked up the platter. "You're going to be up to your wrists in soil very shortly."

Roman took the stoneware from her. "And you've worked all day, then grilled, and stayed up late to bake a cake from scratch since I kept you out late."

"You know, you can be pushy," Marlene said, but she began putting the meat on the platter.

"And you have no problem putting me in my place," he answered.

Samantha watched the interchange with interest. It was easy to see they cared about and respected each other. Marlene had taken a chance, and it had paid off. She might have regrets later, but she'd also have good memories and know that she hadn't let fear rule her. Samantha had to decide if the possible pleasure outweighed the possible pain.

Shortly after nine that night, Dillon pulled up behind Roman's car and honked his horn. Climbing out, he stretched his arms over his head. He and Ricky, his head mechanic, had worked hard to get the husband's Ferrari back in shape.

Before he'd even looked at it, Dillon had told the woman to lose his phone number. He could understand once, but not twice. Sneaking around wasn't the way for any marriage to last. Crying, she had promised she wouldn't drive it without permission again. Somehow, Dillon didn't believe her.

It was her problem now. He had problems of his own. At the top of that short list was Sam. No matter how he tried, he couldn't shake the feeling that he had let her down. He wanted her, but not if it meant helping run Collins. He had his own life.

Using the key, he let himself into the house through the front door. His mother was playing the piano while Roman, arm braced on the top, gazed down at her.

Dillon wondered if they'd heard the horn. "I'm home."

"Hi, Dillon," his mother greeted him.

Roman waved and went back to staring at Dillon's mother as if he'd never get enough.

What happened to her watching him eat? he mused as he continued on to the kitchen. There was no food on the stove or on the countertop. He glanced at the table and saw a note with his name on it propped up against a crystal salt shaker. He recognized the lilac stationery as his mother's. Thinking she'd left instructions about warming the food or where to find it, he opened the envelope and pulled out the note.

Please come to the guest cottage. I'll be waiting.
Samantha

All of the reasoning he'd been doing that day took a backseat to the sudden burst of joy. *They still had a chance.*

Shoving the note into his jeans pocket, he headed out of the kitchen. "Mama, I need to go out. I'm not sure when I'll be back," he called as he hurried through the living room.

"Drive carefully," his mother called, but he was already closing the door.

. . .

Marlene's hands paused over the keys as soon as she heard Dillon's car motor fire up. "I hope they can work it out."

"They will if how fast he left is any indication," Roman said.

"Dillon can be stubborn."

"I wonder where he got that from?" Roman said, the corners of his mouth tilted into a smile.

Marlene lifted a brow. "That coming from a man who kept badgering me when I said no."

Chuckling, Roman sat beside her on the bench, his back to the piano. "Giving up wasn't an option." His hand cupped her face tenderly. "Once I saw you, there was no turning back. Kissing you sealed it for me."

Lowering his head, he brushed his lips across hers, once, twice, then settled.

Marlene was trembling by the time he lifted his head. She felt the same way, but she had reached out once for what she wanted and regretted it ever since. With unsteady hands, she started playing the piano again.

The drive to the guest cottage took the longest five minutes of Dillon's life. Her note could mean she wanted to talk business or put both of them out of their misery and fall into the nearest bed.

Turning into the driveway, he shifted gears and became aware of the engine's noise. The only lights were those on the third floor. He distinctly remembered the landscape lights being on when he'd picked Sam up for their business dinner. It could be a coincidence or . . .

Switching off his lights, he let his eyes adjust to the darkness and drove around the side of the house. He parked off to the side, then got out and followed the path to the guest cottage a hundred feet behind the garage.

He'd barely knocked before the door opened. She wore a dress that bared her exquisite shoulders and stopped above her incredible knees. His mouth dried.

"Please come in."

Somehow he got his legs to move. He closed the door behind him.

"Thank you for coming." She bit her lips, started toward the small kitchen in back. "I know you probably haven't eaten. Marlene sent tons of food."

He caught her arm, felt her tremble, then caught her other arm. "Are you all right?"

"That depends on you."

"Is Evan on your case again?" he snarled.

"No. Thanks to you I can stand up to him and not feel guilty."

"Then why are you trembling?"

"Don't you know?"

His hands flexed on hers, afraid to hope that what he saw in her eyes was desire. "Maybe you should lay it out for me."

"I'll take you for as long as you want me." She leaned against him, her arms going around his waist. "Life has no guarantees. I know that better than anyone. I don't want to waste another minute. I want us to be lovers." She lifted her head. "Is that plain enough?"

Dillon dragged her to him, his lips finding hers. His mouth moved to burn a path to her shoulders and met the top of her dress. He pulled it down and moaned on seeing her bare breasts. If he kissed her there, he wasn't sure he'd be able to stop until he'd made her his again. He picked her up.

"First door on the left."

He didn't waste time getting them to the queen-sized bed. Setting her on her feet, he peeled the dress from her exquisite body. He got harder and hotter as inch by incredible inch, she was revealed to him. He accepted that he'd never get tired of looking at her.

She grabbed the hem of his T-shirt and tugged it over his head, then made short work of his pants. Together they fell into the bed, their mouths locked again in a heated kiss as they touched and tasted each other.

His mouth and teeth closed over her taut nipple. She arched against him. Her hands held him to her as he suckled her, then he moved to the other breast. She twisted restlessly beneath him.

His hand drifted down her body and found her wet and ready. Lifting upward, he sheathed himself and then brought them together. The fit was tight, exquisite. He thrust again and again into her satin heat. She met him stroke for stroke.

Whimpering moans of pleasure slipped past her lips. Or were they his?

He was lost in the pleasure they gave each other. They went over together, with her name on his lips, his on hers.

Their bodies touching from breast to thigh, sharing a pillow, Dillon and Samantha stared at each other. He enjoyed the smile, the contentment, on her face. "I never thought we'd be together like this again."

"My fault." She kissed his chin. "That's behind us now. When it's time for you to leave, I'll be sad, but I'll understand."

Unexpectedly, he felt a stab of annoyance. His eyes narrowed.

She cocked her head to one side. "I'm almost afraid to ask why the scary face."

"We just got back together, and you're ready to wave me good-bye."

Sighing, she stroked his chest with the pads of her fingertips. "I just don't want you to feel trapped. Marlene helped me understand and reminded me that it wasn't too long ago that the last place on earth I wanted to be was Elms Fork. Now, I can't imagine being anyplace else, and I understand now why I never felt content anyplace else. For me, this is home."

"And I can't imagine living here permanently." His hand closed over hers as shadows darkened her eyes. He felt her tremble. "But no woman has ever had me as angry and as mixed up as you have. I certainly never wanted one more."

Sam grinned. "Really?"

He smiled at the pleased look on her face. He liked making her happy. "Really, but don't let it go to your head."

Stern-faced, she shook her head. "Wouldn't dream of it."

Dillon chuckled. "Somehow I don't believe you."

She gave him a quick kiss on the mouth. "Shows how smart you are."

Dillon had always thought so, but becoming involved with a woman he couldn't get off his mind wasn't smart. Yet he was incapable of walking away from her and staying away. He worried about her almost as much as he wanted her. "Did you eat today?"

Her gaze flicked away. "A dozen chocolate-chip cookies. And before you say anything, I was in a funk because we were at odds, and that's how I handled it."

His hand tenderly swept over her hair. He liked touching her, holding her. "You never order them when we get take-out."

"Because too many will go straight to my hips."

Grinning, he ran his hand over her butt. "I'd say you don't have to worry about that. It's my favorite cookie."

"I know. You told me when we met for the first time at the bakery."

"You were with your mother."

Her eyes widened with delight, then narrowed in anger. "And you were with that shameless woman. She was clinging to you like wet tissue paper in those disgraceful short shorts and a nothing top."

"I can hardly remember her, let alone what she had on," he said with a total lack of interest. "How can you?"

She eyed him. "You'll get an even bigger head if I tell you."

His eyes narrowed suspiciously as seconds ticked by. "You had a crush on me."

Sam lifted one shoulder in dismissal. "At thirteen, I was an impressionable young girl."

His finger turned her face toward his. "You were already growing into a beautiful woman like your mother. The night of your prom, even knowing you were trying to seduce me because you wanted to forget you'd lost your parents, it took a hard talk with myself to take you home."

Her eyes shut briefly, then opened. "I missed them, wanted to forget, but despite all the talk about you being related to me, I couldn't get you out of my mind and I was just tipsy enough to be able to blame my seduction attempts on the alcohol."

"Your mom and dad were good people." He screwed up his face. "Unlike Evan and his wife."

"I don't think they even like each other," Sam admitted quietly.

"Probably not. They're both selfish and think they're better than anyone else. They let me know the first time I met them that I was dirt."

Gently, she touched his arm. "I'm sorry."

"Long ago and forgotten."

Samantha wondered. She might have gotten past her bad memories of Elms Fork, but she didn't think Dillon had. "I'm hungry. Besides the grilled chicken, your mother baked an Italian cream cake."

Dillon threw back the covers and got out of bed. "I'll go fix us something."

Samantha took a moment to enjoy the view of all those sleek naked muscles and prime butt before sitting up to hold the sheet over her breasts with one hand while she tried to move the covers around with the other. "I'll help."

"What are you looking for?"

She felt her face heat, but she answered, "Lingerie."

Dillon grunted, picked up his shirt, and handed it to her. "You won't need that until morning."

When dawn came, Dillon quietly let himself out of the cottage. He would have liked to wake Sam up, but that would have led to another round of lovemaking. A kiss on her bare shoulder had to do. There was no way he was taking a chance that Evan would find out about them.

In his car, he slowly turned around and drove with the lights off until he hit the street. He wasn't ashamed to be with her, but if Evan found out, he'd give her grief. If it was in

Dillon's power, he was going to make her life happier. He'd never felt this strong need to protect and keep safe any other woman except his mother.

He wasn't going to worry about his feelings or try to analyze them. He had a feeling he wouldn't be able to.

Turning into his mother's driveway, he drove around back. In all of his craziness while in high school, he'd always managed to drag his behind home before dawn. Cell phones weren't as popular in those days, and with his reputation, he knew she'd worry.

In college he might hang out all night, but never when he came home. He was too aware of the neighbors waiting to crucify him and tell his mother that he was still headed to jail. She had defended him enough to last two lifetimes.

Roman was right about one thing, people in the town really liked her. She'd been able to overcome their harsh and unfair belief about her. He didn't plan to do anything that might change their minds.

Getting out of his car, Dillon wondered if Roman had stayed last night, then decided he didn't want to go there.

He unlocked the back door, went through the kitchen and started for his room, then switched direction to the other wing of the house, to his mother's bedroom. She'd known why he'd torn out of there last night, wouldn't have worried, but still . . .

The flameless candles were off. The little alcove lay in shadows; the bedroom door was open.

He wasn't sure he wanted to go in. He was a grown man, but she'd know what he'd been doing, whom he'd been doing it with. Strangely, his concern was for Sam. It wasn't likely his mother would treat her differently or think less of her. They were both single adults.

The thought had no more formed than it ran through his mind that his mother and Roman were single adults.

"Dillon." Light chased away the shadows in the alcove.

"Yeah." Dillon entered the bedroom. His mother sat up in bed, her eyes searching his. "Is everything all right?"

He sat on the side of the bed, stared down at his shoes. "Sam and I worked things out."

"I'm glad." She brushed her hand over his head as if he were a little boy. "I like Samantha. She's a wonderful and beautiful young woman."

His head came up and he was grinning. "She is, isn't she?"

"Yes, she is," his mother said. "I'm glad you were able to work things out."

"For now." He came to his feet, shoving his hands into the pockets of his jeans. "One day I'll leave."

"Then enjoy to the fullest every second you have with her," his mother said. "Make it count."

He stared down at her. "Is that what you're doing with Roman?"

She glanced away.

He reached for her. "I didn't say it to embarrass you. I just don't want you hurt."

Finally she looked at him. "He's already told me that when the job is over he still plans to see me."

"He said you make him happier. I think it's the same way with you."

"He annoys me at times, and then . . ." She lifted her shoulders helplessly.

"The same with Sam. She tried to outstare me, challenge me, in Vegas," he recalled. "I was ready to leave her in the hotel, but I couldn't."

"You really like her."

"Yeah. You really like him."

"Yeah."

Dillon stared at his mother; she stared back. A word leaped into his mind, but he refused to say it aloud. From his mother's huge eyes, she was thinking the same thing.

"Don't worry about breakfast. I think I'll call Sam and see if she wants to grab a bite at the Golden Griddle. You want to come with us?"

"Roman is picking me up at seven thirty for breakfast there, and then bringing me home after work." She seemed almost embarrassed.

"What? No lunch date?" Dillon teased, enjoying his mother's blushes.

"It's Billy's birthday. We're having pizza."

Dillon laughed, leaned down, and kissed his mother on the cheek. "Whoever gets there first will save a table for four. Deal?"

"Deal."

Seventeen

· · · · · · · · · · · · · · ·

Samantha and Dillon arrived first because he'd called her at six-thirty on her cell phone to make sure she didn't oversleep. They'd quickly decided they'd rather talk face-to-face.

After Samantha disconnected the call, she had hurriedly showered and dressed, glad she'd had the forethought to bring clothes and toiletries to the cottage. She got in her car and hurriedly drove to the restaurant. When she pulled up she saw Dillon, his long, muscled jeans-clad legs crossed, arms folded across a wide chest, waiting for her.

She parked beside him, got out, and he was there. She didn't think, she just curved her arms around his neck and enjoyed the kiss. "Good morning."

"There went keeping this from your uncle." Dillon didn't have to look around to know they'd been seen. The restaurant was a popular place for breakfast.

"Last night I might have wanted to keep this between us,

but not any longer." She grinned. "Besides, you're too yummy to resist."

"Something tells me that you might be a handful."

"Make that two." Taking his hand, she led the way inside the restaurant.

The hostess stared from her to Dillon. Samantha felt like sticking out her chest and saying, "Mine."

"Table for two?"

"Four," Dillon told her. "Another couple will be joining us."

"This way."

Samantha felt Dillon's hand at the small of her back, the stares of the people. Talk of them would be all over town by midday. She couldn't care less. She took the seat he held and accepted the menu. "Marlene and Roman joining us?"

"Yeah. They have a breakfast date. He's also taking her home from work," Dillon said. "I'm not sure if they're going out or staying in."

"Doesn't matter as long as they're together."

"Yeah." He understood that now.

"Good morning. You folks ready to order?" the waiter asked.

"Sam?"

"The breakfast supreme with pan sausages, hash browns, large orange juice, coffee, and lots of strawberry jelly."

"I'll have the same." He handed his menu to the waiter.

"How was the trip yesterday?" Samantha asked, with a grin. "I forgot to ask last night."

He grinned back. "We had our minds on other things."

"I picked up a new client who wants me to work on his Lamborghini and another I hope to see for the last time." He folded his arms on the table and told her about the wife sneaking to drive her husband's car when he was out of town.

"Your drinks." The waitress placed their water, juice, and coffee on the table. "The food will be here shortly."

"Thanks." Sam picked up her juice, slipped off her shoe, and ran her foot up Dillon's leg. He barely kept from jumping. "Surely she can find a time to ask him to drive the car when he'd find it difficult to refuse."

Dillon snatched up his glass of water and took a long swallow. Heaven help him if Sam asked to drive his car while they were in bed. "You wouldn't do that, would you?" She smiled, and he knew if she did, he'd be in danger of giving her anything she wanted. "Sam?"

She placed her glass on the table and sat back in her chair. "I believe in playing fair. You'll let me drive the Ferrari because you want to, not because I asked you in a weak moment. Especially knowing there will be times I'd be just as vulnerable. You can be quite impressive."

"The same goes for you," he told her. She made him hard with just a look.

"Then I'd say we're two lucky people." Sam nodded toward the entrance. "I'd say they're lucky as well."

Dillon followed the direction of her gaze and saw his mother and Roman approaching. While she was smiling, Roman looked annoyed. Dillon stood, holding the chair for her. "Hi."

"Good morning," Sam greeted them.

"Good morning, Samantha," Marlene returned as she took her seat.

"Everything all right?" Dillon asked. His easygoing friend had yet to smile.

"Good morning. Depends." Roman took his seat. "Go ahead and tell him."

Marlene glanced sideways at Roman. "His engine light came on in his car a couple of houses down from mine. It took some doing, but I finally talked him into letting me take a look."

Dillon was puzzled. Roman wasn't a chauvinist. "Mama is a great mechanic."

"I didn't want her getting dirty," he explained.

"That was hardly going to happen," Marlene said. "Your car's engine looks as if it just rolled off the showroom floor."

"Dad taught all of us to take care of our cars on the inside and outside," he murmured.

"It shows," Marlene said. "Without putting it on the machine I can't be sure, but my money's on the alternator."

"If Marlene says it's the alternator, it's the alternator," Sam said. "She diagnosed my problem in no time."

"Is that why you're out of sorts?" Dillon asked. "Because Marlene knew what was wrong with your car?"

Roman asked a passing waitress for two menus before slanting a look at Dillon. "I thought you knew me better than that."

"Then what?"

Roman grimaced. "You should understand. I don't like my car being down. I'm used to driving it, enjoy driving it."

Marlene patted his shoulder in sympathy. "A flatbed wrecker is coming to pick up the Porsche and take it to his dealer."

"The car has never given me a moment's problem since I special ordered it two years ago. Now, when I need it most, it decided to stop," Roman muttered. "Marlene and I had plans for tomorrow. We were going to the nursery after she looked at my yard. I thought we might go the Arboretum. I need my car."

"I can just as easily drive up and we can use my car."

Roman was shaking his head before she finished. "You are not getting on the highway after dark to drive back home."

"I've driven from Dallas after dark before," she said.

He faced her. "You're not doing it this time."

Marlene blinked and her eyes narrowed, but she didn't refute what he said.

Dillon coughed to disguise a laugh and saw Sam trying to disguise her own laugh. His mother usually had her way. It was clear that when it came to her safety, Roman was having his. "I'll take you by the car rental agency before we go to the plant. Hopefully, they'll have an SUV."

"Here's some menus for you folks and water." The waitress took their orders and left. Almost immediately Dillon and Samantha were served their food.

"Please eat while your food is hot," his mother told them.

Sam said grace and picked up her fork. "The rental selection here is not going to be that good."

Roman nodded. "You're probably right. If I can't get what I want, I'll take anything. In the meantime, I'll reserve an SUV in Dallas to use while we're there, then drive the rental from here back."

"Men and their cars," Marlene said.

Roman turned to her. "You think I'm overreacting, don't you?"

"No. You planned the weekend, and now there's a glitch. But things happen," Marlene told him with quiet understanding.

"You shouldn't worry. We're not going to let car problems ruin our day. We'll do everything you planned and then some."

Roman's gaze narrowed on her face, then a slow smile spread across his. He took her hand and kissed her fingertips. "You know, you're amazing."

Dillon fully expected his gossip-conscious mother to snatch her hand away and snap at Roman for the public display of affection. He almost fell off his chair when her fingers curled tenderly over Roman's fingers.

"You're just now figuring that out?" Marlene said with a lifted brow.

Roman laughed and leaned toward Marlene. Dillon cleared his throat. His mother blushed. Roman straightened and grinned.

Dillon couldn't hold back his own smile. Sam was right, his mother and Roman were lucky as well. He couldn't be happier for them.

Shortly after dark, Roman's day was only marginally better. Elms Fork's only car rental agency wouldn't have a car available until closing at nine—if the person returned the car on time. Since he couldn't get a rental till then, he decided to work through lunch to try to finish the audit.

Leaning back in his chair, he stared at the name on the computer screen. The thief who'd systematically stolen over a million dollars from Collins in the past three years. Roman had already called Dillon to let him know the report was finished. He and Samantha were on their way.

Roman reached for his cell phone and punched in Marlene's number. Just the thought of hearing her voice, seeing her later, made the stiffness in his muscles fade away.

"Hi. You ready for me to pick you up?" Marlene asked.

"Yes. Dillon and Samantha are on their way here now. They'll leave the front gate unlocked for you."

The cranky security man at the entrance had made it clear in Samantha and Dillon's joint office, when she'd asked him to stay until Roman was ready to leave, that he had plans and wasn't staying once his shift was up. He was tired of working late because they couldn't get their work done on time.

Dillon had shot up from his seat, but Samantha had waved him aside and stood, her palm faceup as she'd asked for the gate keys. The man had hesitated, then slapped them in her hand with a smirk.

Tossing them on her desk, Samantha had told him that Collins might not be a good fit for him any longer.

His shocked expression had been priceless, his apologies useless. Samantha had told him they'd discuss it Monday at eight in her office, dismissing him by taking her seat. He'd slunk off like a whipped puppy. To Dillon's "Well done," Samantha had said, "I learned from the best. You." Since they were staring at each other hungrily, Roman had gone back to work.

"I'm leaving now. Bye," Marlene said.

"Bye." Roman disconnected the call. It was his problem that he wanted her to depend on him for something, to trust him with her love. She'd freak out if she knew how much he loved her. He'd been falling since the moment he saw her. It had been so easy to love her. She deserved to be loved, pampered, treasured. And she was so afraid to take that final step.

He just hoped he got the chance. Straightening, he moved

the curser to print the file. As the laser printer spit out the sheets, he slid the top on the portable thumb drive that contained backup files of all the information.

Outside his office door, he heard voices and recognized them as Dillon and Samantha. He blew out a breath. This wasn't going to be easy.

"Who is it?" Dillon asked as soon as he and Samantha came through the door.

"Please tell me it isn't one of the longtime employees," Samantha said, her hand in Dillon's.

"I wish I could, Samantha." Roman reached for the inch-thick stack of sheets on the printer. "The embezzlement goes back three years. The reason no one caught on is because accounts payable simply paid invoices. There was no reason for them to check with shipping to ensure that the merchandise had actually been shipped."

"But you did?" Dillon asked.

"Yes. Although Collins had lost a few accounts, production was up ten percent from last year. As you thought, there was no way the company should have been in such a bad financial position." Roman shook his head. "Unfortunately, your grandfather only saw the decline of capital, the lost accounts, and thought the company was in trouble. Without matching shipping to invoices, it would have been impossible to tell someone was embezzling from the company."

"Who is it?" Dillon's voice was cold.

Roman looked at Samantha before answering. "Evan Collins."

Shocked raced across her face. She felt numb and pulled her hand from Dillon's. "No, he wouldn't do that." She rounded the desk to stare at the computer screen. "Someone must have used his name."

His mouth tight, Dillon curved his arm around her shoulder.

"I checked and double-checked, Samantha. I'm sorry," Roman told her. "In the past three years, fake invoices were submitted by your uncle payable to Frazier and Company for well over a million dollars."

Her eyes briefly shut. "That's my aunt's maiden name. She had a business account to be able to go to the Dallas Mart and Design District and shop."

"Since he was V.P., no one questioned him. The same way they paid his expenses without question," Roman told them. "Besides the inflated expenditures, he's given copies of bogus receipts."

"It's hard to believe he'd do that to his own father." Samantha swallowed hard.

"He's stolen his last penny from Collins," Dillon promised. "He's going to jail."

"I think not," Evan said, a gun in his hand.

Eighteen

. . . .

Dillon stepped in front of Samantha. "Put that down."

"I'm not going to jail." Evan motioned with the gun. "Move away from the computer. Samantha, shred those papers. It will be your word against mine once the evidence is destroyed."

Roman handed the paper to Sam. "Do as he says."

Sam took the sheets, but she didn't move. "How could you do this to your father? He died thinking he'd failed."

"Shut up!" Evan shouted, advancing farther into the room. "You shut up. I worked all of my life for Collins. This company should have been mine."

"So no one would ever know you stole?" Dillon asked.

"You have a big mouth. Maybe I should silence it."

"No." Sam rushed to shred the papers. "I'm doing as you say. There's no need to hurt anyone."

"Listen to you, caring for this nothing." Evan wiped perspiration from his forehead. "I thought he was here alone since his truck was outside, but you made your choice."

"The papers are shredded," Roman said. "You can leave."

"Smash that computer," Evan ordered.

Roman didn't hesitate. The monitor crashed to the floor.

"You think I'm stupid?" Evan riled. "I meant the tower under your desk."

Roman reached for the tower. Dillon's hand on his arm stopped him. "Your mother is on her way here," Roman whispered tightly.

"What did you say?" Evan took a step closer. "Try something, and I'll use this gun."

Roman disconnected the wires to the tower and dropped the tower on top of the broken monitor. The crash vibrated around the small room.

"Why?" Samantha asked, her voice quivering.

"I had expenses. Gambling debts." Evan's voice trembled.

"You could have gone to Grandfather." Samantha had tears in her eyes. "You didn't have to steal from him."

"He would have told me to clean up my mess."

"And you should have," Dillon told him.

Evan swung the gun on Dillon. "Shut up. This is all your fault, and that mother of yours."

"You have what you came for, you can leave," Roman told him.

"I have the gun. I give the orders." Evan's hands shook.

Sam took a couple of steps toward her uncle. "We can work this out."

"Sam, don't," Dillon warned.

"You stay where you are!" Evan shouted angrily. "If it wasn't for you, Daddy would have left me the company. You tried to take what's mine, and now you're going to pay."

"No!" Samantha's desperate scream joined that of Marlene's just outside the door.

Evan glanced over his shoulder, then back as Dillon lunged for him. Stumbling back, Evan fired the gun. Dillon didn't stop, his hard fist connecting solidly with Evan's chin. Evan went down and didn't get up.

Dillon turned to check on Sam. His world tilted. She was on the floor, her eyes closed, a ribbon of blood running from her temple.

With a cry of pain and rage, he crossed the room, gently taking her from Roman and wrapping his arms around her. Tears stung his eyes. He was unaware of the passing time, of the sheriff and the ambulance attendants rushing into the room, of his mother telling Roman that she'd arrived soon after Evan and called the police.

"She's alive, Dillon."

He heard his mother as if from a distance. This couldn't be happening.

"The ambulance is here, Dillon. Let them help her."

Faintly he recognized Roman's shaky voice, saw his mother crying beside him. He tried to speak, couldn't. He was afraid to let her go. It was as if, as long as he held her, she wouldn't . . . A guttural sound of pain slipped from his mouth. He couldn't lose her.

"Dillon, you have to let her go to the hospital." On her knees, his mother took his face in her hands. "Listen, Dillon. Let them have her. I know it hurts, but you can't help her this way."

He felt tears slide down his face. His hold loosened. Two sets of hands were there to take Sam and put her on the gurney.

"I didn't mean it. The gun went off by accident. You have to believe me."

The numbness Dillon felt turned to red-hot rage. He came to his feet and went for Evan. Wide-eyed, Evan scuttled back. One policeman reached for Dillon. He batted the hand away, kept walking. Then his mother was in front of him, Roman by her side.

"Samantha needs you. They're taking her to the hospital. When she wakes up she'll want to see you. She needs you."

"Let's roll."

Dillon's head jerked around as he heard the snap of the gurney rising to its full height. The two E.M.T.s rushed past him with Sam, the white sheet up to her neck. She looked pale, lifeless. Dillon felt his insides knot.

"Nothing will save you if anything happens to her," he said to Evan, then hurried out the door to catch up with the gurney.

Directly behind Dillon, Roman held Marlene's arm with one hand and called his brother-in-law with the other. He didn't want his family hearing about the shooting on the news. Then, too, they'd want to be there for Dillon.

"Hello."

Watching the E.M.T.s load an unconscious Samantha into the ambulance, the two police cars with lights running, he talked fast. "The audit I did went bad. Samantha was shot. She's unconscious with a head injury. They're loading her into the ambulance now."

"Oh, God. Anyone else hurt?"

"No. Just Samantha. We need your prayers."

Marlene moved to pull Dillon away from trying to get into the back of the ambulance. "You have to ride up front. Roman and I will be right behind you."

"You know you have them," Nathan said. "We're coming."

Since he knew it wouldn't do any good to tell them there was no need, he didn't try. "I'm not sure where the hospital is located."

"We'll find it."

"Thanks." Roman went to Marlene and curved his arm around her waist as the passenger door shut and the ambulance took off with sirens blaring.

Sam wouldn't wake up. She'd been in the ER for almost an hour, her private room half that time. The sheriff had tried to talk to Dillon, but he'd been too angry and scared and referred him to Roman. Dillon's only focus was Sam getting well. He'd paced the ER waiting room, his thoughts in disarray. He kept thinking how happy they'd been that day, how full of life she was.

Carson and his parents had arrived with hugs and prayers. Dillon had been too restless to sit and carry on a conversation. Carson had matched him step for step, silently giving him his support.

Now, sitting by her bed, Dillon held Sam's hand and prayed. The resident in the emergency room said he "thought" she would be all right since the small-caliber bullet had only grazed her temple. He'd requested a neurological consult for the next day. Dillon didn't plan to wait that long. He eased his hand from Sam's, took out his phone and dialed information.

In seconds he was speaking to Dr. Cade Mathis's answering service. Before he could finish telling her about Sam, the woman said that Dr. Mathis was out of town on an emergency. She wasn't sure when he'd return.

Feeling helpless, fighting anger, Dillon disconnected the call and bowed his head. The door opened behind him. He didn't look up. His mother and Roman had been in and out of the room to check on Sam, and him too, he supposed. He didn't know if Carson and his parents had left or not.

"I called the neurosurgeon I met yesterday. He's supposed to be the best, but he's out of town."

"I heard you needed me."

Dillon jumped up, almost knocking over the chair. "Dr. Mathis."

With him was the resident, staring worshipfully at Cade. "He's the best in the state, probably the nation."

"Call me Cade. Nathan called. Sorry it took so long. I needed to finish late rounds." Cade moved to the bedside and stared down at Sam. "I've already checked her X-rays and CT scan. All look good."

"She won't wake up," Dillon said, watching intently as Cade examined Sam.

Finished, the doctor looked up. "The brain has a marvelous mechanism to protect itself from unpleasant things. It simply shuts down. I understand that before she was injured, your life was threatened."

"Yes." Dillon's face hardened. Evan was going to pay for this.

"How would you describe your relationship?" Cade asked.

Complicated. Passionate. Dillon searched for a word and finally said what was in his heart. "I love her."

Cade smiled as if he knew the admission wasn't easy. "Her

not waking up might have more to do with not wanting to face you being injured more than her own injury." Cade looked down at Sam. "Have you been talking to her?"

"He said to let her rest." Dillon picked up Sam's hand. "I've just held her hand and prayed."

"I thought it best," the resident explained quickly.

"In most cases, but this time I think Ms. Collins needs to hear his voice," Cade said.

"I'll talk nonstop if I have to," Dillon promised.

"I want to order a few more tests before I leave," Cade told him.

Panic hit Dillon. He grabbed the doctor's arm. "You're leaving?"

"I have a seven o'clock surgery that can't be postponed. She should be awake by then, but if not, I'll be back tomorrow after I make evening rounds."

Dillon stared into Cade's face, met his direct stare, and knew he could trust him. "Thank you. Whatever your bill, I'll gladly pay it."

"Getting her well is all the thanks I need. I'll go order those tests."

Dillon retook his seat and kissed Sam's hand when the door closed. "You hear that, Sam? Cade said you're going to be all right. All you have to do is open those pretty eyes. If you can manage before he leaves, not only will I give you a key to every car, truck, and motorcycle I own, I'll teach you how to drive them."

Marlene was in the waiting room with Roman's sister and her family, Dr. Mathis's fiancée, and another couple, Zachary and

Madison Holman, who had come with them. She couldn't thank Nathan enough for having the foresight to contact Dr. Mathis. The way the staff had stared at him, he must be the best.

Seeing Dr. Mathis come through the waiting room door, she came unsteadily to her feet. She felt Roman's arm around her, helping her to keep it together.

Dr. Mathis stopped in front of her. "I believe she's all right. I want to run a few more tests, but I expect her to wake up shortly. If she doesn't, I'll return tomorrow night."

Tears crested in Marlene's eyes. "Thank you. We were so worried."

"I told you, if it was possible for her to be helped, Cade would find a way," said his fiancée, Sabrina Thomas.

Dr. Mathis sent Sabrina a smile filled with love. "My one-man cheering squad. I'll go order those tests."

"Marlene, please drink the coffee Roman brought you," Tess urged.

Marlene turned to Roman and went into his arms, crying softly. "I was so scared."

Holding her tightly, he kissed her on the top of her head. "Me too. You want to go back to her room for a bit?"

Marlene sniffed and straightened, drying her eyes with the fresh tissue Tess handed her. Carson's mother was beautiful, with laughing black eyes; she'd always been friendly and down-to-earth despite her husband's millions.

"Thank you for coming." Marlene took the other woman's hands, her gaze going to Nathan standing by her side. Tall, elegant, and handsome, he was a man you could count on. He'd certainly proven that tonight. "You helped us get through this."

"You know we love Dillon." Tess cut a look at Roman.

"Something tells me you're the reason Roman has been so late returning to Dallas."

"Real subtle, Tess," Roman said, his arm back around Marlene.

"If you don't ask . . ." Tess shrugged and grinned.

Marlene stared up at Roman. "I wouldn't have made it through this if you hadn't been here for me to lean on."

"As long as you need and want me, I'll be here," he said, his voice throbbing with sincerity.

The door swung open. "Ms. Collins is waking up. Her fiancé wanted you to know," a nurse informed them.

Everyone took off. Roman had told the ER staff that Dillon was Samantha's fiancé so he could get updates on her and stay in her room.

In a matter of seconds they were all crowded around Samantha's bed, openly flaunting the "no visitors after eight" rule. Marlene reached for Roman's hand, and his fingers locked with hers.

"Come on, Sam, you can do it," Dillon coaxed. "Keep those eyes open this time if you want the keys to everything I drive."

Carson whistled. "You sure know how to bribe a woman."

Fighting tears of happiness, Marlene watched Samantha's eyelids slowly open. "I won't even be upset that he let you drive them before I do."

"Dillon." His name was the barest whisper of sound, but he heard it.

"That's right, baby. I'm here, just waiting for you to wake up."

"Head hurts. I—" Her eyes widened as she tried to lift her hand toward his face. "The gun went off."

Dillon caught her hand, kissed her palm. "I'm all right."

He looked at his mother for guidance. He didn't know how much to tell her.

"The bullet missed Dillon and grazed your head," Marlene said softly.

Her unsteady hand lifted to the bandage on her head. "The last thing I remember is Dillon going for my uncle." She frowned at him. "Stupid."

"It's my fault you were hurt," Dillon managed. "I'll never forgive myself."

"Uncle Evan's fault, not yours."

"Looks like the patient woke up." Cade stood at the foot of the bed. "How are you feeling, Ms. Collins?"

"This is your doctor, baby," Dillon told her.

"Head hurts. A bit groggy," she answered.

"I've ordered you something for the headache. They'll bring it as soon as it comes from the pharmacy." Cade moved to stand beside Dillon. "Follow the light. How many fingers? What's the date? Good." Cade slipped the penlight back into the pocket of his lab coat. "You're going to be fine. I see no reason why you can't go home in the morning if everything continues to progress this well. Just take it easy for the next few days. The headaches and any dizziness should be gone by morning."

"Thank you," Samantha said.

"You're quite welcome. You can visit for ten more minutes, then she needs to rest." Cade looked at Dillon. "Yes, I'll clear you to remain."

"Whatever your car needs for a lifetime, it's on me." Dillon kissed Samantha's hand again.

"Very generous, but that won't be necessary." Cade spoke to Marlene. "I wonder if I could see you alone for a moment."

"Of course." Marlene left the room and followed Cade back to the waiting room. The only people there were the Holman couple and Cade's fiancée. "I can't thank you enough for coming. You went out of your way to help us."

"I would have come anyway, but there was another reason," Cade said.

Lines radiated across Marlene's brow. She noted that Zachary Holman had come to stand beside the doctor.

"Is there anything familiar about us?" Zachary asked.

Her puzzlement grew. "I don't understand."

"I don't think there's an easy way to say this," Cade said. "Is Dillon's father A. J. Reed?"

Marlene gasped, swayed. Both men reached for her, then eased her down in a chair Madison quickly pushed over.

"We don't mean to embarrass you or hurt you," Cade told her. "A. J. is Zachary's father, and mine. He's an unpleasant, mean-tempered man who cares nothing for us. We were blessed to have good women like you for our mothers. Zachary grew up with his, but I didn't find mine until several weeks ago. If we have other brothers or sisters, we both want to know."

She shook her head. "I don't want that part of my life brought up. Not now."

"Because of Roman, the man with you?" Sabrina asked softly.

"I'm thankful for what you did for Samantha and Dillon, but I don't want to talk about this." Marlene came unsteadily to her feet. She didn't want to be reminded of the shame, to remind Roman and his family of her stupidity. "I need to get back."

Cade handed her his card. "Our information is on the back. If you change your mind, please call."

"I won't. Good-bye."

· · ·

Roman was waiting for Marlene in the hall. Seeing her pinched features, he quickly went to her. "What is it? He give you bad news about Samantha?"

"No." Marlene started to walk around him. He caught her arm.

"What is it?" She was trembling. She wouldn't even look at him.

"Nothing. I'm just tired. I'll say good night now. I'm going to sit with Dillon before I leave," she told him.

"What happened between the time you left and now?" Roman asked. "Three minutes ago you couldn't get close enough, now you can't get away fast enough."

"Please let it go." Her voice trembled.

Roman saw Dr. Mathis, his fiancée, and the other couple come out of the waiting room. They paused, looking at him and Marlene, then turned the corner for the elevator. "Maybe I should ask Mathis."

"No." Marlene's nails dug into his wrist. "Please. Just stay out of this." She released him and hurried down the hall.

She was scared. No way was he letting this go. Not by a long shot. He went to the elevator, but they were already gone. He pushed the elevator button to go after them. By the time he reached the parking lot, he didn't see them. He turned and went back to Samantha's floor. Tess, Nathan, and Carson were just leaving her room.

"You ready to leave?" Nathan asked.

"I'm staying." There was no way he'd leave Marlene while she was upset and scared.

"Maybe it's for the best," Tess said. "I think all of this has finally gotten to Marlene. She was shaking like a leaf. I don't think Dillon noticed, he's so caught up with Samantha."

"Drive carefully." Roman hugged his sister and gave a one-arm hug to his brother-in-law and his nephew. "I'll call tomorrow with an update on Samantha."

"One on you and Marlene would be nice as well." Tess glanced back at Samantha's door. "I don't think she's going to be easy to reel in."

"But I have no intention of losing."

"You can go home tomorrow." Dillon kissed her hand. "We'll put you up in the guest bedroom at Mama's house where I can keep an eye on you."

"Dillon, I'm going to be fine." Her fingers tightened on his. "The medicine helped the headache."

"I'm not taking a chance." His eyes closed briefly. "I thought I'd lost you. It was the worst feeling in my life."

"I'm sorry if I frightened you."

"Stop saying that or I'm going to go back on my promise of giving you keys to my rides."

"You weren't joking?" she asked.

"I meant every word, but I'm going to make sure you can drive them before you get out on the highway," Dillon said. "I finally understand Cade wanting to make sure his car was ready before his fiancée drove it. You take care of what you love."

"W-what?"

Dillon leaned down close to her face. "I love you, Sam. I didn't realize how much until I almost lost you. You're the one thing in life I don't want to live without."

"Dillon," she murmured, tears cresting in her eyes. "I've loved you for so long. I was afraid you'd never love me back."

"I do, hopelessly." He kissed her tears away. "I guess my roaming days are over—unless you can come with me. I'm not letting you out of my sight for the next hundred years."

"I'm holding you to that." Her voice trembled.

"You better."

Marlene slipped quietly out of the room. She breathed a sigh of relief that Roman wasn't there until she rounded the corner and saw him waiting by the window next to the elevator. He looked unwavering.

Slowly he came toward her. It was all she could do not to back up. "We're going to talk, Marlene. We can do it here or at your home in privacy. Your choice."

She could have alerted security, but she would only put off the inevitable. "My house."

Both were silent on the elevator ride and the drive to her house. He got out of the car and went to wait for her on the porch. She opened the front door and went inside.

"Say what you have to say and then leave."

"I love you."

"What?" She couldn't be hearing correctly.

"I love you." He caught both of her arms. "Nothing is going to change that love. Not your past. Not your trying to push me away."

Her stomach muscles tightened. "I don't want you to love me."

"Because you think I'll use you like Dillon's father?" he snapped. "Do you know how much it hurts when you look at me and I know you're thinking of him? He might be out of your life, but you can't let the memory go."

"Leave me alone."

"If I could, I would," he snarled. "Do you think I like loving a woman who doesn't know if she wants to drag me to bed or run for the door? You're it for me. I love you despite you making me so angry I could spit. I love you because of your strength, your courage. Love you even more because, for some crazy reason, you think you can't be loved."

Her eyes widened. Shame hit her. Her lips quivered.

He jerked her to him, his mouth taking hers until she was weak and pliant in his arms. "I thought I knew what love was. I didn't until I met you. You, and only you. You touch my heart and soothe my soul. It tears me up that I can't do the same for you." His face fierce, he stepped back.

"I can't make you love me. I can't make you feel the pride and love I feel for you. Looking at defeat, especially in the eyes of the woman I love, is not something I'm sure I can handle." His hands fisted at his sides. "When you can trust and love me, give me a call."

Marlene watched Roman, shoulders slumped, walk to the front door. Without looking back, he opened it and closed it softly behind him.

He was gone. She'd never have to worry about her past coming up, never feel that sharp stab of shame.

And she'd be alone with her fear. With a cry, she rushed out the door. "Roman!" she screamed, hurrying off the porch. "Don't go. Please, don't go." She couldn't see him. There was no moon, and in her hurry to leave earlier, she'd forgotten to turn on the porch light. She stumbled, went to her knees.

"Roman."

"I'm here. Honey, I'm here." He pulled her into his arms, held her tightly to the solid warmth of his body.

"I love you. I love you so much," she cried.

He tensed, then picked her up and carried her back into the house. He didn't stop until she was in his lap in the den. "Now tell me again."

She sniffed. "I love you. You were right. I let the past over-shadow any possible future with a man. I was so proud of my relationship with Dillon's father. I told anyone who'd listen how wealthy he was, the nice restaurants in Dallas we dined at, the expensive car he drove. Then, when it was over, all those prideful boasts came back to haunt me. I was the talk of the town and not in a nice way."

"Now, the town respects and watches after you," Roman said, brushing her hair back. "You're a remarkable woman. Why can't you see what others see?"

"I finally figured out it was because I was stuck in the past. No more. I want life, love, and I want them with you."

"Marlene," he breathed, his warm lips parting hers.

She nestled against him and told him about Cade and Zachary being Dillon's half brothers. "In a few days, when Samantha is better, I'll talk to him about it, but I already know he'll want them in his life. Love opens your heart."

She turned in his arms. "You opened mine." Her lips brushed across his, once, twice, before hovering above his. "Make love to me, Roman. Make me yours."

"First, I have to ask you something and your answer will determine if we make love or not," he told her.

She felt the bulge beneath her hips and moved against it. His breath hissed through his teeth. "Don't do that."

"Then ask your question." She bit his ear.

"Mercy," Roman breathed, then blurted out while he could still think clearly, "Will you marry me?"

Marlene went still. She simply stared.

"If you love me enough for us to make love, you love me enough for us to get married. I'd planned to wait until we were married for our first time, but I don't think I can make it." He took her trembling hand. "Once you said you wouldn't get married even if your life depended on it. Well, mine does. Marry me, Marlene."

"There's only one answer." She leaned down and captured his mouth with hers, letting fears and regrets fall away, leaving love and passion and trust. "Yes."

"Thank God." He pulled her to him, his heated mouth devouring hers. Lifting his head, he gathered her in his arms and strode to the bedroom. All the time she was biting his ear.

In the bedroom he placed her on her feet. Silently she turned away and pulled back the covers. Roman toed off his shoes, unbuckled his belt. When she faced him again, his hands settled at her trim waist while his mouth pleasured them both. "I need to see you."

Stepping away, he gathered fistfuls of the flared skirt of her sundress and drew it over her head. Air stalled in his lungs. He'd thought she'd be perfect. She was so much more. The rose peaks of her breasts tempted him through the sheer bra. Her slightly rounded stomach, her woman's softness, long legs he couldn't wait to feel around him. "You're even more beautiful than I'd imagined."

"Let's see if I can say the same." She pulled his polo shirt over his head, then unsnapped his pants and shoved them over his hips.

Roman hardened even more as her hungry gaze ran over him, her hand following, cupping him. Air whistled through his teeth. He moved her hand away. "I'm too near the edge."

She wound her arms around his neck. A shudder racked her body. "I almost lost you."

"You didn't." His mouth went to the tempting peak of her breast, suckled, delighted in her long moan. He released the bra, letting it fall, then placed her in bed with him over her.

He took the peak again, his hand kneading the other breast before sliding downward. He found her wet and hot.

She twisted beneath him at the twin assaults. Her body was on fire, the need building as his mouth moved to the other breast. Then his mouth slid downward, teasing, kissing as he went. Helplessly she twisted as he pleasured her.

He moved back up, his mouth and hands on her body gentle and demanding, passionate and restrained. She welcomed each new sensation rippling through her.

She realized that she had never known this gentleness in intimacy—demanding, yes; gentle, never. If she'd had any lingering doubts about him, they slipped away as he loved her.

Every nerve screaming for release, she dragged his head back up and their lips fused, hot and urgent. With greedy urgency, she ran her hands over the heated muscles that flexed and rippled.

"Please. Now."

Lifting her hips, he joined their bodies with one sure stroke. Moans of pure delight rippled from their lips. Her hands clutching his shoulders, her legs wrapped tightly around him, she yielded to the desire burning out of control.

He was on top of her, inside of her, surrounding her,

possessing her. He stroked her, gliding in and out with increased power. She felt her body coil and tightened her arms
around his neck.

They shattered together. His breathing as ragged as hers, he
buried his face against her throat, brushed his lips there. It was
a long time before either could speak.

"Finally, you're mine." Roman pulled her closer. "I love
you, Marlene. I'll never stop."

Her hand cupped one side of his face. "I know that now. If
you don't mind, I think I'd like a short engagement. I've spent
enough nights without you."

"You read my mind."

Dillon was holding Sam's hand when dawn broke the next
morning. Bowing his head, he gave thanks that they had a
chance to watch countless dawns together.

"Dillon."

Instantly alert, he came to his feet and leaned down to her.
"You all right? You need something?"

She moistened her lips. "I dreamed . . ." Her voice faltered.

His frown deepened as his hand tightened. "You're gonna
be all right. Cade is the best."

"Then he was here?"

Finally understanding, he kissed her lips. "That he was,
and as soon as the nurse checks on you again, I'm signing you
out and taking you home. I know women like big weddings
that take a lot of planning, but I'm hop— Honey, don't cry.
What is it?"

Sam blinked back tears. "I thought I dreamed you asking
me to marry you."

He grinned and kissed her. "You're not backing out. You're mine, and as soon as you feel like it we're heading to the jewelry store to find you a ring."

"I love you so much," she said.

"And I love you right back." He leaned over to whisper in her ear, "As soon as Cade gives the okay, I'll be sharing the bed with you."

"You think you can call him now?"

Dillon lifted his head and gazed into Sam's serious eyes. His chest tightened with love and thankfulness. "I love you, Sam, now and forever." He brushed his lips across hers. "Cade had surgery this morning. I'll call him around noon."

Epilogue

. . . .

Brothers. He had two brothers. Dillon still found it hard to believe that Cade and Zachary were his brothers.

"Are you all right?" Sam asked from beside him.

"As long as you're by my side I am." His finger ran over the five-carat diamond engagement ring he had insisted she get. He planned to spoil and love her every chance he got.

"I feel the same way," she whispered.

Leaning over, he kissed her on top of her head, then drew her closer to him, his gaze trained on the street in front of his mother's house. In the back, she and Roman were grilling and probably doing some kissing of their own.

Their wedding was only six weeks away. He'd heard from more than one source that the women of Elms Fork had almost come to blows on who was giving her a shower. They'd finally settled on four with different themes. Like Roman said, the town loved his mother, and with Roman by her side, she realized that now.

Luckily for his sanity, he and Sam were getting married in

three months. Carson's mother had been invaluable in helping acquire the Mansion on Turtle Creek for their garden wedding and reception.

"I can't wait to meet them. Our children will have loving aunts and uncles, cousins," Sam said. "They'll have what we didn't have."

Dillon's head snapped around. She laughed. "No, I'm not pregnant. I'm talking in future tense."

A black truck turned the corner, followed by a Lamborghini. He, Cade, and Zachary had spoken on the phone twice, but this would be the first time they'd seen each other since Dillon found out a week ago they were related.

The truck and car stopped in the drive. Men piled out the passenger's side as the women got out of the driver's side.

"I'm going to like my future sisters-in-law." Sam started for the small group. A little girl of about five ran to meet her, followed by a grinning male toddler.

"Are you my auntie?" the little girl asked, smiling up at Samantha.

Sam squatted down to eye level. "That I am."

Both squealed and hugged her.

Dillon grinned, imagined Samantha with their own children. The women hung back as he met the men on the walkway. "Now I know why you were staring at me. Mama says I look like him."

"But you're nothing like him." Zachary pulled out his wallet and flipped it over to his driver's license.

Cade did the same. "So far I'm the youngest."

Dillon produced his license. Grinned. "I'm the youngest. That means I get to drive your cars, and since I promised Sam she could have keys to my rides, that means yours."

Zachary and Cade shared a look, then grinned back. They had another brother. "Fair enough," Zachary said.

"You got it," Cade said, reaching out for Dillon and Zachary with his long arms. "Welcome to the family."

New York Times bestselling author

FRANCIS RAY

really knows how to heat things up!

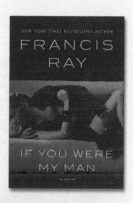

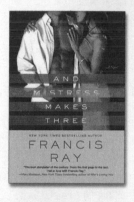

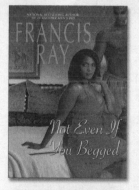

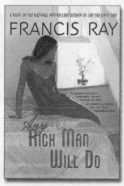

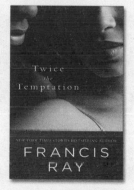

FALL IN LOVE WITH
New York Times bestselling author
FRANCIS RAY's
Grayson Family & Friends Series!

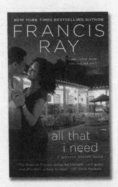

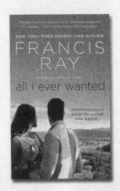

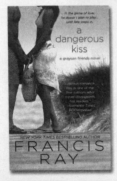

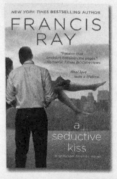

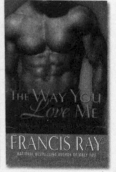